Chicago Lightning

Kaye Spencer

Lasterday Stories, L.L.C.

Chicago Lightning

Cover Design – Kaye Spencer

Published by Lasterday Stories, LLC
www.lasterdaystories.com

Public Domain Song – 'After You've Gone' by Henry Creamer and John Turner Layton, Copyright 1918, New York.

ISBN: 979-8-9930823-0-1
LCCN: 2025924611

To Brakelle Beth

because...

Roaring Twenties and Gatsby

Chapter One

Chicago, Illinois – Valentine's Day 1929

Belly down on cold concrete, Ceara Rocchelli fought her way to consciousness. Stale cigarette smoke mixed with garage odors accompanied her slow ascent into disoriented awareness. Blinking away double-vision, her foggy brain recognized the thin yellow glow in the dim distance as light peeking from under a closed door. Something on the other side of that door mattered, but what it was became mired down in her muddled thinking and sank into obscurity. Her lips were sticky, and she tasted blood when she swallowed. A wish for water faded under the tantalizing lure of sleep. She was bone-deep cold and so tired. So tired...

Ceara jerked awake. She held her breath, listening. *There— Voices. Angry voices. Men's voices in the other room*. A cautious check left and right revealed darker shadows of things she couldn't make out, but she felt no sense of another person.

Chancing she was alone, she pushed upright, despite every part of her body protesting. The chink and rattle of chain scraping on the concrete didn't register in her cobwebbed mind. How long had she been out? Minutes? Hours? When she tucked a strand of her blonde bobbed hair behind her ear, her attention locked on the ring of metal around her right wrist. Puzzled, she trailed her gaze along the chain attached to the metal ring to where it wrapped around the back axle of a Model-T a few feet away.

She stared dumbly for some moments. Then it hit her.

Panic blazed hot and fast like a wildfire in high winds. She yanked the chain and tore at the cold circlet of steel. Useless, her mind said. Stop fighting. Desperate seconds ticked until her tenuous hold on rational thought got the upper hand, and she wrestled her terror into submission.

Think! Think! How did I get here? Why am I chained?

Wading through the quagmire of muddy memories, fleeting snippets flashed like blinking neon letters on a sign. The other side of that door...a street-front office with a blackened window. She swept her gaze floor to ceiling, squinting into the shadows and peering around the concrete pillars rising through the ceiling and the vehicles in various stages of repair to see the telltale dark shapes of wooden crates stacked near a tire rack and a lone metal desk butted up against a wall. Her visual journey stopped at the far end of the warehouse. Although she couldn't see details, she knew a row of small windows ran along the top of double-paneled cargo doors and an iron bar dropped across the doors to keep them closed. She also knew those doors opened into an alley? Why did she know that?

Like cogs falling into place on a turning wheel, memories spun in her mind, gathering coherence. Still, there was something missing. Something critical. No! Not something. Someone. Whipping around, she stared at the office door. So close. She'd been so close to freedom.

Hagen.

Almost her liberator.

Please, please, let him be alive.

Tears assaulted her wall of courage. Her stubborn Irish blood kept that wall from crashing and crushing what remained of her dream of a new life without Eddie. It was too late for self-pity and regrets. Hagen had known the risks as well as she. But the risk she hadn't anticipated, and what she hadn't seen coming, was falling for him. And, oh, how she'd fallen.

She'd known from the beginning she had to forget him and bury her feelings in the same dark place where the mother in her grieved for her dead child. Well-meaning people assured her the grief of losing a baby would eventually become bearable, but she didn't believe them any more than she believed her love for Hagen would ever die.

Lifting her hand to wipe the bitter tears that slipped past her barricade of fortitude, her arm caught on her metal tether—a cruel reminder that her attempt at freedom had failed. A spasm of shivering brought her back to her harsh reality, and she scooted to lean against the side of the Model-T. Drawing her legs up to her chest, she put her forehead on her knees and hugged her legs for the little warmth it provided.

This wasn't the first beating she'd taken, nor was it the worst. Eddie had the honors for that one. Pain didn't concern her, either. Pain was a reminder she was alive, and alive meant there was still a chance. That tiny scrap of hope was the nudge she needed to avoid giving in to despair. This was her first attempt to leave Eddie, and the planning had been sketchy at best. Right then, she promised herself she'd find another way out of her prison-marriage.

Her fighting spirit gained strength with her mental pep talk. She relished the thought of Eddie's manhood taking a solid hit to its pride when he discovered the real reason she'd been caught running off with his new mechanic.

Mechanic. What a laugh.

The doorknob grated an ominous warning. Ceara threw herself face down on the filthy floor with one arm draped over her face. It was a crazy idea, but maybe they'd leave her alone if she appeared unconscious.

Stark white light from a high-powered overhead electric bulb illuminated the room, causing her to squint even under the cover of her arm. Although she couldn't see the faces of the men walking toward her, she saw their polished shoes and pressed trousers below their long overcoats and that two men dragged a third man between them.

"Dump him beside her."

There was no mistaking Paul Carta's deep, raspy baritone, and the image of his jowly, ruddy face came readily to her mind. He was Eddie's right-hand man and accustomed to giving orders and having them followed to the letter without question, which was why Eddie trusted him above the others. Even if the opportunity arose, there was no use bargaining with him.

A body dropped with a dull thump and rolled against her. The heat radiating from him felt like she'd left the shade for the sun on a hot summer's day.

"He's not going anywhere, but we'll play it safe. Leo, you've got the key. Run the end of the nippers through the chain ring to hook him to her. They wanted to be together. Well, now they are." Paul grunted a mirthless laugh.

Hagen! Ceara's heart swelled. She stopped her smile before she gave herself away.

Paul went on while Leo Passero handcuffed them together. "When I called Eddie and told him they'd been caught sneaking off together, he said to give them a good Broderick so they'd know he means business. So that's what we did. We put the screws to them. That was a smooth move on his part to have us hire some unknowns to do it, too. It keeps our hands clean. Now, let's get outta here."

"What? Leave them with only Gilbert and Lenny in charge? I know Eddie's repaying a favor, but they haven't been on payroll long enough to know if they can handle a job like this. For all we know, they're still scared of the dark and the

Boogieman. If someone shows up before we get back, they may blow the whole shebang."

Ceara perked up at the concern in Leo's voice, little as it was. He'd always been fatherly toward her, and she was fond of him, as well.

"Naw. They're too scared of Eddie to do any thinking on their own. Their job is just night watch while we catch a few *Z's*. We'll lock the front door, and I'll send them home before the real fun starts. If these two wake up and make a fuss, the boys'll gag 'em. Their one and only job is to keep them quiet."

"It's not right to leave them on the floor like this," Leo persisted.

"Have you gone soft in the head? Who cares? You know Moran called Eddie back early from St. Louis to meet him at ten thirty in the morning. He's made a deal for three hijacked shipments of Capone's Old Log Cabin whiskey. They're the biggest shipments yet. Fifty-six bucks a case for first class, uncut stuff. It's too hot to sit on. Moran wants it out of here pronto." Paul nudged Ceara with his boot. "You know Bugs and Eddie are *simpatico* on everything. We'll oversee the transport after payment."

"Scarface'll blow a gasket when he finds out he's lost more whiskey."

The nasally whine in Aldo Jucca's voice felt like centipede feet crawling along her skin. She caught a whiff of cigarette smoke just before something small and compact pinged off her shoulder. Jucca was Eddie's gofer, his trigger man with a fondness for knives, who did all of Eddie's really ugly work. The way Jucca's thin-lipped sneer pulled over his small nicotine-stained teeth when he looked at her always left her feeling sullied and in need of a bath to wash off his residue. The gleam in his piggy-black eyes hinted of something inhuman and without conscience peering back—not unlike Eddie's eyes when he was that other man, the one with an uncontrollable temper.

"Don't let Capone hear you call him that. You know he hates it." There was caution laced with a good dose of respect in Paul's voice.

Jucca made a rude snort as he squatted beside Ceara. "I ain't skeered of him. We work for Eddie. Moran and Capone are peanuts."

The stench of Jucca's cheap cologne tickled her nose. Anticipating his touch, she controlled her urge to flinch when he placed his palm on the small of her back then drew downward in a slow, kneading motion. Revulsion churned in her stomach, but she held still.

"I'm counting on Eddie letting me have a go at her. She's an uppity dame, but a real looker. Me and her just need a little time alone. I'll get that out of her easy as cake."

"Leave her alone, Aldo. If I had to put money on you or her, I'll take odds on her cleaning your clock any day of the week."

Ceara wanted to hug Leo.

"There ain't a woman alive who's a match for me."

Jucca's high-pitched, weasel-whiney laughter prickled the hairs on her arms. He rubbed his palm along the length of her thigh and across the back of her knee where he bunched up the skirt of her nurse's uniform and snaked his fingers under the hem. She feared they could hear her heart hammering.

"I said knock it off! She's not yours." Leo's voice held a sharp warning as he jerked Jucca back.

Ceara sent more thoughts of gratitude out to Leo. Another few seconds, and she'd have come off the floor fighting.

"Eddie'll let me have her when he's done. I'll teach this Sheba who's boss. You just wait and see."

Leo grumbled, "Ah, what's Eddie's beef with these two, anyway? He does plenty of his own fooling around. There're rumors he's got him a woman out in Cicero."

Paul snorted. "Yeah? Well, you ask him if you want. Me? I'm keeping my trap shut. It's none of our business how he treats his old lady. For the last time. It's almost one. I'm beat."

"Wait," Leo said.

"Criminy, Leo. Let's call it a night."

A car door creaked open and closed.

Annoyed, Paul asked, "What are you doing?"

The slapping snap of a blanket shaking out brought a shower of dust sifting down. Ceara forced back a sneeze.

"Ah, come on, Paul. She's never said an unkind word to you or anyone else. You know it as well, and better, than most. She came to your house every day for a month to help out when Bernice was down with pneumonia. She's a good kid. You've said so yourself. You're no happier about her being treated like this than me, and it's damned cold in here. Eddie wants her alive. She's been in here for close to an hour. Laying unconscious like she is, she'll freeze to death for sure."

"Ah, go tell it to Sweeney." Paul uttered a scoffing laugh that didn't quite ring true.

"Know what I'm gonna do?"

Jucca's sniveling chuckle raised the hairs on her arms again.

"No one cares, Aldo."

Leo sounded as tired as she felt.

"I'm gonna carve my name on his forehead before I kill him."

Ceara's arm jerked when Jucca kicked Hagen in the side.

Paul groused, "Well, you're not doing anything to him before Eddie puts the screws to him. When Eddie takes him for a ride, you can do all the carving you want. Until then, you'll do what I tell you. Let's blow. It's nearly two, and we've got to be back here before Eddie shows."

Darkness returned with the turn of the light switch as the last man left the warehouse. Ceara remained motionless through the count of one hundred then, careful not to rattle the chain and with one eye on the door, she sat up, rolled Hagen onto his back, and cradled his head on her lap.

"Hagen. Wake up."

His head merely lolled in response to her urgent whisper and light taps upon his cheeks. His breath was warm and soft as lamb's wool against her hand.

"Thank you for trying to help me."

She traced the long, strong line of his jaw, her fingertips lingering on his lips. Then she pressed her lips to his. He needed a shave, but she didn't mind. She only cared that she'd always have this one cherished moment, even though he'd never know she'd kissed him.

Shivering interrupted her wishful musings as a reminder of how cold she was. The effort of maneuvering Hagen's inert body onto the edge of the spread-out blanket warmed her somewhat. Snuggling against him with the free edge of the blanket drawn over them captured their combined body heat and her shivering subsided. In the moments before fatigue became sleep, Ceara's memories drifted back to New Year's Eve outside Eddie's favorite of his two swanky restaurants.

Eddie's prized Phantom 1 Rolls-Royce, parked in his reserved space, had failed to start when they were ready to go home. From the backseat, she'd noticed the stranger walking on the opposite side of the street. Eddie's raging, arm-waving, foot-stomping outburst caught the stranger's attention, and he watched the show for some time before crossing over to offer assistance. She'd rolled down her window for a clearer look at the stranger from his cowboy hat and worn bomber jacket to his faded blue-jeans and scuffed boots. Eddie had asked his name and what he was doing in the neighborhood.

Her life changed when Hagen said his name and where he was from. Their gazes locked in unspoken, mutual understanding. Wrapped up in his temper fit over the car, Eddie hadn't noticed Hagen's slight nod or the reassurance in his easy, confident smile that went straight to her heart. His eyes said it all, and she'd understood with the certainty of the sun rising in the morning this man embodied her hopes and dreams. And she knew with the same certainty she could never have him.

Despite her continued stoic pretense as the dutiful wife to a man she loathed, she diligently concealed her growing love for a man for whom she had no business feeling that way. Hagen would walk out of her life once he fulfilled his duty and, for all she knew, he'd return to a wife and children.

For weeks, she'd yearned to speak more than a few polite words to him. The hastily scribbled escape notes they'd passed under Eddie's nose were as precious to her as love letters, but they didn't go far in softening the fact that she was now chained to a truck and to the man J. Edgar Hoover had sent to help her.

She clung to Hagen as tightly as she clung to the hope they'd get away before Eddie arrived. It meant curtains for them if they didn't.

Chapter Two

From the depths of his chest and with everything he had, Hagen Kane used his last breath to yell like Granddad Kane showed him. Sand pinned his arms, burned his eyes, filled his mouth. His ears rang; head pounded. No one knew where he was. They'd never find him. He'd never ride his horse again or go to school or play with his new puppy. His mother would cry. Consciousness faded...

Jerking awake from the depths of his recurring nightmare, Hagen rolled onto his back. He stared into the murky shadows, while his racing heart slowed, and the terrible memories of being buried alive eased from his mind. With a shaking hand, he swiped the perspiration beaded on his forehead then craned his neck for a look around.

Although distorted, like peering through a sooty windowpane, there was enough light to make out a car up on blocks and other vehicles parked along the walls. A narrow metal ladder reached vertically to a loft area. A desk and chair butted up against another wall with a water pipe running along at shoulder height. A myriad of early morning city noises made their way into his foggy stupor. Cars puttered. A truck backfired. A rooster crowed. Horns honked. Doors slammed. The sound of muffled talking and intermittent radio static came from somewhere close, but he couldn't pinpoint the source. Maybe from the other side of the door—

It all rushed back like a freight train on a downhill grade. He lurched up, but his arm caught.

"What the hell?"

He yanked his arm to free it, but only succeeded in causing the metal ring around his wrist to gouge into his skin and the chain attached to it to clang and rattle. "Son of a bitch!"

A hand clamped over his mouth at the same instant someone hissed at his ear. "*Shh*! We've got guards out front. I'd rather not be gagged."

Ceara! "I was afraid I'd never see you again."

He drew her into his arms, and she clutched handfuls of his shirt, her head nodding against his chest.

"I thought the same of you." Her whispered words held a tremor of held-back tears.

How he'd longed for this moment. How he'd dreamed of holding her, to tell her his feelings, to kiss her. But that was fantasy, and this was cold, hard reality. He released her, and scooted back a respectful distance. This wasn't personal for her. She expected him to do his job, even though he'd crossed the line between love and duty the instant he'd laid eyes on her. In one blink of her baby blues, he'd gone from impartial lawman to a man in love with a crime boss's wife. In his profession, that was a hell of a shitty place to be stuck. And he was stuck so tightly, he couldn't see a way out unless she went with him, and that wasn't going to happen.

Speckles of blood dotted her white nurse's uniform and apron like dirty splatters from stomping in a mud puddle. *Damn that mealy-mouthed Jucca and his flick-knife.*

Voice low, he asked, "How badly are you hurt? They worked you over pretty hard."

That was an understatement. When the two thugs were done haranguing and playing rough with her, Jucca had put his hands on her in places he'd no right, leering and promising total violation of her body. Hagen swore he'd wring the slimy little bastard's chicken-neck for every illicit touch. But she'd taken everything Rocchelli's apes had dished out, and she hadn't cracked. She was a woman of singular steel and mettle, and she deserved a better life than the one she was trapped in.

"I've been better, but it's nothing that won't heal." The forced levity in her voice fell short of funny. "You?"

"Other than my head feels like it's been squeezed in a vice, I'm all right."

"I figured out their game early-on that they weren't going to kill me or seriously hurt me. I wasn't so sure about you."

"I wasn't so sure about either of us."

"I must have fainted. I don't remember how I got back here."

"It was a good thing you did. After they dragged you off, I mouthed off one too many times, and Jucca let me have it." Hagen rubbed the knot on his head. "Any idea where we are? Looks like a garage."

"I think this is Bugs Moran's booze warehouse on North Clark Street in the Lincoln Park area. If it is, there will be a sign on the front about a shipping and hauling business. I recall a boarding house or apartment building across the street and a bakery and grocery, maybe a delicatessen just a quick walk away. It's a typical busy Chicago neighborhood."

"Obviously, you've been here before."

"Once with Eddie. He left me out front in the fake office while he came back here, but I peeked and eavesdropped. It sounded like he was finalizing the transport of a hijacked load of whiskey."

Mindful to keep the noise down, Hagen took a firm grip on the chain, braced a foot for leverage, and pulled for all he was worth. Nothing. Not an inch of give. "Any idea what time they brought me in here?" He checked his watch and turned the stem a few times.

"Around two." Ceara related what she'd overheard.

"It doesn't take a fortune teller to predict what Rocchelli's got in mind for us when he gets here."

"Men like Eddie aren't known for their understanding natures, especially when it comes to their wives running off with other men." Ceara fiddled with the band of steel around her wrist.

"Yeah. I know. He's got a short fuse and the chops to back him up. He wields some real power in Chicago. He's a rising kingpin. He's bullied-out most of the small-time bootleggers and racketeers, which means he's setting himself up to give both Capone and Moran competition. If they aren't careful, Rocchelli will run them both out of town, too, or make them conveniently disappear and take over their territories."

"When you combine all of that with his inheritance, Eddie could be unstoppable before either Capone or Moran realizes what's happening."

Hagen rubbed both hands over his face then scrubbed his knuckles into his eyes as he heaved a tired exhale.

"I'm sorry."

"For what?" Hagen asked.

"For everything that's gone wrong. The security guard at the station wasted no time turning us over to Eddie's henchmen once he recognized me."

"Hey, we gave it a shot and got caught. It happens. Now we know what won't work, so we'll make a better plan." It wasn't much of a condolence, but it was the best he had.

"When Eddie finds out his accounting ledgers are missing, he'll know I took them. If he figures out you're a Bureau agent and that we planned this together..." A shuddering, breathy, almost-sob caught in her throat. "He'll kill you to punish me."

Her words, tinged with unshed tears, reached out and squeezed his heart. "I've gotten myself out of tight spots before, so don't put me in the grave just yet. There's a crime boss's wife I want to take to dinner before I die." It was a lame attempt to ease her worries, but seeing her little smile was worth it.

"I'm holding you to that."

Lord, how he wanted to kiss her. He could give her such a life—a life built on love and respect, not one endured in fear and regret. But she wasn't his, nor could she be, even if they managed to get out of this alive. He was a lawman sworn to protect and deliver a witness in possession of incriminating evidence into J. Edgar Hoover's keeping. His personal wants and wishes had no place in this situation.

Clamping the lid down on his feelings, he asked, "What's the earliest Rocchelli will know his ledgers are gone?"

"Sunday afternoon if he sticks to his routine."

"Three days." Hagen worked that around in his head. "It might go easier on you if he knew before that. Use them to bargain with."

"You want me to tell him?"

"If you can work it to your advantage. He respects ambition, and he understands negotiation from a position of power."

"He does, but he also has a temper that turns him into a raving madman."

"I know. I've seen it first-hand. He was sparring with a guy with better boxing skills." Hagen exhaled a long, tired breath.

"The guy rubbed his nose in it, and it took four of Eddie's men to pull him off before he beat the poor chump to death."

He didn't explain the real purpose of the row of tightly-set rubies on half of the wide silver band Rocchelli wore on the middle finger of his right hand. The rubies were a special cut for slicing an opponent's face to shreds. Normally, he wore the ring with rubies on the palm side. With a quick twist, the rubies were as deadly as a set of brass knuckles.

"Boxing and prizefights are his passions. He spends hours at them, either watching or participating. He drops a lot of money into it. When he's in the boxing ring, or when he's backing a fighter, he intends to win."

"I've sparred with him twice. I know how he fights."

He had boxing experience, and it had taken him only a few minutes to know Rocchelli's technique was rough-edged and without discipline, especially when he got mad, which happened at the drop of a hat. Rocchelli was a street brawler with the strength of a bear. He carried solid, meaty muscle in his chest, shoulders, and arms with stout, thick tree-trunk thighs that rooted him to the ground. Opponents underappreciated his shorter-than-average stature relative to the power that fueled his fists. His compact stature was a deception he used to his advantage, for he moved with cat-like grace when it suited him.

"Every winning streak eventually runs out. Ask anyone who bets on the ponies." Hagen scowled at their handcuffed arms. "I don't have to tell you this, but we've got to get out of these cuffs and off the chain if we're going to have any chance to escape."

"If I had a bobby pin, I could pick the locks."

"You pick locks?"

"Any Five Points girl worth her salt can. Handcuff locks are not at all sophisticated, and these are old, which makes them even easier to open."

Hagen made a production of checking his pockets and his hair. "Sorry, I'm fresh out of bobby pins."

Ceara patted her hair. "It seems when I lost my uniform cap, the bobby pins went with it." Her smile faded when she shivered.

"Hey, come here. We've got a blanket. Let's use it."

Working around their common tether, they huddled under the blanket with their backs against the truck door. Hagen put his arm around her shoulders and drew her closer.

"The personal service in this joint stinks."

Hagen chuckled. "Breakfast would hit the spot, all right. I can at least buy you a cup of joe when this is behind us."

"First dinner and now coffee. I'd like that."

Their combined body heat eased some of his soreness, and he relaxed. In a few minutes, Ceara's head dipped forward, and he snuggled her into a more comfortable position to hold her while she slept. Closing his eyes, he rested his cheek against her head and let his lawman's planning mind go to work.

***

"*Ohhh, no,*" Ceara moaned. "We're still in the warehouse." She shifted position. "I'd hoped it was a bad dream."

"Nope, not a bad dream, but it is Valentine's Day, if that helps."

"Quite a gift, wouldn't you say?" She lifted their chain-connected arms. "His and Hers matching jewelry. I would have preferred a box of chocolates."

Hagen grinned. "I'll keep that in mind."

"What time is it?"

"Coming on to ten. They're starting to show up. The two boys out front have been skittish as bachelors at a Sunday box social. They've checked on us every few minutes for the last two hours. I asked for breakfast, but the hospitality in this place is lacking."

"You'll have a chance to complain to the management when Eddie gets here."

Hagen chuckled. "I'll do that." He stretched his back and shoulders to lessen the ache. "Do you know where the Bureau office is?"

"No. Why?"

"If you get out of here without me, do you think you could find it?"

"Probably."

"When you do, tell them you need to contact Wes Lansing in Amarillo. He'll handle everything."

She responded with a half-hearted nod.

"What does that mean?"

"I'll think about it."

"While you're thinking, tell me what you did with the ledgers."

"If you don't know, then Eddie can't force it out of you."

Hagen grunt-scoffed. "He can't get anything out of me. I'm a whole lot tougher than Hoover's pretty boys. Most of them can't even use a gun."

"What do you mean? Can't or don't? That seems a rather crucial distinction in relationship to our survival."

"It's like this. Hoover has two types of agents. The ones he's most proud of are his college boys. They tend to have law or accounting degrees, and they hail from respectable, moneyed families. They don't drink booze or use tobacco and, on the whole, they stay away from women. More importantly, they don't carry guns. It's against Bureau policy. Even if they did pack iron, most of them wouldn't know which way to point the business end to keep from shooting themselves in the foot."

"Oh, that's just swell." She threw her hands up.

Hagen chuckled low in his throat at her exaggerated reaction. "Those boys represent the image of sophistication, education, honesty, and integrity Hoover puts out for the public. They're his gentlemen investigators. They do the legwork on cases. Once it's time for the arrest, they're done, because that's where their authority ends. The local police take over."

Ceara's eyebrows puckered into a deep frown. "So, Hoover sent me a pathetic namby-pamby over-educated do-gooder who can't use a gun?" She drew her knees to her chest and locked her fingers across her shins.

"No. I said I wasn't one of them. I'm a Texas boy, born and raised. I'm in Hoover's other group."

"Hoover has categories of agents?"

"Yeah. We're what he calls his no bullshit cowboys—Pardon my colorful language. We're Texas and Arizona Rangers or veteran lawmen from the southwest. We've got the reputation and philosophy Hoover admires, but can't publicize or admit to. When we show up, Hoover looks the other way, so we can break the rules of Bureau etiquette without him owning up to it. We take care of the problems in ways the Bureau can't."

"Which are you? Ranger or lawman?"

"Texas Ranger. Hoover needed a new face. Someone who'd never taken a Bureau case and who wasn't likely to be recognized east of the Mississippi. My orders are to get you and Rocchelli's accounting ledgers to the nearest Bureau office. From there, you'll have Bureau protection all the way to Washington, D. C."

"But not by you."

He hoped his off-handed shrug masked his regret. "I'm the cavalry, not the escort brigade. My authority ends when I get you to Hoover's men."

"I see."

Was there disappointment in those two words, or was he just hearing what he wanted in her tone? "But I need the location of the ledgers."

"No."

"If you're dead, and no one knows where the ledgers are, then all you've been through has been for nothing."

"They're in a safe place. They won't be forgotten."

"Where?"

"Just...a safe place."

"Listen!" Hagen raised a silencing hand. The outer office door opened, closed, and voices rose in animated conversation. With an eye on the door, he spoke out of the side of his mouth. "Other than staying alive, our goal is to get loose from the chain and out of these handcuffs."

Ceara bobbed her head that she understood, her gaze glued to the door.

Hagen advised, "Whatever happens, play along until we get our break. There's always a way out, unless we're dead, and I'm not ready to die. Not by a long shot. And especially not at the hands of a mobster known as *The Roach.*"

Chapter Three

Ceara dreaded as much as wished whatever was going to happen would get going. From the sound of the voices, there could have been five or fifteen men in the office. She thought she recognized one of the voices as the optician-turned-gambler who had come to dinner just two weeks ago, but she couldn't recall his name. A dog barked and received a sharp *Shut up!* The telephone rang.

Then, just like that, the waiting was over. Hagen gave her a hand up as Leo entered from the front. Leo remained at the side of the door where he had a good view of the warehouse, his Browning automatic rifle balanced in the crook of his arm like it was an extension of his body. Seconds later, the bar across the panel-doors at the back lifted from the outside. The doors parted in the center overlap, and Paul came in, his scowl as unpleasant as the Thompson submachine gun he carried.

"So, how'd you two lovebirds make out last night?" Paul chuckled at his joke.

"Finer'n frog hair," Hagen drawled. "But it was a long night. I need to use the john."

"Ooh, I need to go, too. I thought you guys would never get here." What hadn't been a problem suddenly became an urgent necessity.

"You can wait."

Certain she'd get nowhere with him, Ceara gave Leo her best pitiful-face plea as she wiggled foot to foot. "Please." No surprise. Leo gave in.

"It won't hurt to show them some decency. There's plenty of time to lock them back up before Eddie gets here."

"Are you jingle-brained? Eddie'll skin us alive if we lose them."

"He won't know from nothing if we don't tell him." Leo passed his B-A-R to Paul then dug into his trousers pocket for the handcuff key. "You're a good egg, Hagen. Don't make me regret this." He inserted the key into the hole, gave it a turn to release the teeth, and the ring opened. The chain slipped free and clanged on the concrete.

Hagen rubbed his wrist. "I won't promise anything, but I'll remember the compliment."

Leo almost smiled. "Do that. It's the only one you'll get from me." He worked the key into the slot on Ceara's handcuff, turning the key this way and that. "It's jammed, Sis, but it won't get any tighter. Think of it as an ugly bracelet."

"Thank you. You've always been kind to me." Nice words couldn't hurt.

Despite his position as Eddie's second-in-command, she liked Leo. She couldn't help it.

Embarrassed, Leo *hrmpfted* a dismissive grunt, retrieved his rifle from Paul, and motioned toward the back of the warehouse. "The john's in that little room. Make it quick." He kept them both under casual rifle cover to keep them honest.

Paul blocked Hagen's way. "I told Eddie you were trouble when he hired you. I haven't changed my mind. Don't try anything funny. Eddie didn't say we had to keep you alive. Just her." He pushed past Hagen and went into the office.

Ceara pulled the lightbulb chain hanging over the sink, cupped water into her hands, and drank her fill despite the tinny flavor. The john was as cold as it was filthy, but Ceara ignored both. She dawdled until Leo rapped on the door.

"You've got to come out sometime, Sis."

She waited outside the door under Leo's watchful eye until Hagen emerged, then Leo herded them toward the front. Paul returned carrying a cup of coffee. The pungent aroma combined with the rising steam reminded Ceara's stomach how empty it was, which gave her an idea.

Paul explained, "The guys out front think Eddie's taking care of a couple of double-crossing snitches for Bugs, so don't think that yelling for help will do you any good. Get my drift?" He gestured with his Thompson. "Leo, chain them up."

"Hagen, you saw how they came off. Hook yourself to her."

Ceara collapsed at Leo's feet.

Hagen dropped to his knees beside her. "What's wrong? Talk to me." Ceara winked on the sly. Hagen caught her meaning. "She's fainted. Bring me that blanket."

"Ah, crap," Paul groused. "Get her up."

Hagen tapped her cheeks. Ceara blinked and made an overblown attempt to sit up while passing her hand over her forehead as she fell back into Hagen's arms in a dramatic swoon.

"It's so cold... I haven't eaten..."

"You dizzy dame. What the hell are you doing? Leo, cuff them. *Now*!"

"Please," Ceara pleaded. "Let me rest here for a few minutes."

"You can rest while you're chained—"

The sound of car tires crunching on gravel in the alley cut Paul off. Striding to the panel-doors, he cracked them to peer out.

"Eddie's here."

Not unkindly, Leo coaxed, "Nice try, Sis, but no more games. Better get up."

Cecil Murra, Eddie's favorite among his stable of personal bodyguards, stepped partway inside the warehouse and gave it a quick once-over. Satisfied all was kosher, he made a curt all-clear wave. Taking his position beside the doors, Cecil crossed his arms over his chest and stood like a stone gargoyle guarding palace gates. A car door in the alley opened and closed. Her hatred had a name, and he was coming through those doors.

Edoardo Giovanni Vincenzo Rocchelli entered the warehouse with the bearing of a king receiving supplicants. In spite of herself, Ceara's breath hitched. He cut a fine figure of a man who reeked of seedy sophistication all wrapped up in an aura of lethal confidence.

Aside to Cecil, Eddie said, "Keep an eye on the alley. Phil stays with the car."

"Sure, Boss." Cecil went outside.

Although dark glasses masked his eyes, Eddie swept his gaze around the warehouse in a manner that appeared bored and uninterested. He idly brushed the dusting of snow from his shoulders and opened his double-breasted overcoat. Ceara wasn't fooled at his apparent disinterest. Eddie missed nothing.

As he strolled toward her, she took in his appearance from his tailored suit and one of his many custom-make eight-hundred-dollar silk vests that served as body armor, to his gleaming, patent leather wingtip oxfords. The silver tips were only slightly less brilliant than his diamond-studded platinum watch chain. His black felt fedora, perched at a jaunty angle, added another layer of arrogance, power, and affluence to his formidable presence. It was no wonder men and women looked twice at him. It was impossible not to.

His promenade of power ended in front of her. He took his time tucking away his dark glasses in a vest pocket while giving her the up and down. Removing his white leather gloves one slow finger pull at a time was another intimidation strategy she'd witnessed with a back-talking snitch.

"I see you sweet-talked your way out of the handcuffs."

She flinched, expecting to feel the gloves on her face. "Only half of them."

"Boss, we were—"

Eddie silenced Paul with a brusque wave. "Paul tells me you gave my boys the slip at the hospital and made it to Union Station before someone spotted you. How'd you get by them?"

"They're stupid."

"What's the grift, babe?"

Feigning innocence, Ceara said, "I'm not trying to pull anything."

"Don't give me that line. You think I'm some sort of patsy? A weak sister? You stole something of mine, something private, and I want it back." He rhythmically tapped the gloves against the palm of one hand.

So much for hoping he wouldn't miss his ledgers until Sunday. Begging forgiveness was as demeaning as it was futile to deny his accusation. Reaching into the depths of her well of survival, she grasped hold of her courage, and looked her husband squarely in the eyes.

"I assume you're referring to the accounting ledgers of your clandestine dealings, and your personal journal that shows the transactions and shipments of booze you've been skimming from Moran and Capone and some lesser crooks. The books that list names of every person you have on the take or on your payroll right on up the political and law enforcement line?" Gaining steam, she propped her hands on her hips. "You mean those books?"

A corner of his mouth twitched. "What did you do with them?"

She flashed him a saucy smirk to fuel her sassy-mouthed fire. "I made a deal with the *Lakeshore Daily News* for twenty grand. It's enough so I can live in style, get a new name, and a new life. You'll read all about it in tomorrow's edition."

"Don't crack wise with me. Try again, kitten." He slapped her with the gloves.

Ceara pressed the back of her hand to her lips. She could make it easy on herself or, at least easier, but her Irish temperament wasn't about to cooperate.

"I mailed half of the ledgers to Capone and half to Moran along with a personal note. No doubt they'll crack your code. I did. You'll hear from them by tonight." She lifted a *wait-a-minute* finger. "No. That's not quite true. I didn't send the journal of your running notes. I anticipated needing bargaining leverage, so I kept it and put it in an especially safe place."

The leather gloves packed a punch this time. Eyes watering, she gingerly touched her fingertips to the hot welt rising on her cheekbone. She laughed. He had a knack for bringing out the fight in her.

"What's wrong, Eddie? Scared of what they'll do when they find out you've been playing them both for suckers? If I were you, I'd be more scared of Capone than Moran. Capone is sneaky when he gets even. He'll send goons after you when you least expect it. Moran is right out in the open with his revenge, and he just keeps coming. He'll have men gunning for you in broad daylight. You may think you're hard-boiled, but you'd be wise to keep your back to the wall, or maybe even leave the country."

"What's she talking about?" Leo asked. "What books? I thought this was about them running off together."

Eddie snarled, "Shut up. She's just flapping her gums. Her smart mouth is gonna get her in trouble one of these days. All you need to know is things have changed since I got back to town."

Jucca came in from the office. "Hey, Boss. We need to talk."

The two men moved aside and stood with heads together, Jucca's voice too low to distinguish words. Eddie listened without comment, but the beady-eyed sidelong glances that Jucca threw toward Hagen sent Ceara's heart into her throat and her hands sweating. The telephone rang. Someone shouted at the barking dog. Eddie turned on his heel and came toward her. The change in his countenance was subtle, but evident for someone who knew the signs, which she did. It was in his eyes, plus he was calm, too calm, which meant he was killing mad. She'd experienced this Eddie first-hand, and it had almost killed her. Small talk was over.

Jucca trailed at his heels like the cur he was. Eddie snapped his fingers. Jucca grabbed her arm and wrenched it behind her back. Searing pain burned between her shoulders. Jucca's tobacco breath and the steely edge of his flick-knife hovered at her cheek. Paul blocked Hagen from intervening.

"Think twice, buddy-boy."

"Yeah, *buddy-boy*," Jucca goaded. "Give me a reason to carve my initials on her pretty puss."

Hagen took a step back.

Eddie lifted Ceara's left hand. "Where's your wedding ring?"

"I tossed it into a gutter. It seemed only fitting." She uttered a cry of pain when Jucca twisted her arm again.

"Want me to fix her smart mouth, Boss?" Jucca moved the tip of his knife to the corner of her mouth.

Eddie waved Jucca off as he released her hand. He took a step closer to Hagen. "What's the story, cowboy? Why were you running off with my wife?"

Hagen dragged his gaze from Jucca to Rocchelli. He shrugged. "She offered me money to help her leave you."

Eddie gestured for Hagen to lean closer. Tone hushed, lips tight, he asked, "Where are my fucking ledgers?"

Hagen slapped him on the shoulder like they were old buddies. "I don't fucking know." His smirk spread to a full, mocking grin, but his eyes were steel-steady.

"Aldo. Help him remember."

Ceara dropped her right shoulder and clamped her hand in Jucca's crotch with a violent twist. He squealed and swiped at her face as she tore free of his grip.

Red-faced, clutching his crotch, Jucca snarled, "You'll pay for that, bitch. I like to make naughty girls beg and scream."

Ceara felt blood trickling down her left cheek before she noticed the pain. She pressed her cheek to her shoulder, which left a bloody smear on her white uniform.

"Enough games." Eddie looked at Hagen. "Aldo will take her apart slice by slice until one of you comes clean about my books. Ya follow?"

"If that weaselly bastard touches her again, I'll gut you like a fish just before I cut out his fucking heart and feed it to him." Hagen's voice, deep and hard, held the promise of his words.

Jucca sneered. "Shee-it. You pansy-ass daisy—"

Hagen shoved Paul and planted a smashing fist into Jucca's face, sending his flick-knife skittering on the concrete and Jucca to the floor. Jucca rolled to his feet, swept up his knife and held it low at his side, his gaze hot to get even.

"I'm gonna fill you with daylight, pretty boy."

"Not today." Hagen went for him.

"Knock it off!" Leo stepped between them his Browning aimed at Hagen's midsection.

"This ain't over." Jucca stabbed the air in mock attack.

Eddie grabbed Ceara's arm and yanked her around to face him. "Cut the Dumb Dora routine. Where are my ledgers? I'll know if you're lying."

Something inside her shifted. She was in an all-or-nothing fight for her life. There was no reason to continue hiding the circumstances that brought them to this confrontation.

"On the level? All right. I'll give it to you straight. I lifted the ledgers from your desk right after you left for St. Louis. I mailed them in two packages to Washington, D. C. with general delivery to me."

A slow, smug grin moved the cruel hard line of Eddie's mouth. "That wasn't smart. It's nothing for me to get them."

"I'm way ahead of you. I also sent a letter to a friend who lives there with instructions to claim the packages. If I don't make it to D. C. by noon on Monday, she'll know I'm dead, or I wasn't able to get away from you, which is the same thing. She'll deliver the packages to the person I contacted to trade your ledgers for protection and my freedom."

"You gonna tell me who?"

Ceara took her time savoring this moment. "J. Edgar Hoover."

Saying his name was like candy in her mouth—sweet and satisfying. The few seconds it took Eddie to comprehend were the most gratifying moments of her life. Then, his face turned dark and ugly.

"It's payback time, Eddie." Ceara allowed herself a self-righteous smile.

"Payback for what?"

Silence fell like the eerie quiet after the first shovelful of dirt on a coffin.

"A baby's life."

Chapter Four

Ceara was determined to get her story out before Eddie stopped her. "Leo, remember last August when men broke into the house to kill Eddie, and they attacked me?"

Leo nodded. "It was the same gang that made the drive-by in July when you two came out of his Cicero restaurant. They missed that day, so they made a hit on the house. Eddie got off a few shots. We combed the place, but never found them. We beefed up security after that."

"Aldo!" Eddie snapped his fingers. "Shut her up!"

Hagen planted himself in front of Ceara before Jucca could reach her. "You'll have to go through me, little man. Let her talk." Hagen locked Jucca with a hard gaze that dared him to make a move.

"Everyone take it easy." Leo swung his Browning in a general way that might have been meant for Jucca, but it also served as an indirect warning to the other men. "Go ahead, Sis. I've had questions about that night."

"She's got nothing to say." Eddie threatened, "I won't take your guff, Leo. I own you. Your wife. Your kids. New grandson. Remember that."

Leo stood firm. "I want to hear what she has to say. Her side."

Eddie exploded. "She has no fucking side! And you have no questions. She's stalling to save herself." Through clenched teeth, he hissed, "This conversation is *over*."

Silently thanking Leo, Ceara blurted, "The failed hit at the restaurant gave Eddie the idea for the lie he concocted to cover up what really happened. No one broke into the house. I walked in on him while he was cooking his books, although I didn't know it at the time. He thought I'd seen something I shouldn't have." She leveled a hot glare of loathing on Eddie. "But I hadn't seen anything."

Ceara left Hagen's well-meant, but unrealistic protection to stand in front of Eddie. This was between them now as husband and wife. She would speak the truth before she died.

"You'll have to kill me to keep me quiet now. Since that's what you're planning, I have nothing to lose." Confidence blossomed within. "While I lay in the hospital all those days, I mourned the death of our baby—my baby who didn't have a chance at life, because of you." With her loathing for Eddie as the weapon, she beat down the choking sobs welling in her chest as those all-too-raw memories rushed back.

"The only reason I wanted to live was to get even with you. My hatred gave me strength. I was determined to find out what you were hiding. When I found it, I knew it was my ticket out of town. I made a deal with Hoover for your ledgers and my sworn deposition in exchange for a new life where you'd never find me."

"You double-crossing, fucking bitch!"

Eddie swung a wicked backhand that rocked her to her toes. She teetered, but kept her feet.

Paul stopped Hagen. "Stay put. This isn't your party."

Ceara wiped the back of her hand over her bloody lips. "Your men... Look at them. They're remembering that night and putting it together." Acid, corrosive and malignant, dripped from her words.

Eddie's eyes frosted. She saw her death in his icy glare the instant before he clamped his meaty hands around her neck. He dug his thumbs into her throat. She clawed his hands; her lungs burned. Hagen yelled her name, lunged for her. Paul knocked him down. Spots floated in her vision. Blood roared in her ears. Voices became hollow echoes. After all she'd been through, it was too cruel to die this way. Darkness descended in her mind. Consciousness faded. She drifted into nothingness...

A violent jerk brought her back. On her knees, she clutched her throat while sucking in great coughing gulps of air.

"—can take her for a ride later and make it look like she pulled a Dutch act, but you're not going to kill her in front of me."

Eddie broke from Leo's grip. He grabbed a handful of Ceara's hair and yanked her head back. He bellowed, "How did you contact Hoover? I made sure you were never alone. Not even when you went back to work."

Almost sobbing, Ceara clawed his hands to break his powerful hold on the top of her head. "You're not the only one with connections. You made enemies. I used them."

Paul pulled Eddie off her. "No more, Eddie. No more. Not here, like Leo said. You've got other business to take care of. Moran and the whiskey will be here any minute. This will wait."

Paul's level-headed insistence got through to Eddie's maddened mind, and he discarded Ceara like she was so much trash as he wheeled on his men.

"Which one of you palookas is the traitor?" He raked an accusing glare over the men then he cut a suspicious look toward the alley. "Cecil? Phil? Who?"

"Lay off, Eddie. It wasn't them. They're loyal to you." Ceara clambered to her feet, rubbing her bruised neck. She exchanged a fleeting glance with Hagen. He swiped at the blood trickling into his eyes while managing a reassuring half-grin as he got to his feet.

"Then who was it?" Eddie demanded.

"You can go to hell wondering." Ceara braced herself for the assault.

"Then I'll get it out of your boyfriend."

There was no surprise in his threat. "He's not my boyfriend. He doesn't know anything. We had a business arrangement. I paid him to help me get out of town. He said it was time for him to move on, anyway."

Eddie considered for several moments. "That so, Cowboy?"

"I'm always looking for a few extra *simoleans*, and the price was right."

"You been ninety sixing my wife?"

"We got pinched before I had the chance." Hagen flashed Eddie a grin that begged to be squashed. Eddie accommodated him with a fist to his belly that doubled Hagen over.

"Aldo nosed around. He says your name is Hagen Kane, and you're a private dick. A no account gumshoe that my cheating, whoring wife somehow hired to get her and my books to Hoover."

Bent double, his hands braced on his thighs, and his head cocked, some seconds passed before Hagen straightened to his full height. Then he rolled his shoulders and flexed his fingers. With a self-satisfied grin, Hagen said, "Jucca is as stupid as his informant. I'm a Texas Ranger."

Two more wicked punches to his belly put Hagen to his knees. Eddie loomed over him.

"If you're smart, cowboy, you'll stay down." Eddie swung his attention to Ceara, a dark, sinister sneer of triumph on his face. "Call off Hoover, and I'll let your family live."

He expected her to crumble under his superior position. She saw it in his eyes, but what he didn't understand was she was beyond that. Her mocking, scornful laughter echoed in the cold warehouse.

"That's an empty threat. You know where I come from—the same place where Capone earned his reputation. Five Points. We're tough, and we know how to survive. All my life, my parents have payed-out honest money to corrupt cops and strong-arm thugs just like you. You're nothing, Eddie, nothing but a small-time fish who wants to swim in the big pond with the barracudas. Capone and Moran are going to chew you up and spit you out. Wait and see."

"Boss... The whiskey," Paul reminded.

Eddie listened to Paul this time. "Shut them in the john. Tie and gag 'em. I'll deal with them later."

Jucca snorted a laugh. "Yeah, and I'm gonna help him." He held his knife low and close at his hip, his lips pulled back in a snarl from his tiny, yellow teeth. "And I'm gonna hear you beg, bitch. Beg for more."

The sound of his sniveling chuckle crawled along Ceara's arms like a scurrying centipede. If he got his hands on her, the beatings she'd taken from Eddie would be cakewalks compared to the unspeakable torture Jucca could dredge up from the depths of his demented mind.

Hagen tackled Jucca like a coiled rattler striking unwary prey, wrenching the knife from his hand as he rolled to his feet. Jucca scrambled up.

"I want my knife."

Paul stepped between them, the barrel of his Thompson aimed at Hagen's midsection. "Knock it off! Kane, you're pushing me. Drop the shiv and get over there."

Hagen lowered the knife. "Sure thing. Let's see if he can fetch."

With a lunge and a swipe, Hagen nicked Jucca's right ear as he sent the knife flying toward the cargo doors. Jucca howled and clutched his ear. Blood oozed between his fingers. Hagen slapped the Thompson away as he lunged at Jucca and planted a fist on his jaw that dropped him on the spot.

The cargo doors parted, drawing Paul's attention from Hagen. Cecil came in ahead of two men. One man pulled out a pump action shotgun from inside his trench coat. The other did the same with a Thompson. Paul and Leo closed in around Eddie, their weapons ready. Eddie's right hand slipped inside his suit coat where he kept his gun.

Cecil waved off their suspicion. "It's all silk, Boss. I know them. They're regular. The Markley brothers. Bart and Willis. They're with the Stokowski Gang out of Kansas City. They've got business with some of the guys out front. Doesn't have anything to do with your business."

"All right, Cecil. I'll take your word." Eddie spoke a low warning to Ceara. "Not a peep, not a wrong move, or when Aldo comes-to, I'll turn him loose on you with his shiv. That goes for you, too. *Capisce*?"

Leo hauled Jucca to his feet and shook him like a dog playing with a rag doll. "You dim wit, Aldo. Wake up."

Jucca blinked without coherence, but he stayed upright when Leo released him.

Cecil returned to his post in the alley. The Markley brothers walked up to Eddie.

With a knowing wink, Bart said, "We were surprised to see your boiler parked in the alley. Simplifies things for us."

Hagen cut his gaze toward the cargo doors in answer to Ceara's eyebrows-raised, *What do we do now?*

Paul cautioned, "There's something hinky—"

Eddie squelched him with a hard glare. Eyeing the Markleys, and guardedly curious, he asked, "Something wrong with the whiskey shipments?"

The brothers laughed like he'd told a funny joke.

"Whiskey...*riiight*." Willis winked and clicked his tongue. "We're not interested in what's going on back here, but all of you in one place is like icing on cake. You follow what I'm saying? Now, here's the dope. Some of us will be going out the front like we own the joint." As an afterthought, he added, "And when the *coppers* show up, don't count on them caring what happens, because they won't, if you get my meaning."

"Thanks for the tip." Eddie made another silencing gesture to Paul and Leo as the Markley brothers assumed positions on either side of the closed office door.

Eddie checked his watch. Voice low, he said, "Bugs'll be walking through the front door right about now. We're the shotgun messengers for the whiskey, which will arrive right after Bugs gets here. He'll have men with him to transfer the cases to the trucks parked at the back doors. We'll move them out to distributors before anyone gets wise." He jerked a nod toward Ceara. "Lock her in the john with Kane." He walked to the office wall and pushed aside a pin-up calendar in order to peer through the peephole.

Paul motioned to Ceara with the Tommy gun. "You heard him. You, too, Kane. Get moving."

The street door banged open and a booming voice laid down commands that rang loud and clear to the cargo doors.

"Police raid! Drop your weapons! Hands up. Move to the back. Line up against the wall."

"It's a hit!" Eddie stumbled over his feet in his frantic retreat, his face white as death. "Downing's Rats! Chopper squad. *Scram*!"

Ceara sidestepped Eddie's wild grab, which threw him off balance. He slammed into Leo who plowed into Paul, and they all went down in a heap. Leo's Browning skidded. Hagen snatched it up in almost the same motion as taking possession of Paul's Thompson right out of his hands.

"Rocchelli! How's it feel to be a patsy?" Bart Markley bore down on Eddie. "Here's a goodbye message from—"

Eddie fired twice, and he didn't miss either brother.

Ceara, already dodging and ducking her way around the crates and vehicles on a run toward the doors, spied Jucca's knife. She scooped it up on the fly, folded the blade, and dropped it into her apron pocket. She burst through the center of the doors and hit Cecil full-on. Her momentum took them to the ground. She scrambled on hands and knees, but he snagged her ankle.

"Not so fast, cookie!"

The heel of her shoe to his face smashed his nose in a spray of blood and crunching bone. She kept kicking until he released her and her last kick caught him in the throat. He collapsed on his back, gasping, and she scrambled over him, helping herself to his gun as she went.

Behind her, Hagen yelled, "*Ceara*! *Get down*!"

She dropped. Phil charged around the front of Eddie's car, bearing down on her with a double-barreled shotgun. His trousers caught on the bumper, and he fell flat just as Hagen fired. Hit or not, Ceara couldn't tell as Phil rolled under the car, his shotgun on the ground out of reach.

Another bellowing command came loud and clear from inside the warehouse. "*Give it to them, boys! Give them some Chicago lightning*!" A deafening roar of shotgun blasts and the *rat-a-tat* staccato of submachinegun fire further shattered the frigid morning air.

"Drive!" Hagen hauled Ceara to her feet and shoved the Browning into her hands. "Don't lose this!"

Running, she glanced over her shoulder to see Eddie flee the warehouse with Paul right behind him and Leo dragging Jucca like a sack of potatoes. Hagen sent them diving for cover with a strafing spray from Paul's Thompson. Her moment of hope that Eddie had collected some of those bullets was dashed when she saw him using Jucca as a shield.

Ceara yanked the passenger door open and slid across the brocaded upholstered seat. She dumped the B-A-R on the floorboard, stuffed Cecil's pistol under her right thigh, and ground the gear shift into gear. She stomped on the accelerator as Hagen jumped on the running board, bracing himself in the open door, and gave the warehouse another round of bullets. The big car roared out of the alley with the back tires kicking up gravel like a blast of birdshot from a shotgun. She caught a glimpse of Cecil and Phil running the other way down the alley.

Ceara hit the street too fast and over-cranked the steering wheel. The tires squealed when they grabbed pavement. The passenger door slammed against Hagen, pinning him to the door frame. Ceara righted the front end and gunned the engine. The door swung wide, and Hagen dropped onto the seat as he leaned out to pull the door closed.

"Hagen!" Ceara screamed.

Eddie leaped onto the running board with a wild, swinging, meaty right fist that missed Hagen's head and connected with the door frame. Hagen rammed the butt of the Tommy gun into Eddie's gut, but Eddie deflected the blow and wrenched the Thompson from Hagen's hands, then flung the gun into the street.

Hagen yelled, "Keep going!"

Driving in the wrong lane, Ceara looked back to the street just in time to jerk the steering wheel in order to dodge an oncoming car that took to the sidewalk at the last moment before head-on impact. Her sharp turn dropped Eddie to the seat and on top of Hagen. Accelerator to the floor and the engine wrapped tight in a too-low gear, Ceara yanked the steering wheel back and forth, which sent the big car into a zig-zagging, curb-to-curb skid with the passenger door flapping like a window shutter in a high wind.

The yelling and cursing, grappling and thrashing all jumbled into a cacophony of physical chaos that trapped her against the door. Eddie's punch at Hagen's head missed and glanced off her shoulder. Eddie grabbed the wheel when Hagen came up with a head-butt to his forehead that didn't faze him, but he let go of the steering wheel and clamped his hands around Hagen's neck.

"Pull over!" Eddie yelled at Ceara. "Or I'll fucking kill him!"

Terror blazed through her. She knew the power in those hands. She grasped for Cecil's gun as Eddie yanked the steering wheel down, and her head smacked the window. The violent veer threw Eddie off balance. Hagen reared up, his voice exploding on the air with a sound neither human or animal. It was fierce and guttural, rising with a deep-throated, quavering howl that built to a blood curdling crescendo. Hagen's momentum propelled both men through the open doorway and onto the street.

The engine chugged toward death and coughed to a standstill when she slammed her foot on the brake. Just before the engine died, she remembered to depress the clutch. Grinding through the gears, she found reverse, alternately craning her neck to see in the mirrors and over her shoulder through the narrow rectangular back window. Weaving and jerking the steering wheel like a drunkard driving home on a Saturday night, when she skidded to a stop beside Hagen, it occurred to her she should have just turned around. Hagen yanked open the passenger side back door, hefted an inert Eddie up by his coat collar and seat of his trousers, and heaved him inside.

"What are you doing?"

"He's going with us. Find an alley and pull in. Too many witnesses here." Hagen slammed the back door and got into the front as Ceara took off. He held the sprung door to keep it closed while flexing the fingers on his left hand.

"Broken?" Ceara glanced at his hand.

"Naw. I got in a lucky punch after the back of his head hit the street. Must have primed him when I head-butted him. I've never seen him so much as stagger from any punch."

Three blocks farther, Ceara turned into an alley. Hagen made quick work of manhandling Eddie's bulk from his belly onto his back, but not before he relieved him of his custom grip 1903 Colt .32. He stuffed the gun into his waistband before he gagged Eddie with his own monogrammed handkerchief, buckled his leather belt around his ankles, and tied his hands behind his back with his silk tie.

Hagen got back in the front with a hard yank that partially latched the door. "Now get us the hell out of town. We don't want to get caught up in whatever happened back there. We can't tell the good guys from the bad guys." He took up the Browning from the floorboard and checked it over.

With a white-knuckle grip on the steering wheel, Ceara found her way onto a southbound street that merged easterly onto a two-lane blacktop. She was functioning on raw nerve and instinct that pointed her toward New York where her heart yearned to be—home.

Once the skyscrapers of Chicago were merely dark specks behind them, Hagen said, "Back off on the speed. We don't need extra attention."

Ceara slowed, brushed a trembling hand through her hair, and blew out a shaky breath. "I don't ever want to do that again." Her gaze darted from mirror to mirror. She raised in her seat to see her face in the mirror and dabbed the underside of her sleeve cuff at the thin line of crusted blood on her cheek.

"It was a hell of a ride, but we made it. As long as we stay alive, we can deal with the challenges of staying that way."

She made a hasty glance through the sliding glass window partition between the seats for reassurance that Eddie was still unconscious and tied. "It doesn't make sense. Eddie said it was Downing's Rats. They were a St. Louis gang that fell apart a couple of years ago when most of the gang went to prison."

"Whatever it was, we got out there alive thanks to that bullet soiree."

"What are we going to do with him?"

"Keep him where we can see him. It's safer that way. Now. Let's talk business. We need a telephone. Chicago isn't safe now. The nearest Bureau office is in Columbus. I'll call and tell them we're on the way. Agents in Washington will pick up the ledgers at the post office or from your friend if she's already claimed them."

Ceara exhaled a swift breath on another nervous glance over the seat.

"What's wrong? You're twitchy as a cat watching a bird on a low-hanging branch. He's out cold."

"The ledgers aren't in Washington. I had to give Eddie something reasonable to make him think I was too afraid to lie to him."

"A diversion."

"Yes."

"Where are they?"

She hesitated, fought with her conscience to lie again, then gave in to a partial truth. "New York City."

"Post office?"

"No. I sent them to a place of sanctuary within easy walking distance of where I grew up. It's even closer to where my parents live now."

"That's no help at all. Just tell me."

"I can't."

"Why not?"

"Stop pushing me! You're the special investigator. You figure it out."

"This is bullshit!" Hagen slammed his fist against the window.

Ceara ducked and flinched. Cowering against the door, she stared at the highway. How could she have misjudged his willingness to help her? He'd been so quiet and considerate, and now she was little better off with his temper than she'd been with Eddie's.

"Ceara—"

Shaking her head, she turned her shoulder to him. She had nothing more to say.

Chapter Five

"Ceara—" Hagen cast a scowl over the seat at the still unconscious Rocchelli. "I won't hurt you." *Damn Rocchelli for making her believe all men are bastards.* "Look at me...please."

Not a glance.

"I'm sorry."

Shoulders hunched, chin down, she retreated into a cocoon of silence. He wished he could take back his words and his lame-brained window punch. Combing his fingers through his hair, he cussed his big mouth.

"We'll stop at the next town and find the police—"

"No! No cops. Especially not small-time locals looking for their big break to make front page news."

Damn it. No matter what he did or said, he was wrong. It took him another couple of miles before the rough edges of his impatience smoothed out enough that he thought he could avoid getting a permanent cold shoulder.

"We have to have a plan to work with. We can change it as we go. Don't shake your head. Hear me out. We won't involve the law. We'll head straight for the Bureau office in Columbus. Soon as we find a telephone, I'll make a call and alert them to our status and location."

Encouraged that her lack of response wasn't an outright refusal, he dropped it. It wasn't a point they had to settle right then, so he circled back to the question that had gotten him sideways with her.

"Tell me about the ledgers. Something—anything—that'll help me."

She was shaking her head before he finished. "I'm not turning those books over to anyone now. Not even you. Once they're out of my control, I've lost all bargaining power with whomever I need to negotiate for my freedom and my family's safety, whether it's Eddie, Moran, Capone, Hoover, or someone else. You heard Eddie. He'll hurt my family to get what he wants out of me. His ledgers are all I have to keep me and my family alive."

"Things have changed. We have Rocchelli. When we get to Columbus, you'll press charges that he authorized your kidnapping and torture. That's enough to keep him locked up until Hoover steps in."

Her response was slow in coming. "I'll think on it."

Impatience pushed him to play his wild card. "Those ledgers are government evidence." He leaned toward her to drive his point home.

"No, they're not. They're my ticket to a new life."

"You're knowingly obstructing a federal investigation by withholding evidence."

Her unladylike scoff didn't suit her.

"Hoover didn't know there was anything to investigate until I contacted him. I'm not under subpoena, and there's no warrant. I'm not obstructing anything."

"Hoover knows about the ledgers now. I'm authorized to—"

Ceara slammed on the brakes as she cranked the steering wheel toward the side of the road. Hagen braced a hand against the dashboard as the big car skidded along the shoulder kicking up dirt as the engine coughed to an abrupt, chugging halt. She turned on him with a wildfire of anger and fear blazing behind a shining sheen of tears.

"Get out! If you're not going to help me, then get out! And take him with you." She made a dismissing wave toward Rocchelli. "You can have him arrested. I'll go to New York by myself. I've been beaten, choked, cut with a knife, shot at, and...and...all because I— All because I slept with the wrong guy. I'm no better than the floozies I've seen fawning over him. And what's worse, I married him. I just want to be free. I don't want to be scared anymore." She wiped tears with the heels of her hands.

Hagen accepted her verbal onslaught, weighing his words before he responded. "You're free now. You have the control. Rocchelli has nothing on you. It's over."

"You're wrong. It's not over. This is the calm before the storm. I thought taking his ledgers was my way out of the hell I was living in. Instead, all I've done is gotten myself into a deeper level of that same hell. I'm only safe as long as he stays unconscious...or dies. He won't stay in jail long. His attorney will have him out like that." She snapped her fingers.

"His influence runs through every police department in Cook County and it reaches out to other precincts and neighboring counties, which means he's got favors he can pull in right on up the line. He'll be angrier than ever, and revenge will be that much sweeter to him. My only chance at any kind of life is to get my family out of the country. We'll change our names." Ceara pounded her fists on the steering wheel. "I'm such an idiot. Why didn't I see that sooner? I have to warn them. I have to get to them before Eddie does."

"Telephone them. Tell them what happened and that they have to get to a safe place to wait this out."

"They don't have a telephone."

"Call a neighbor. There's got to be someone you can leave a message with. Where does your dad work? Call there." He took her rapid nodding to mean she was working through names of neighbors and friends.

"My parents own a grocery and dry goods store, but there's no phone there."

"Then phone a police station. Hell, send a telegram."

"And say what? *Your son-in-law is a Chicago mobster, and he may show up to torture or kill you. Please take all necessary precautions.* My dad would never believe a message like that even if it was actually delivered which, in Five Points, is as unreliable as the police are untrustworthy. Corruption runs every bit as deep in New York as it does in Chicago."

Hagen's impatience roared back. "Damn it! Those are excuses, not solutions. I understand you're worried about your family. I do. I heard Rocchelli's threat. But we need help." He pressed her. "Look. I'm a lawman. No. I'm a Texas Ranger. There's a difference. A difference that matters. I'm here, because I swore I'd protect you and get you and those ledgers to a place of safety. And I aim to do just that."

Her eyes pinched at the corners; her mouth tightened into a thin line.

"I know you've had it rough, but don't give up now." With his eyes, his voice, his heart, Hagen reached out with every ounce of his feelings for her. "Let me help you."

Slowly, reluctantly, she nodded. "I'll go to Columbus to turn Eddie in. You call whoever you need to get protection for my family. But I won't give up the location of the ledgers. I'm getting them myself, which means I have to go to New York just as soon as Eddie's in jail. I want you to go with me." She hesitated for the space of a breath. "I need you to go with me."

He didn't want to refuse her anything, but in this, he had no choice. "I can't promise that."

"Why?"

"You know why."

She nodded slowly. "Your job ends when you deliver me to Hoover's agents. Because that's what I am to you." She mouthed the words on a whisper. "Just a job."

It she'd have cut his chest open and pulled out his heart barehanded, it wouldn't have hurt as much as those three words knifing through him right then. She'd never been just a job to him, but he couldn't tell her how he felt.

"I'm not going to Columbus or any other Bureau office where I'll be held captive again. I'll be nothing more than a hostage to the legal system under the guise of protection. I'm going to New York. After you turn Eddie in, you can go back to Texas and get on with your life."

She was right. That was exactly what she faced in Columbus, but she was wrong about him getting on with his life. He didn't want to return to Texas, unless she went with him, but that wasn't in the cards Fate had dealt them. His life was every bit as empty as hers. He wasn't at liberty to tell her how he felt, how she'd touched him forever, how the thought of a future without her in it was no future at all. He swiped his hand over his face as he exhaled a deep breath.

"Let's tackle one problem at a t—"

Hagen stared at Cecil's gun—a Savage 1907, 10-shot semi-automatic pocket pistol—leveled at his belly and the slender, steady hand that held it. There was likely a cartridge in the chamber, so she had eleven chances of hitting him, which were eleven chances too many. Few things scared him, but the cold metallic click of the hammer pulling back was right at the top of that list. She couldn't miss. He searched for mercy, but found none in her glacial-cold stare. With that expression, she'd make a hell of a poker player. There wasn't a hint of bluff in her granite-hard expression. But damn, it riled him to have a gun pulled on him. Slowly, he raised his hands in truce. She didn't have a killer's mentality, which was worth the gamble that he could slap the gun aside before she put a bullet through his liver.

"Your conscience won't let you commit cold-blooded murder, or you'd have killed Rocchelli already. I don't doubt you'd pull the trigger if you were defending yourself, but not now. Not eye-to-eye like this. And not me."

"Would you let anything stop you from protecting the people you love?"

That took the wind out of him. *The people I love...or the woman.* Damn. She'd hit him where he lived. Nothing was more important, or stronger, than love.

"No. You're right. There's nothing I wouldn't do."

Tense seconds ticked off before she eased the hammer down and stuffed the gun under her thigh. She started the car, took a rough first gear, and pulled back onto the highway. The stubborn set of her jaw told him she was through talking, which meant short of commandeering the car and hog-tying her, which still wouldn't get him the location of the ledgers, he decided going along with her was his best option. They were headed in a generally easterly direction, which could, at any opportunity, take them southerly toward Columbus or northerly toward New York. There was still time for him to make the Columbus decision for them.

Miles of silence rolled behind them with no indication she'd ever speak to him again. Needing to interrupt that possibility, Hagen said, "You're not a floozy."

No response. He rested his head against the seat and stared at the highway ahead.

"You used to call me Mrs. Rocchelli."

"What?"

"You've used my first name several times today."

"Do I need to apologize for that?"

"No." On a noncommittal, lips-pursed shrug, she admitted, "I like it."

"I like it, too. And I like that you've called me Hagen instead of Mr. Hagen."

"You gave Eddie one name when he hired you. I played it safe and added 'mister', so he wouldn't suspect we were chummy. Thank you for helping me."

He almost said he was just doing his job, but caught himself. They'd already danced around that conversation. "You're welcome." He needed to say more, wanted to say more, but everything that came to mind felt too personal or too much like a lawman, so he opted for changing the subject.

"Would you have shot me?"

"Well, it *was* a heated moment, but you backed down before I had to make that decision."

Any other time, being accused of backing down from a fight would have rubbed him the wrong way. Now, he just chuckled. "I'm glad we got that cleared up."

She smiled. "I sent the ledgers to a person who works in a building you've recently become reacquainted with. I included a letter with instructions and that you or my father can pick up the packages on my behalf."

He resisted asking why she hadn't told him this to begin with for fear she'd stop talking.

"Part of what I told Eddie was true. This person will hold the packages until Monday and then send them to Hoover."

"That's encouraging."

"What is?"

"You trust me enough to include me on the approved claim-the-packages list. What about the person you sent them to? You must have a lot of faith in him...or her."

"Faith." A little smile softened her expression. "Interesting word considering who it is. Any yes, I have complete faith that my instructions will be followed religiously."

"So, how does a person become reacquainted with a building?"

"You're the special investigator—"

"Yeah, yeah, yeah. Figure it out myself. I heard you the first time." Frustration reared its impatient head again, but he bulled it down. At least she'd shared this much, cryptic as it was. He scrubbed his knuckles against his chin stubble.

"How did you get the ledgers out of the house without getting caught?"

"As soon as Eddie left Tuesday morning, I removed them from his desk, split them into two boxes, wrapped them in colorful paper with ribbons and bows. Paul, and my bodyguard of the day, not only carried them to the car when we left the house, they carried them into the hospital assuming they were exactly what they appeared to be—gifts."

"Right in plain sight." He chuckled, impressed with her ingenuity.

"I re-wrapped the boxes in plain brown paper, tied them with string, and sent them from the hospital's business office."

"Simple plans are the best."

"Is that so? It was a simple plan to meet at the train station and look how that turned out." She cast a teasing scowl his way.

Hagen chuckled at her effort not to smile. "I didn't say they always work. Simple is easy to remember and execute. How did you leave the hospital without getting caught?"

"I joined a group of student nurses and their two nurse-instructors as they walked from the hospital to an off-premises classroom three blocks away. We walked right along the sidewalk where Eddie's men waited in a car to take me home at the end of my shift. Once I was out of their view, I left the group and walked on toward Union Station until I flagged down a cab."

"Other than Leo and Paul, Rocchelli's men don't have the brains God gave a goose."

Ceara giggled. “Undoubtedly, those men are also soon to be unemployed.”

“I’m not suggesting I’m in favor of the idea, but how far is it to New York?”

“From Chicago… I suppose eight hundred miles or so.”

He worked through the logistics. “The maximum speed limits will range from forty-five to reasonable and proper, depending upon the state and the particular road. Stopping for fuel and food and if we don’t hit bad weather…” He calculated and added twenty percent. “We’re looking at a good fifteen or sixteen hours under perfect conditions, which never happens. When a person’s in a hurry, all sorts of things go wrong. We can count on it.”

“At least the fuel tank is full.”

“It won’t last long in this hay-burner. We might make a hundred and seventy-five miles on a full tank. Two hundred is pushing it.”

“How will be pay for more fuel? I have no idea what happened to my handbag. I only had five dollars, anyway. Do you have any cash?”

“Jucca cleaned out my pockets, but I’ve got a few bucks salted away that he missed. It’ll get us a couple tanks of gas and a sandwich.”

“Well, that’s something in our favor.” Ceara turned the heater knob to the high setting. “I’d give a lot for a coat.”

“I can’t help you there, but I can turn up the heater in the back. One of my first jobs working on this baby was installing an extra floor heater to keep Rocchelli's feet warm. It won't be much, but with the divider open, the air will circulate."

He slid the glass, leaned through the opening, and adjusted the heater knob. An idea hit him, and he hung upside down over the seat and rifled through the cocktail cabinet and the other nooks built into the mahogany panel of the front seat.

"Pay dirt."

"What?"

Back in the front, Hagen dropped two boxes of ammunition on the seat, then he showed her a leather flap-fold wallet.

She perked up. "How much is there?"

He opened the wallet and fanned the bills. "Three grand, more or less, depending upon the day and Rocchelli's mood. He mixes large and small bills and arranges them face forward in smallest to largest denominations with the second bill upside down, then two the right way, one upside down, and so on. The last bill is always upside down and backwards."

"How do you know that?"

"I've counted it a few times."

"Why?

"Curiosity. There were some benefits to being his mechanic and part-time chauffeur. I had a lot of time alone with this car. He deliberately left the wallet where it was accessible. The money is for pay-offs and insurance to keep his men honest. The pattern is always the same, but the amount changes whenever it strikes his fancy. He's got a suspicious streak a mile wide."

"He certainly does. He's crazy-suspicious."

"This ammo works in Rocchelli's Colt and the gun you've got." Hagen shook the partially full box with .32 shells and replaced the two in Rocchelli's gun. When he checked the 20-round box magazine in the Browning, it was full, just as he'd anticipated, but there weren't enough .30-06 cartridges for a full reload. He'd have to be frugal with his shots and keep track of each one. "We'll refuel at half a tank and get something to eat. The fewer stops, the better."

"I'm looking forward to food and something to drink."

He weighed his curiosity against pushing her too far and took the chance. "Now that we more or less agree on a plan, will you tell me more about that night? The night you lost your baby."

Chapter Six

Hagen understood her silence now came from a different place inside her than the stubborn silence when he'd pushed too hard for information about the ledgers.

"Want me to close the divider?"

"I don't care if he hears."

"I'll close it anyway." Hagen pulled the sliding glass into place.

Still, she didn't speak for some moments longer. "Eddie has a reputable accountant for his legitimate business finances, and he dutifully pays income taxes."

"For his two restaurants and the tugboat business."

"Yes, but he keeps separate, meticulously detailed accounts of all his financial affairs—legal and under-the-table. He also has a Victor safe built into a wall in his den that I'm not supposed to know about, but I do now. I didn't have time for the combination."

"He's such a suspicious bastard that he probably memorized it and will take it with him to his grave rather than let anyone know what it is."

"I think you're absolutely right. But there are ways to open a combination lock if you have the patience." She winked.

Hagen shook his head, chuckling lightly. "You can tell me that story some other time. Finish the one we're on."

"Every Sunday after church and lunch, he retires to his den. The den is always locked when he's not in it. Sometimes, he locks himself in. Most of the time, though, he doesn't.

"Sundays were wonderful. So quiet and peaceful. I could listen to the radio or read, go out to a movie when I wanted, take a walk in the park down the street. It was the only time that was my own even before..."

Her mouth tightened into a pained, hard line.

"It was storming that Sunday evening. The electricity flickered for an hour before it finally went out. I had oil lamps readied, and I went to the den to see if Eddie needed one. Everyone in the house had instructions not to interrupt him on Sundays unless it was so important it couldn't wait until Monday morning. I decided this was one of those times. I knocked, called his name, and announced myself. I opened the door just a peek and stayed at the threshold. He had a lamp going, so I apologized for bothering him. The electricity came on right then.

"He came at me like a madman—I don't know how else to explain it—arms flailing, fists clenched. He accused me of spying on him. I backed to the other side of the hallway, still apologizing. He grabbed the lamp and bashed it against the wall beside me. How the house didn't catch fire..." She shrugged and didn't speak for a few moments. "He dragged me into his den by my hair and threw me down. His fists— He—" She shook her head in place of words, sucking in a breath that she exhaled slowly.

"I was just into my sixth month. More than the pain, I remember the blood. There was so much blood." Again, she fell silent. "The only thing he was sorry for was that I had made him angry enough to hurt me." Her eyes welled with tears. "He blamed me for losing our baby."

"I've seen it happen. It's... There're no words for it. Heinous isn't strong enough." As a lawman, Hagen had dealt with all manner of criminals and hard cases. He could handle what adults did to each other, but when it came to children—to mothers and babies—that was a different story. It tied him in knots.

"Eddie is someone else when he's in that rage. It's like his mind takes him someplace dark and evil. When he came to his senses and saw what he'd done to me, he went into his performance. He threw furniture and fired his gun. Then he picked me up and ran down the servant's stairs shouting for someone to get his men to the house. Outside, he bowled over Phil and ordered him to stay behind and lead the search for the intruders that had broken in and attacked me. Eddie drove like a maniac to the hospital." She cut a glance at Hagen. "But not to the nearest hospital."

"What? What do you mean?"

"The nearest hospital is the one where I worked and was on a leave of absence from. He drove much farther to a hospital where no one knew me."

Hagen held up his hand. "Hold on. He deliberately bypassed the nearest hospital knowing you might bleed to death? What kind of husband...man...does that? Never mind. Go on."

"Somewhere along that breakneck drive, I told him I was leaving him, which was a mistake. He became that other man again. He said the only way I'd ever leave him was in a hearse. It wasn't until weeks later that I realized why he'd driven me himself and why he'd bypassed my hospital."

"He was already isolating you from anyone who might suspect what had really happened."

"He told the medical staff I'd been attacked at home during a foiled kidnapping and robbery. He posted a two-man, around-the-clock guard outside my room for my *safety*."

A spattering of sleet danced on the windshield. Hagen flipped the wiper knob.

"The physician who attended me, Dr. Alan Swain, extended my convalescence at the hospital. I didn't learn the reason until my pre-discharge examination. Dr. Swain minced no words. He told me straight-out he knew Eddie had beaten me. He kept me in the hospital as long as he could, so I'd be well on my way to fully recovered when I left.

"I sobbed my way through the story. He helped me plan a way to leave Eddie. He said my freedom hinged on whatever Eddie hadn't wanted me to see. It was so obvious once he said it. I could think of nothing else but discovering what Eddie was hiding."

"Weren't you afraid to go home?"

Ceara pursed her lips in an almost smile. "Oddly enough, no. He couldn't risk hurting me. Concocting another story to cover another beating would have been too suspicious. So, in that respect, I gained the upper hand, but I was also careful not to abuse my newfound control. He was often cruel with his words, but that didn't bother me. I didn't care what he said.

"I moved into my own bedroom, still insisting on a divorce. He reminded me Catholics don't divorce. I countered with annulment and a promise of dismemberment of certain body parts he was proud of if he ever touched me again. Neither of us was willing to test the other, but it was soon evident that I'd returned home with empty confidence. I was his prisoner. It didn't take long before I was stir-crazy with boredom at being confined to the house and grounds."

"In Texas, we call it cabin fever. Being stuck inside days on end when the weather's too bad to do anything outside. Day after day. Or it hits you when you're sick. You can't sleep anymore, because that's all you've done. You've read all your books...twice. Your thoughts play games with your rational thinking."

"That's exactly it. I had to get out and do something—anything. So I choked down my pride and asked to return to work, with bodyguards, of course, in exchange for resuming my responsibilities of running the household and playing hostess at his parties and such. He agreed I could go back to work a few days a week if I'd donate my wages to the less fortunate of Chicago—the elderly and indigent, needy children. I already did volunteer work on Saturdays at the church's food store. He liked the image of his wife more involved in charitable activities."

"In essence, he also took your paycheck from you."

She shrugged. "I didn't lack in spending money from him. In that, he was generous. He just didn't like not being in control of my money, little as it was compared to his. I'd been saving a good deal of my wages to give to my sisters when they go off to college. That was one of our marital disagreements. He didn't care that I was saving for my sisters. He didn't like that I wouldn't relinquish control over my own money."

"How did he manage to swing having bodyguards roaming the hospital corridors?"

Ceara rubbed her thumb against the pads of her fingertips. "Money. Everything with him revolves around money and control. The administration looked the other way while his men roamed the premises or sat outside the doors from the time I arrived to when someone picked me up. He didn't allow me to go out on the ambulance. Since I didn't want to jeopardize losing what I'd gained, I complied. He also viewed my change of attitude as acquiescence to his rules and demands."

"But you had an ulterior plan."

"I did. We settled back into a bearable living arrangement. It wasn't long before he pressed me to move back into our bedroom despite Dr. Swain's strict instructions to leave me alone—to put it delicately—for at least a year while my body healed.

"I had no intention of ever being that close to Eddie again, but I agreed on the condition that I could return to work fulltime without bodyguards. That made him mad. Our negotiations reached impasse."

"When, and how, did you find his ledgers?"

"A few days before Thanksgiving, Bugs Moran sent Eddie on a three-day job out of town. I asked permission to measure for new upstairs draperies, including his den. The only person allowed in his den when Eddie isn't there is our fulltime, live-in housekeeper. She's worked for Eddie for at least twenty years. Eddie approved my request as long as Mrs. Monterro never left me alone, and that she'd keep the door locked at all times, even when we were inside the room."

"You were casing it out." He nodded approval of her strategy.

"Mrs. Monterro and I finished all of the measuring by the end of the first day. The second night, which happened to be Mrs. Monterro's weekly evening off, I broke a water pipe in the basement where it's difficult to repair. The mess occupied the entire household staff and my bodyguards long enough for me to go through Eddie's desk and read the ledgers."

"How did you get into the room?"

"The same way I would have gotten us out of the handcuffs."

Hagen grinned. "You picked the lock."

He'd never seen such a smug, satisfied smile.

"I used gloves, and I was so careful, especially when I saw the little pieces of paper stuck in a crack at the side of the drawers."

"Old trick to tell if someone has snooped."

"That night, I memorized how the ledgers were arranged, so I could put them back exactly as I'd found them. When I went back to get them to mail, I left the ledgers with his legal business dealings, which included employee payroll, household and living expenses, charitable donations, and so forth. They were no use to me, and I'm certain his accountant has the same information. The books I took are his two double-cross dealings with Capone and Moran, the three detailing his illegal business transactions—gambling, booze, racketeering, and so forth—and his personal journal of running notes related to his illegal business.

"I think the information is damning, but I can't judge whether it's enough to send him to prison. He might just get hit with a fine and more taxes. Much of it is in a rudimentary code that would deter the casual reader, but it's not difficult to decipher. I came up with more complicated ciphers when I was a kid."

"What did you find out?"

"Basically, Capone pays Eddie for inside information on Moran, but what Capone doesn't know is it's Eddie who frequently intercepts Capone's whiskey shipments for himself, and he tells Capone that Moran is responsible for every single stolen shipment. He's also changed the price of intercepted whiskey shipments and gotten more money out of Moran. Eddie has his fingers in parts of Capone's business, too."

"That shindig back at the warehouse makes more sense now."

"The hard part was pretending I knew nothing about his ledgers, while I figured out a way to use them."

"I considered telling Moran and Capone what Eddie was doing behind their backs, but that would make me nothing more than a woman who didn't keep her place or her mouth shut and, worse, a wife who couldn't be trusted. If I'd rat-out my husband, who's to say I wouldn't do the same to them?"

"Contacting Hoover was a brilliant move."

"Dr. Swain suggested it. Besides being under guard day and night, to show the public and his employees what an exemplary husband he was, Eddie accompanied me to my twice-monthly medical appointments, which Dr. Swain insisted upon after my discharge as a way for us to talk without arousing Eddie's suspicions. He denied Eddie's presence during our appointments, and Eddie didn't argue. That was *women's business.*

When I told Dr. Swain what I'd found in Eddie's desk, he advised me to hand it over to Hoover in exchange for protection and a new life. Dr. Swain made the arrangements with Hoover."

"Clever man. Clever plan."

"A few days later, Dr. Swain invited us to participate in a blood testing research project involving married couples. Eddie was more than willing, since this would hit the newspapers as yet another one of his Good Samaritan endeavors."

"Good Samaritan? Eddie Rocchelli?" Hagen grunted his contempt.

Ceara laughed lightly at his reaction.

"Eddie's careful with publicity. He makes sure his name and photograph show up in the papers only when he benefits. He bought the front pew at our church so the entire congregation can see how pious he is. He gives thousands of dollars a year to the St. Helena Catholic Church. He goes to mass on Sunday morning and Wednesday night and on all of the holy days, even when he's out of town. He believes this promotes his public image as a perfect husband, legitimate businessman, and unselfish supporter of the city."

"It's an effective disguise until someone lifts the mask."

"Meaning that someone is me?"

"Well, there's a saying about if the shoe fits... Go back to the blood tests."

"Dr. Swain presented the paperwork to sign along with a brochure explaining the procedure and the purpose. Tucked inside my brochure was a note from Hoover himself. Eddie never caught on."

"That was slick. You know, for all his pomp and blow-hard personality, Rocchelli isn't observant or he'd have caught on to our planning that we did right in front of him."

"I've thought of that, too. He is so confident in his power over people, that it blinds him to what he doesn't want to see. Eddie donated ten thousand dollars to the hospital to show his appreciation for the care I received. The *Lakeshore Daily News* ran an article with a photograph of Dr. Swain shaking hands with Eddie as he accepted the donation with me at Eddie's side. It was big enough news to hit all the major newspapers."

"Nice irony."

"Yes, it was, and it still is." Ceara pursed her lips in a smug grin.

"What did that note say?"

"I call it my Freedom Letter." Dipping her fingers into the *V* of her bodice, she produced a folded, dainty white handkerchief and handed it to him.

His eyebrows arched. "Secret pocket?"

"Brassiere. It's a hiding place Eddie didn't have access to."

Hagen grinned as he opened the handkerchief and unfolded a small paper.

Ceara—my dearest niece,

It is with eager anticipation that I await your upcoming visit. I am pleased you are relocating to a more hospitable location. Our quaint town of Kane should meet all of your expectations.

I am confident you will find the apartment on Hoover Avenue satisfactory. My assistant, Mr. Hagen, will oversee your travel arrangements. You may put your complete trust in him. Mr. Hagen is qualified to handle the transportation of your personal effects, including the more delicate items of which you have expressed particular concern for their safety. While you are undoubtedly anxious to know the exact day and time of Mr. Hagen's arrival, I can assure you he will show up at his earliest possible opportunity.

With fond thoughts, Uncle Edgar

"Lots of hints if you know what you're looking for." He handed back the note.

"I remember every detail of the night you showed up. It was cold and calm with a skiff of snow. Eddie had extra men on guard it the restaurant. We'd parked in his reserved space. He told Phil and Cecil to wait down the block as long as they had the Rolls warmed up and ready to go at midnight." Ceara glanced at Hagen. "It was highly entertaining the way they fretted and carried on trying to get the Rolls started. You did something to it, didn't you? How did you not get caught by the other bodyguards?"

"The night was cold. His men spent most of the time inside the restaurant with only an occasional check outside. It was easy enough to slip unnoticed around the side of the building where the car was parked. I jimmied with the ignition wiring."

"Eddie reacted in his usual raging fashion at their ineptitude, alternately threatening to fire or shoot them. You seemed quite amused as you came over to help. When you told Phil this car's model was known for ignition problems, I thought his seams would burst when you said you could get it running. I remember your exact words when Eddie asked your name and where you were from. *Just call me Hagen. I'm from Hoover, Texas hitchhiking my way to Pennsylvania to work for my Uncle Edgar as a mechanic in his filling station. My money and my ride ran out here.*"

Hagen nodded as he recalled those moments, too. "I saw recognition in your eyes." He'd seen more than recognition. It was hope, and it had gone straight to his heart like an arrow shot from Cupid's bow.

"How did you keep from being spotted? Eddie has spies everywhere. He pays them to keep him informed of strangers and goings on around town. You completely fooled him."

"Another Ranger drove me up from Amarillo the Saturday before Christmas. We hauled along an old beat-up Indian motorcycle that I rode into town when he dropped me off about thirty miles out. I'd read what little information the Bureau had on Rocchelli, so I had somewhat of an idea how he operated.

"Hoover had arranged a room on the second floor of the boarding house a few blocks from your house. With binoculars, I could see the comings and goings from your front gate. Hoover also had a job for me on the water line project on your street. On Sunday, I prowled around to get the lay of the neighborhood. Then I reported for work on Monday morning—Christmas Eve. I had Christmas Day off, which I spent watching your house from the big Sycamore tree in the park. I took a sack lunch, thermos jug of coffee, and a book. It was a nice day sitting there in the sunshine. Then I went back to work on Wednesday and kept an eye on your front gate."

"You didn't see much activity, did you?"

"No, and that was a problem. I asked the other workers about who lived in the mansion, and they were more than willing to tell me all about Eddie Rocchelli and his fancy car and his money. New Year's Eve arrived, and the guys got to talking about their evening plans, and I asked where rich people like Rocchelli celebrate New Year's Eve, and they said he always has fancy parties at his two restaurants, and the one he always attended was the *Lake Shore Rocchelli*. They nudged each other and winked about both restaurants being the most high-class speakeasies in Chicago. I managed to get one of the guys to tell me the address without being obvious about it. We got off work an hour early, which gave me plenty of time to find the restaurant, stash my motorcycle, and wait."

"You certainly impressed Eddie when you accomplished what Phil and Cecil couldn't."

"I had to infiltrate Rocchelli's gang to get close to you. I'd already wasted a week trying to figure out how to make contact. I hadn't expected he'd offer me a job on the spot, but it played right into my hands."

"What was your plan if he hadn't offered the job?"

"Show up on the doorstep and beg for a job—driver, mechanic, groundskeeper, dog walker, dish washer. Anything."

He liked that his exaggeration made her smile.

"Eddie was incredibly successful in controlling my life." She checked traffic in her side mirror, tapped the brake, and hugged the shoulder as she made the right turn onto an intersecting two-lane asphalt road.

"Is someone coming up on us?" He dipped his head to see into his side mirror then twisted around to peer through the narrow back window, bracing himself against her jerky, engine-chugging downshift, while chalking up her stiff shifting to the Rolls' naturally temperamental transmission.

"No. Eddie brought me this way for the grand opening of the Columbus Zoological Gardens." She smiled, but didn't look at him. "You said you'd figure out a way for me to get to New York once Eddie is in jail. I'm trusting you to make that happen."

His frown changed to a satisfied smile. Things were looking up. His next challenge was getting in the driver's seat so he could get them down the road with some real driving. One little victory at a time.

As nonchalantly as he could muster, he offered, "I'll drive when you get tired."

He slid the partition window open to make a quick check on Rocchelli and to get the heat circulating again, then he stretched out his legs as best he could, given the limited room. But he wasn't complaining. Just about any place beat where they'd been. He compared the dash clock against his wrist-watch. With any luck at all, Rocchelli would be locked up by dark, and Ceara's family would be safe with police protection.

Ceara paid him no mind when he studied her for several moments as he contemplated his duty as a lawman. Not entrusting her into Bureau custody was a direct and wanton violation of Hoover's orders, but the farther he got from Chicago, the less important that became. He wasn't Hoover's man. He was a Texas Ranger, and he lived by a different code—a code of the head and heart—and where Ceara went was where he had to be.

Besides, from a certain point of view, New York was just the long way around to Washington, D. C.

Chapter Seven

Ceara turned off the highway for fuel and parked under the canopy at a gas pump. Hagen shoved his shoulder against the passenger door, and forced it open despite the metal-grating protest from the bent hinges. The attendant, a high school-aged boy wiping his hands on a grease rag, hurried toward them.

As he got out, Hagen said, "I'll come around to your side. The boy won't see much through the smoky tint on the windows, but we don't need an over-enthusiastic grease monkey getting a peek at Rocchelli. We also don't know what he might or might not have heard about that shooting, so roll your window down an inch or two and listen. If I say 'Texas', that's your cue to get the hell out of here. Don't wait for me to get in the car. If I can't jump on the running board, I'll be sprinting and dodging down the street like a jack rabbit running from a coyote. You can circle around and pick me up."

Ceara laughed. "That's something I'd like to see." She cracked her window, noting with some amusement that the boy's steps slowed as he gave the car an envious, and appreciative, once-over.

"Want me to fill'er...um...up? I'll wash the windows and check the oil and tires, if you want." The kid's darting gaze moved from Hagen to the Rolls and back, his eyes widening with suspicion.

"Just gas." Hagen leaned against the back window. "It's not stolen."

"Wh—what?"

"You think I stole it, because I don't look the sort to drive a fancy car like this."

"Well, no offense, mister, but it crossed my mind. My boss requires payment first. We've had a few too many drive-offs from people passing through."

"Understandable." Hagen handed him a five.

The boy lifted his cap, scratched his head, and settled the cap in place. "Car's sure got some dings on it, and I heard the trouble you had with the passenger door. Sounded like it's sprung." He inspected the dent in the front fender.

"I got it cheap. The owner had some bad luck with it."

Ceara smiled at Hagen's sarcastic understatement.

The kid laughed out loud. "Bad luck. That's a good one." Appeased, he went about fueling. "You and your missus traveling far?"

"My miss—?" Hagen caught himself. "Yeah. We're heading for Louisville. Her family's there. I need a telephone or telegraph to let them know where we are."

"There's a telephone inside, but it's for local calls only. The telegraph is in the Penny and Dime down the way three blocks, but Henry only sends messages between eight and noon."

"Then how about a place to eat?"

The young man waved in a 'that way' direction. "Ralph's Diner. Best food in the county. Just keep going to the edge of town. It's on the right. Plenty of parking in front."

Hagen made small talk about the weather while the boy finished fueling. When he replaced the nozzle in the holder, the boy said, "I'll be right back with your change."

"Keep it, and add this to it for a tip."

"Gosh, mister. Thanks." The kid stuffed the tip in his pocket as he trotted to the office.

Hagen got back inside, but the door resisted his efforts to latch it, so he rolled the window down and held onto the frame to keep it from swinging open.

"To Ralph's Diner?" Ceara asked.

"Yes."

The parking area was empty, so Ceara took a spot in front of the plate glass window and turned off the ignition.

Hagen cranked up his window. "We're going to chance leaving our weapons in the car. We can't parade into a restaurant armed like we're going to rob it." He tapped Ceara's dangling handcuff. "Do what you can to hide that."

Ceara unbuttoned her cuff and tucked the ring and short chain inside her narrow sleeve. “It bulges.”

“It’s better than it was.”

She brushed at the bloody stains on her uniform then made a quick check of her face in the center mirror. “I look wretched. People are going to stare.”

“Can’t be helped. Ready?”

“More than ready. I’m hungry, and I need a restroom.”

“That makes two of us.” When he got out, he lifted the open end of the door against the sprung hinges and closed it with a hard shove.

Ceara checked over the seat at a still unconscious Eddie before she got out. When she came around the front of the car, she said, “You know, the way you slammed the door, it probably won’t open again.”

“Better than having it swing open or rattle while we’re driving.”

Hagen put an arm around her, and she turned her face to his chest to buffer the biting, icy sting of the wind as he escorted her to the door. A host of familiar aromas welcomed her when she stepped inside and, for a few moments, she was back in her mother’s kitchen, safe, warm, and surrounded by her family’s love. A sharp pang of regret for moving so far from home plucked at her determination to keep her emotions from melting into a puddle of memory tears.

“Take this window booth. Slide in on this side so the handcuff is to the wall.” He slid onto the booth across from her.

A radio played somewhere in the back. The only other person in the restaurant sat on a stool at the far end of the long lunch counter, his coat and hat on the stool beside him. He nursed a cup of coffee while reading the newspaper. A tendril of smoke rose from his cigarette.

Ceara said, "There's a pay-phone in the hallway."

"No privacy. We'll find another."

A waitress came with two cups and a pot of coffee. "Hi, folks. My name's Maddie. You want coffee?"

"Yes, thanks," Hagen said.

Maddie sized them up as she filled the cups. "You look like you're having a rough day."

Ceara nodded, her eyes downcast.

Hagen answered, "You might say that."

"I saw you pull up in that fancy car. We don't see many of those come through. You don't quite fit the picture of folks who can afford a Rolls-Royce. You're obviously a nurse, and I'll bet you know car engines inside and out."

"You have a good eye." Hagen picked up his coffee cup.

"It's part of the job. You wait tables as long as I have, you eventually see it all. After a while, it's easy to peg the profession. Wherever you came from, you must have left in a hurry."

"Why's that?"

"Most people wear coats and hats on cold winter days."

"They're out in the car."

From the narrow slant of her eye, she clearly didn't believe him. "So...passing through town or needing a place to stay?"

"Passing through. Headed for Louisville to see family."

A man called out, "Hey, Maddie. Order up."

She spoke over her shoulder. "Thanks, Ralph." To Ceara, Maddie observed, "From the looks of your face and the blood on your uniform, you'll want to clean up. The restrooms are just off the kitchen."

Ceara didn't look up. "Thank you."

"You just missed the lunch crowd. We've still got a couple of specials left. Meat loaf and mashed with apple pie baked fresh this morning. It's hot and quick. You can get on down the road in a jiffy."

"Thanks. It sounds good." Hagen asked Ceara, "Okay with you?"

She nodded.

"Two specials and keep the coffee coming. Couple of glasses of water when you have the chance."

Hagen took his break when Ceara returned. She divided her attention between the Rolls and the hallway, anxious for Hagen to return. Maddie brought their food as Hagen slid into the booth. Ceara couldn't remember when her least favorite meal tasted so good. When they finished, Maddie refilled their coffee cups, placed the pot on the table, and sat down beside Ceara.

Her voice low, she asked, "You're in trouble, aren't you?"

Hagen said, "We had a run in with some *desperadoes*."

"I thought so. You're jittery as June bugs the way you're keeping an eye on your car. It's like you're expecting someone you don't want to see. I think you know something about the shooting that happened in Chicago."

Hagen eased back. "Shooting?"

"It's on the radio. It's big enough it'll make the front page above the fold."

Goosebumps prickled Ceara's arms.

"Sounds bad. What's the scoop?" Hagen asked.

"Some say it was Frank Nitti or Jack "Machine Gun" McGurn. Others are sure it was Al Capone who hit George Moran's booze warehouse in the Lincoln Park area of Chicago's north side this morning."

Ceara stole a quick glance at Hagen. He toyed with his coffee cup, seemingly only mildly interested. "So what else is new in Chicago? What's the story on this one?"

"They're calling it the St. Valentine's Day Massacre. Seven of Moran's men were gunned down execution style. Two vehicles made up like Chicago police cars pulled up in front of the warehouse, right on the street. Witnesses say four men, maybe more, got out. At least two were dressed in police uniforms, and they waltzed right in."

"In broad daylight? That takes guts."

"Apparently, they took everyone by surprise. Somewhere in all the shooting, witnesses saw a car leaving out of the alley behind the warehouse. They didn't get the license plate, but they described the car as a light-colored Rolls-Royce four door sedan with three or four people in it. There's disagreement on that. Some say there were two men standing on the running board. Others say just one. And maybe another person in the back seat." Maddie's scrutinizing gaze settled on Ceara. "But they all agree the driver was a woman."

"A woman?"

Maddie nodded. "She was described as a strawberry blonde with a bob, and she was wearing a white nurse's uniform or an evening dress."

Hagen talked around a mouthful of pie. "Makes a person wonder what a woman was doing there."

Maddie snorted on a soft chuckle. "I wonder."

Ceara's heart pounded at where Maddie was going with her veiled interrogation. Her body tensed in preparation to flee. Fearing she'd reveal their secret if she looked up, Ceara suddenly found the inside of her empty coffee cup to be the most interesting thing she'd ever seen.

"It's quite a coincidence that we're driving a similar car but, as you can see, it's just the two of us."

Maddie almost smiled at his diversionary tactic. "I guess the laugh's on Capone, though. If he was after Moran, he never showed. No one's seen him. The only survivor is in a bad way, and he's not talking. In fact, he's not expected to live."

"Survivor?" Hagen asked.

"Frank Gusenberg, one of Moran's men. The cops are also on the lookout for Moran's chief lieutenant, Eddie 'The Roach' Rocchelli. They think he's taken to hiding and laying low. Logical place is with Moran. It seems there's evidence that another scuffle was going on in the back of the warehouse just before the shooting happened. Cops aren't saying if they're related."

Hagen whistled through his teeth. "Sounds too crazy to be true."

Maddie grunted in agreement. "Isn't that the truth? Regardless, the cops gave out a description for Rocchelli's car. The Cook County police department, the Chicago radio stations, and local newspapers are taking tips from callers. There's a reward for information that leads to the apprehension or arrest of anyone connected with the shooting."

Panic washed over Ceara like waves crashing upon the beach.

Hagen looked straight at Maddie. "Have you called yet?"

Maddie smiled lightly. "No."

"Are you going to call after we leave?"

"No."

"Why not?"

"Interesting as this is, I figure it's none of my business." Maddie drew her gaze from Hagen to Ceara. "A man roughed me up once. Roughed me up bad. I was lucky enough to survive and learn from it. I left the lousy no-good scoundrel, because someone helped me when I needed it most, no strings attached. Something tells me that's what you're doing...or wanting to." She swung her gaze back to Hagen. "My advice is you'd better dump that car fast. You've got the law and probably some bad men looking for you from all directions. Eddie Rocchelli is hot potatoes."

Ceara cast a wary look around the diner. Satisfied the lone customer was only interested in his lunch and newspaper and that the kitchen staff weren't lurking, she took a gamble.

"All right. Here's the story. My husband is Eddie Rocchelli. I was—am—leaving him. He caught us and held us in the back of that warehouse. When the opportunity showed itself... Well, his car was handy."

Maddie nodded toward Hagen. "He your boyfriend?" Hastily, she added, "Mind you, I'm not making judgments."

"No. It's not that at all." Still, Ceara's cheeks warmed. How could anyone think otherwise?

Hagen came to her defense. "I'm a lawman assigned to bring Mrs. Rocchelli in to testify against her husband." He placed his hand palm down on the tabletop then lifted his thumb just enough to show his badge. "When Rocchelli found out, he wasn't keen on the idea."

If surprised, Maddie didn't let on.

Palm down, Hagen passed folded bills across the table. "Here are five double sawbucks for coats and hats. I'll match it for sandwiches and water to take with us."

Maddie deftly pocketed the money as she stood and gathered up the empty plates. "Food for the road coming up."

When she'd gone, Ceara whispered, "Jucca searched you. How did he miss your badge?"

"I've got a pouch sewn inside each of my boot tops." He grinned. "A man doesn't generally pull off another man's boots when he frisks him and a quick pat-down will miss it."

"Ooh, that's clever. What else do you have stashed in your boots?"

"Couple hundred in cash. Gun in an ankle holster."

"A gun? It must be a tiny thing to fit inside your boot top."

"I wouldn't call a 1908 semi-automatic, single action, six-shot Colt pistol tiny."

Ceara giggled lightly. "That is certainly more information than I ever hope to need." Sliding out of the booth, she said, "I'll be right back. Another quick visit to the restroom before we leave."

When she returned, Hagen was buttoned up in a double-breasted overcoat and adjusting the fit of a homburg. Ceara caught a glimpse of the man who had been sitting at the lunch counter as he left the restaurant, hatless and coatless.

"Here, honey. This is mine." Maddie held a brown wrapper coat with fur collar up to Ceara to eyeball the fit. "It'll do. We're about the same size."

Handling the coat, while simultaneously keeping the handcuff tucked inside her sleeve, ended in clumsy failure when the clatter of metal against tabletop clanged like shattering glass. Stricken, Ceara gathered the handcuff to her body in a fumbling attempt to hide it.

"I... It's..."

"It's such a bother to find just the right outfit for that kind of jewelry, isn't it?"

Ceara could have hugged her. "Yes, it is."

"Here's my hat. Gloves are in the coat pockets."

"Thank you for not turning us in."

Maddie waved her off. "It's nothing. I know what it's like to be down and out. It feels good to help others." She gave Ceara the bulging paper sack filled with food. When she handed a beveled glass gallon jug of water to Hagen, he slipped his index finger through the glass ring on the neck and passed money into her hand, which she deftly tucked into her apron pocket.

She winked. "Thanks for the tip." Wiping down the table, she said, "See you folks around. Hope you have a good trip."

On the way out the door, Ceara whispered, "How much more did you give her?"

"On top of the two hundred, another three C-notes for her trouble."

"Five hundred dollars. Oh, how I'm enjoying spending Eddie's money."

Heads bent into the wind, they hustled to the car. Ceara grasped the driver's side handle, but Hagen put his hand over hers.

"I'll drive. You rest."

She hesitated, suspicion rising. "Where will you take us?"

"There's more than one road to Washington, and sometimes, the scenic route is the most entertaining."

Ceara relinquished the ignition key. "Thank you."

"My pleasure."

Ceara scooted to the passenger side and situated the food and water on the floorboard at her feet before she checked on Eddie. He wasn't conscious, but he'd rolled from his belly to his side. She watched him for some moments. She liked people. Their welfare was important to her. Even at their worst, she could see past their momentary slips of humanity to the decency within, but her well of compassion for Eddie was bone dry. Now that he was trussed up like a Christmas turkey gave her more than a little satisfaction.

Hagen started the Rolls and let it idle. "Count out two full reloads for Cecil's pistol and put them in your coat pockets and give me all of the rifle ammo."

Once they were on the highway, Ceara hunkered in to the heavenly warmth of Maddie's coat, her thoughts drifting toward her family as her mind and body relaxed. In a few hours, she'd be on her way home, and all of this nastiness would be behind her. Still, worry niggled in her mind. The opportunity for Hagen to make the phone call that would send police protection to her family had yet to show itself. Even with Eddie tied up in the back seat, her worry couldn't rest despite her mother's advice that worrying only wasted time better spent on productive thoughts.

Her head nodded forward. Hagen tugged her sleeve.

"Lay down."

She rested her head on his thigh with her knees drawn up, Cecil's gun clutched in her hand, and went to sleep.

Chapter Eight

False dusk arrived under low clouds with occasional episodes of fog and snow. Sporadic sleet plinked on the windshield. Hagen smiled at the tight grip Ceara had on her handgun as he tucked the imitation fur coat collar around her ear and over her cheek. While they were in no danger of freezing, even with the partition window open and heat flowing both ways, they were none too warm.

This was the second time in just a few hours he'd enjoyed having her snuggled up to him while she slept. What he wouldn't give to be on their honeymoon someplace secluded and romantic with nothing but time on their hands and making love on their minds. There was no sense torturing himself with these impossible dreams, but he couldn't help it. Truth be known, he didn't want to help it. He was a traditional guy at heart. Always in the back of his mind was the hope of meeting the right woman to share a life with so they could grow old together and enjoy spoiling their grandchildren in their golden years.

Too bad he'd met the right woman at the wrong time.

Rocchelli's moaning nudged Hagen from his wishings as a reminder they weren't alone. It wouldn't be long before Rocchelli woke, and that would bring new challenges.

Hagen didn't think anything of the vehicle he saw in the mirror coming up behind them until a second car pulled out from behind to drive parallel with it and take up both lanes. An oncoming car took to the ditch to avoid hitting head-on.

"Damn." He squeezed Ceara's shoulder. "Wake up. We've got company."

She bolted upright, instantly searching for trouble. "What's wrong?" Her gaze fell upon Eddie. "Oh. He's conscious." Disappointment colored her words.

"He's not our immediate problem. Behind us. They're gaining fast. I gassed up in Ft. Wayne. Someone must have recognized this car and made a call that set the dogs on us. Here. Take the steering wheel and slide over me. Put your foot on the accelerator and keep it steady. Don't touch the brakes. Mind the road. It's rough. There's been more dirt stretches than asphalt."

They made the switch, and Ceara placed Cecil's gun on her lap. "What are you doing?"

"I'm going to show them how we say *adios* in Texas. Back off to forty-five."

"Slow down? You want them to catch us?" Something nearing terror rose in her voice.

"Yes. Listen up. This is what's going to happen." Hagen watched the cars approaching in the side mirror. "They're on a fishing trip, which is why they're making a slow, but steady approach."

"A what kind of trip?" Ceara's gaze darted in nervous jerks as she checked mirror to mirror.

"Fishing trip. They're not sure this is the car they're looking for. I didn't get out when I stopped for gas, so they don't know who's inside. They're following just close enough to make us nervous. If we run—"

"Then they'll know."

"That's right, but we're not going to run. When they reach the end of their patience, the outside car will come up beside us and keep pace. The other will ride our ass to box us in. If we don't pull over, they'll force us off the road, but they won't open fire unless we give them no choice."

"Let's outrun them. Eddie brags about the horsepower in this car. He says there's nothing faster, not even Capone's Cadillac."

"Rocchelli's all hat and no cattle."

"What? Speak English, not Texan."

"He's a blowhard. This car can't hold a candle to the engine power of Capone's Cadillac. With the extra weight of the armor plating and bulletproof glass, this car *might* hit seventy going downhill with a cyclone pushing it. Those cars coming up on us aren't built like this lumber wagon."

Out the corner of his eye, Hagen saw Rocchelli struggling to get on his knees to see out the back window. Hagen rolled down his window.

"Keep the tires on the road and the nose of this baby headed east. I'll take it from there."

Ceara muttered, "Great plan. I especially appreciate all the details."

Grinning at her grousing, Hagen removed his hat and coat then scrunched down on the seat as far as he could to stay below window level with Leo's B-A-R across his chest and the barrel pointing out the window. He lifted his head just enough to see a car pulling abreast.

Her gaze on the road ahead, Ceara talked out of the side of her mouth, "They're waving me over." She dipped her left shoulder.

"Ignore them and keep it steady. Don't roll down—" *Damn it! Too late.*

"I can't hear you." Ceara yelled across the gap between the cars.

"Pull over!" A man yelled back.

"What?"

"Pull over. We want Rocchelli."

"Who?"

"Rocchelli! The Roach."

"Who wants him?"

"Friends who missed him in Chicago."

"He doesn't have friends."

"We know he's in there. Pull over!"

"Here?"

"Pull over, or I'll blow your goddamned head off!" The man pointed a gun at Ceara.

"Blow this!" Extending her left arm out the window, Ceara emptied the magazine into the car.

The car veered, backed off, then surged forward. Hagen came off the seat in a fluid motion and up into the window frame. Perched half in and half out, he brought the B-A-R down over the roof and fired into the car. Glass shattered. The car slammed into Ceara's door, sheering off the side mirror, and forcing the Rolls toward the shoulder amid a hail of submachine gun fire from the second car. Metal screeched as the two cars battled for dominance on the highway. The edge of the asphalt caught the passenger side tires and pulled the Rolls onto the dirt with teeth-jarring jolts as Ceara fought to get all four tires back on smoother ground.

Hagen braced himself as he swung the B-A-R behind and fired at the trailing car then fired immediately into the other one, effectively forcing both cars to back off. Ceara wrenched the Rolls back onto the highway. The tires grabbed asphalt, which sent the big car into a fishtail. Hagen sensed the car lifting to turn turtle, and he dropped inside for the flip.

"Hang on! We're going over!"

The trailing car rammed them at the driver's back fender, knocking the Rolls back down on all four wheels. The jolt of tires connecting with the road slammed Hagen against his door and propelled the heavy glass jug of water torpedoing across the floorboard.

The car beside them roared past. Hagen balanced in the window again, and took aim at the passing car's front passenger tire as it moved in to run them off the road. His aim was true. The car went into a spin that sideswiped the trailing car. The two cars joined in a tangle of screeching metal as they rolled and bounced end over end.

"Put some miles behind us!" Hagen dropped to the seat and cranked up his window. He made a quick check on Rocchelli who lay in a heap on the floor with his head wedged in a corner. Hagen chuckled at the mental image of Rocchelli pinging around the back seat like a steel ball in a pinball game.

Reloading the Browning, Hagen asked Ceara, "Are you hurt?"

Ceara rolled up her window then brushed at her wind-blown hair with a trembling hand. "My ears are ringing. I'm fine if you call being shot at twice in one day being fine." She managed a weak smile. "Are you all right?"

Hagen returned her smile. "No damage. You can slow down now."

She nodded and blew out a rough breath. Leaning forward, she peered through the windshield. "The headlamp on this side isn't working."

"That was some fine driving. I couldn't have done better."

"Thank you. Today is only the fourth time I've driven a car and the first time faster than thirty miles an hour."

"Come again?" Hagen wasn't sure he'd heard right.

Ceara's light giggle smoothed out the ragged edges of what had just happened. "I'd never driven a car until Leo took me driving when Eddie was gone."

A disapproving grunt emanated from the back seat that she either ignored or didn't hear.

"I'm damn glad he taught you. No wonder you had troubles shifting and regulating the speed when we blazed out of Chicago. I chalked it up to the Rolls having a temperamental transmission. Hand me your gun. I'll reload. Did Leo also teach you to handle a gun?"

"No. My father did, but with a stern warning that if I ever pointed it at someone, I had to be tough enough to pull the trigger and not stop until the gun is empty. He cautioned that a gun is no use as a defense if you let it be taken from you. He said the same about anything that can be used as a weapon."

Hagen nodded approval. "I like him. Sounds like something my dad and both granddads would say."

"Cut the chit-chat crap. Where are we, and where are we going?"

Ceara whipped a look over her shoulder. "I liked it better when you were gagged."

"Too bad. Banging around back here had some advantages."

"Apparently," she muttered.

"I asked where we're going."

"Jail," Hagen replied. He returned Cecil's gun to Ceara.

"No jail can hold me. One phone call and I'll be out."

"Jail may be the only place you're safe. Someone wants you dead." Ceara adjusted the center mirror to see Rocchelli's face. "In case you didn't hear, the man said whoever intended to kill you in Chicago wants you badly enough to send goons out to hunt you down."

"I heard. I've got men to protect me."

"They can't protect you in jail. Whoever wants you dead will find a way to get to you."

"I've got money and connections. It'll never happen."

"You're not untouchable. Nobody is..." Her voice faded.

"Where's the jail you're taking me to?"

"Does it matter?"

"Since you haven't turned me over to the coppers yet, that means we're going all the way to D. C. You'll get my ledgers and hand them, and me, over to Hoover in one tidy package."

Her moment of hesitation gave her away. Hagen heard it in Rocchelli's low, irritating chuckle.

"Yes. D. C. That's the plan." Ceara's cheeks pinked.

Hagen intervened. "We're going to Columbus. There's a BOI office there. They'll take you off our hands. Then we'll go on to Washington and settle her business with Hoover."

Rocchelli chuckled low in his throat again. "I'll have your job—your badge as a trophy—before this is over. I'll get you for kidnapping. Wrongful imprisonment. Stealing my car. Transporting my wife across state lines for immoral purposes."

Hagen grinned. "Not likely."

Ceara asked Hagen, "Now what? We still need to make those calls."

"Yeah. There's bound to be a telephone— *Listen*!" Hagen cocked an ear and pigeonholed the sound. "Metal rubbing. "Throw it in neutral! Pull ov—"

The blow-out shook the car.

Hagen grabbed the steering wheel just as the car jerked toward the centerline. "Tap the brake. Go on slowly to a crossroad. Shouldn't be too far."

Low chuckling rose from the back. "Things aren't going so swell."

Ceara grumbled, "As I said… I liked it better when he was gagged."

Lose tread slapped a regular rhythm against the fender as Ceara maneuvered the Rolls off the highway and to a stop.

"Set the handbrake. Keep it running for the heat. And keep an eye on Rocchelli. If he tries anything, shoot him."

Rocchelli grunted. "Cold blooded murder's not her style."

Hagen asked, "Are you sure enough to test her?"

Rocchelli didn't respond.

"That's what I thought." Hagen chuckled as he stuck the barrel of the B-A-R through the open window and crawled out.

***

Ceara stuffed Cecil's gun into her right-hand coat pocket before she reached across the seat to roll up the passenger side window, while simultaneously keeping an eye on Eddie and an ear tuned to the tire-changing noises.

Eddie kicked the back of her seat. "How's about a drink of water from that jug?"

She didn't look at him. "I won't untie you, if that's what you really want."

"I'm thirsty. Hold the jug to my mouth. I'll do the rest. Show a little compassion, doll."

Ceara scoffed. "What do you know about compassion?"

He leaned forward. "I know compassion and kindness are your weaknesses. You can't deny what's in your nature."

"Common decency isn't a weakness."

A car approached from behind, slowed, then went around. Ceara watched until she couldn't see the taillights, and Eddie watched her. She saw it peripherally, while willing herself not to acknowledge his taunting smirk. The Rolls' left front end rose with the jack's choppy, but steady lift.

"How about that drink?"

Irritated with herself that she couldn't deny him a drink, Ceara grasped the narrow-necked bottle at her feet and removed the cap. “Come closer to the partition.” She held the jug to his lips.

Eddie gulped then swiped his chin on his shoulder. Ceara put the jug on the floor then grasped the partition glass to draw it closed. Eddie shoved his head and the point of one shoulder through the opening and stopped her.

“Give me my ledgers, and I’ll give you a divorce, a hundred grand, and the deed to my beach house in Miami. We’ll be square.”

“We’ll never be *square*. How convenient for you to have such a short memory.”

“My memories are crystal clear. I won’t forget how you blabbed your mouth in front of my men, but I’m willing to let that slide.” He pressed his body against the back of the seat, his broad shoulders filling the opening.

“You were nothing until I married you, nothing but a poor Irish street girl—a slum brat. I gave you my name. Social standing. My family money. A house. Fancy clothes. Diamonds. Parties. You had a duty to love, honor, and obey me and give me sons. You haven’t held up your end.”

Bitter grief boiled in the cauldron of her hatred. It constantly simmered just under the surface of her emotional control.

“My end? Because of you, our baby died. How can you expect me to react any way other than as I have? You promised to love, honor, and cherish. Instead, you gave me heartache. Your idea of a wife is a woman who willingly lives as your prisoner while offering blind obedience to the Lord and Master.”

He laughed. "Be a little more grateful, babe. You didn't have it so bad. You knew what you were getting into when you married me. You liked what I offered. You wanted it, just like you wanted what I gave you in bed."

Ceara looked at him a good long while. Slowly nodding, she said, "You're right. I did know and, for a while, I convinced myself it wasn't important who you were under your guise as an upstanding citizen. I'm grateful your mother isn't alive to hear your lies and to see what you've become. She'd be ashamed. She'd point her finger, her eyes would spark, and she'd give you the dressing down you deserve. I can hear the disappointment in her voice. *Sei un verme*, she'd call you. She often told me how good I was for you, and that she hoped I'd marry you to keep you out of the trouble she saw you were headed for."

Eddie's face went dark. "Leave her out of this. My offer for a divorce is only good until Cowboy gets back in the car."

"And if I decline your generous offer? What then?" She didn't give him time to answer. "I'll tell you what. It won't matter. You'll be in jail, and this will all be behind me." There. She'd said it. She hoped for it. But she didn't really believe it.

"That's a laugh. You know jail won't stop me. Someone's gonna pay a visit to your family—might be me, might not—but from this day on, you'll look over your shoulder every minute, always wondering where I am, what I'm planning, where I'll strike, and who I'll take out. You won't be able to stand it. You'll crack and come crawling back. And when you do, you'll learn your place—in and out of our bedroom. I want my ledgers. My offer is your only way out."

God, how she hated his cocksure smile.

"You know it's true."

The barricade of defense she'd erected around her courage was too strong for his assault.

"No. You're wrong. Your ledgers are my way out, as long as they remain in my control. I intend to make sure they stay that way."

"You've got a gun. Now's your chance to get rid of me for good."

Ceara turned the door handle and shoved the door open. As she got out, she looked back at him. "You are right about one thing."

"What's that?"

"I *am* going to divorce you."

"Not a chance, babe. I'll be coming after you and the cowboy. Watch your backs."

"A fanabla!"

The car teetered precariously on the jacked-up front end when she slammed the door to cut off the unbearable sound of Eddie's smug laughter. Hagen put a steadying hand on the fender.

"Used all his charm at once, did he?"

She stomped toward the center of the highway then returned to Hagen. "I know better than to let him bait me, but he has such a mouth. And that nervy grin—"

"He's got a way of getting under a person's skin even without opening his mouth."

Hands trembling, Ceara wiped tears from her cheeks. It was an impossible situation. Living in the shadow of Eddie's threats was no life at all. Not for her, not for her parents, and certainly not for her sisters.

Drawing the sides of her coat together, she hugged herself against the biting wind. "He's offered me a divorce, cash, and property in exchange for his ledgers."

"Did you take it?"

"No."

"Why not?"

"I don't believe him. When I divorce him, it will be on my terms, not his." Calmer now, she noticed the bullet holes and dents in the side of the car. "This poor car is a wreck."

"She took a beating, but she's a tough gal."

"Why did the tire blow out?"

Hagen pointed. "The fender below the armor plating got shoved in against the tire when they rammed us, and a jagged piece of metal dug into the sidewall." He let the car down and removed the jack.

"Where are we?"

"I think just inside the Ohio state line."

"Hagen— There's a car coming."

"I see it." Hagen picked up the B-A-R from the ground and handed it to her on his way to the toolbox on the driver's side to replace the jack and wheel iron. "Put this behind your back, but be ready to show it if they're too nosey or not friendly."

The car slowed, came abreast, and stopped. The passenger rolled down his window, and the driver leaned over to see Hagen and Ceara.

"You folks need help? Did you see that awful wreck back a few miles? Looked like two cars hit. Both of them caught fire. No one survived. People are trying to move the wreckage off the road. I drove down in...in the...ditch..." The man's words slowed and faded as his eyes widened when he got a better look at the Rolls and realization that he'd come up on something he wasn't sure he wanted any part of. He dragged his gaze from the car to look at Hagen.

"Well... I'll...uh...stop at the next town and report the accident." The passenger hastily rolled up his window, and the car continued on.

Hagen took the rifle from Ceara. "I'll drive." He opened the door and stepped back for her to get in.

"Gotcha!"

Chapter Nine

Ceara's right cheek smashed against the doorframe. Lights burst in her head; searing pain spiked across her face. Hagen seized her coat and spun her out of Eddie's grasp with a shove that sent her stumbling. Her feet tangled, and she fell, leaving skin from knees and palms on the asphalt.

The engine revved; tires squealed. Hagen grabbed her around the waist and half-dragged her to the ditch where he dropped her into the snow-dusted dirt and weeds. The strident whine of a car engine faded in the distance.

"Stay down." Hagen stood over her, an ear cocked to the wind, and his gaze locked on the direction Eddie had driven off. "He'll come back under a full head of steam. Chicago's behind us. He needs his men, and he needs them fast. This highway is the most direct route to them."

Dazed, all she could manage was to follow his gaze and squint into the foggy veil of blustery snowfall. Hagen shrugged out of his coat and walked to the center of the highway. He planted his feet like he meant to hold his ground in a last stand face-off with the B-A-R diagonally against his body, his left hand holding the barrel, and his right hand on the stock.

An eerie quiet descended. Seconds dragged on before she heard the hum of a car approaching way down the highway. One dim, blurry headlamp grew ominously brighter. Terror rooted her to the ground. Her gaze darted from the on-coming car to Hagen and back. The gap between the looming monster and its target narrowed, yet Hagen stood like a granite statue in the face of the charging three-ton iron beast.

Too close! Too close! Jump! Hagen, jump! A scream rose in her chest, but caught in her throat in a soundless plea to save himself.

In that instant before too-late-to-dodge, Hagen lifted the rifle to his shoulder and fired several rounds into the front of the Rolls. Ceara was certain the car's fender clipped his heels as he dived out of Eddie's path. Hagen hit the edge of the highway on his shoulder and rolled, sliding to a stop on his belly. The big car careened side to side, then straightened out and zoomed away.

Ceara crawled to Hagen. "If you were trying to kill him or stop him, your aim was off."

"My aim was dead on. I slowed him down. I want that car."

"Slowed him down? How? The car has bullet-proof windows and armor plating."

"The plating and windows are to protect the people inside, not the engine. I aimed just below the Spirit of Ecstasy."

"The what?"

"The bonnet ornament figure." Hagen got to his feet and gave her a hand up. He put his coat back on and talked while he reloaded the B-A-R from the cartridges in his pocket. "With any luck at all, I managed to put a couple of holes toward the top of the radiator, which will cause the car to overheat. In a few miles, he'll be flat-footin' it down the highway just like us. If we can get a ride, we'll either find where he's abandoned the car, in which case, I'll see if it still runs. If it doesn't, we'll go on into Ft. Wayne and figure out what to do then. Either way, we might get to a police station and get the cops looking for him before he makes it to Chicago."

"I heard a *luck*, an *if*, a *might*, and *before*. That's not encouraging. And neither is backtracking." She pointed. "New York is that way."

"It's all I've got. We need a car, and I want his. I'm gambling he'll pull over before the engine gives out. He's helpless when it comes to car trouble. When steam rolls out from under the bonnet, he'll ditch that baby. He won't know what else to do. No doubt, he's got pockets full of cash, so he can buy a ride or steal one, if he has to. He won't stay stranded long, but he'll be pissed when he realizes I took his .32. He's probably got a hide-out gun as backup. Likely a derringer with two shots."

"He's got more going for him than we do," Ceara muttered as she looked both ways and saw nothing but fog and empty highway.

"We're getting nowhere by standing here. Come on." Hagen grabbed her hand and took off at a brisk walk toward Ft. Wayne. "How's your face?"

"Throbbing." She gingerly touched her fingertips to her cheek. "It's already puffy."

"Well, now your cheeks match."

"Flatterer. Hitting the door frame knocked me for a loop."

"It's a wonder it didn't knock you clear out." Hagen mumbled, "Where are all those cars that went by when we didn't need a ride?"

"You really think anyone will give us a ride when they see your rifle?"

"Might use it as persuasion."

"Showing your badge might be a friendlier inducement."

He simply grinned.

A gust of wind swirled powdery snow around their feet, and the sudden onset of sleet stung exposed skin. Without breaking stride, Hagen clamped the B-A-R under one arm while he dug out his gloves.

"I've never been so cold in my life since I've been in Chicago, and I've been in some hellacious blizzards. The air's always wet here, even when the sun's shining. Snows like hell for five miles then clears off for ten. Then, out of nowhere, we run headlong into a wall of fog and this freezing rain. There's something crazy-wrong with your eastern weather. I'll take hot Texas winds and big old prairie thunderstorms any day."

"Aren't you Mister Gloom and Despair all of a sudden? We've been beaten, shot at, and the car we stole was stolen from us. Now, winter weather upsets you? Wait until we get to New York. You'll have some really crazy weather to complain about, then."

Her chastisement made him smile. "Can't wait." He took hold of her hand again and stepped out in a half-walking, half-trotting pace.

Trudging in silence, ten minutes and two cars passed. Ceara couldn't keep up any longer. Tugging to slow him, she said, "Please, Hagen, I have to catch my breath."

"Sure. Sorry. Here. Stand in front of me. I'll be your windbreak."

She rested with her back against his chest. Deep bone-weary fatigue loomed right on the edge of not able to take another step. He put one arm around her and dipped his head so close the warmth of his breath caressed her cheek when he whispered, "We'll make it. We're in this together until the end. Don't give up now."

His words were the boost she needed. The few minutes they stood together with his body offering its little bit of warmth renewed her strength. She heard the uneven puttering hum of an engine in the same moment Hagen gave her a parting squeeze. He held the B-A-R at his side, masked in the shadows of his coat as he moved to the middle of the highway while waving his other arm for the car to stop. The driver of the flatbed freight truck saw him just in time to swerve into the on-coming lane as Hagen jumped out of the way. The truck pulled back into the westbound lane, and the brake lights shone like welcoming beacons on a stormy sea.

Hagen held Ceara's hand as they trotted to meet the car backing toward them. He opened the passenger door and walked along with the truck until it came to a halt.

"My God, son, I just about hit you. You scared five years off my life that I can't afford at my age." An elderly man dressed in heavy coat, overalls, and a woolen cap with ear flaps pulled down shined an old-fashioned hand-torch in Hagen's face.

"Sorry. My wife and I need a ride." Hagen pulled Ceara forward and shoved her into the cab without waiting for an invitation. "We had a flat some miles back, and some hoodlums stole our car. Roughed my wife up. Show him, honey."

The man saw her swollen face well enough, and his indignation made him an instant ally.

"Well, I'll be—"

"They stole her purse, too. Good thing she wasn't carrying all our money."

From the corner of her eye, Ceara saw Hagen stow the rifle between the crates stacked on the flatbed.

"They stole your purse? Seems no one's safe these days. I can give you a ride as far as Ft. Wayne."

"Much obliged." Hagen got inside and closed the door.

"I'm Harry Longley."

"John Jones. This is my wife, Jane."

Three people made it a snug fit on the narrow bench seat, but it was warmer and certainly faster than walking even at the truck's twenty-five-miles-per-hour puttering. Ceara was grateful the cab had real glass in the side windows and not canvas curtains.

"Where are you kids from?"

"Texas." Hagen leaned forward to talk around Ceara.

"Texas? Well, I'll be. I thought I heard a twang in your voice. What brings you so far from home?"

"Her mother passed on. We're headed back home from the funeral."

"Oh, that's too bad. I'm sorry to hear it." The man clicked his tongue. "I don't care how old you are, you never get over losing your mother. I recall when my own dear mother died. God rest her soul..."

Harry took advantage of his hitchhiking, captive-audience and droned on. Ceara nodded, and Hagen grunted polite responses at the appropriate times. When they came upon the charred wreck of the two cars, Ceara exchanged a glance with Hagen as Harry slowed and maneuvered around the cars and people gathered to clean up the mess. More tongue clicking and a general lamentation of the world going to hell in a handbasket with these new-fangled fast cars followed for the next several miles.

Hagen saw the Rolls a moment before Ceara. She sat up a little straighter and peered through the dirty windshield.

"Harry. There's our car. Pull in behind it."

"Well, no wonder it was stolen. That's some fancy car you've got there. It looks like it has a flat on the back, though. Do you have another spare?'"

"One more, but that's it."

"Here, take this." Harry gave him the hand-torch. "I'll pull up so the headlamps give you some light to work by."

"Thanks. I'll see if it starts. No sense changing the flat if it's out of gas. We were driving on fumes and hoping we'd make it to Ft. Wayne before we ran dry."

"That's a good idea."

"Janey, honey. You wait here."

"Whatever you say, darling." Ceara smiled at their little charade.

She followed the light of the hand-torch as Hagen made a circle around the car before he got into the front seat. He came out with the water jug, went to the front, and folded up the bonnet. After a minute or so, he returned to the driver's seat, and turned on the ignition. The car started. He let it idle for a few seconds, then he turned it off and went to work changing the tire. When he came to the truck, Ceara opened the door, and he reached across her to return Harry's light.

"She's purring like a kitten. Thanks for the help, Mr. Longley."

"Glad to help. You two take care."

Hagen slipped a folded bill to Ceara and made a meaningful nod toward Harry. She placed the money on the seat on her way out. Harry pulled onto the road as Hagen retrieved his rifle from the back.

Walking to the car, Ceara said, "Lucky for us Eddie didn't take the ignition key."

"He probably figured the car was done-for when steam started rolling out."

"It seems too much of a coincidence to have two flat tires."

"It would, but it looks like he shot the tire in a fit of rage when the radiator spewed." Hagen opened the driver's side back door. "See what you can find that might be useful."

"Such as?"

"Anything. You never know what might come in handy in a pinch." Hagen closed the back door, latched the bonnet, then got behind the wheel. He swung across both lanes and resumed their easterly route.

Ceara searched all of the drawers and cubby holes in the mahogany inlay that outlined the back seat area. "It's a mess back here. Things are strewn everywhere."

"I hope he was searching for his wallet." Hagen patted his coat pocket.

"There's a flask, camera, chewing gum, hard candy. Here's a cigar case. Brass knuckles. Cigarettes in a monogrammed case. Book of matches. Coins." She left the whiskey and the camera and put the rest of the menagerie into her apron pockets. "No money or guns." She wiggled through the divider and over the seat. "I should have taken off my coat. I barely fit through here. How in the world did Eddie manage?'

"Desperation creates ingenuity."

"Is this the radiator cap?" She picked up the circular piece of metal on the seat.

"Yes."

"Doesn't this need to be on the radiator to keep the water from coming out?"

"Usually, but since I shot holes in the radiator, the cap stays off to keep pressure from building up. We'll have to add water as often as we can find it. I don't know how long or how far I can keep this girl running, but she'll get us a few more miles down the road."

"And then what? What do we do if it quits? We've lost so much time, and who knows where Eddie is."

"We'll find a different way to keep going. I'll baby her along to keep her running through the night. Before day-light, we have to have different transportation. We got away with stopping for fuel, because the news of the Chicago shooting hadn't spread that far yet. By morning, just about everyone who listens to the radio or reads a newspaper will be on the lookout for this car."

"Don't we have enough money to buy a car?"

"Yeah, but strangers showing up in town without a car and wanting to buy a car is suspicious."

"We could steal one."

Hagen laughed. "It wouldn't be our first. We stole this one."

Ceara laughed with him. "Yes, we did. Twice."

"Our other choices are bus, train, and hitchhiking again. An airport won't do us any good at night, and I'm not traveling unarmed, so a daylight flight is out." He patted the Browning. "We won't be welcome on a bus, either."

"Busses are slow and not at all private. Someone's bound to wonder about us."

"That leaves hitchhiking or the train. In the daylight, people will be reluctant to give us a ride when they see your rifle. It was luck that you were able to hide it in the back of Mr. Longley's truck."

"The train is our best option. It's slower than driving, but no faster than a bus—probably even slower—but a train offers more privacy. I'll come up with a way to take my rifle onboard that won't make anyone suspicious." Hagen nodded as he thought. "If we don't leave tracks, we can't be tracked."

"At least Eddie didn't get off with our sandwiches." Ceara handed a wax paper-wrapped sandwich and an apple to Hagen then took out the same for herself. "There's nothing that works-up a girl's appetite like hitchhiking in a snowstorm."

He chuckled. "Yep. A good, brisk walk before supper helps with digestion. Gets the blood circulating. Clears the lungs."

"Speaking of clearing the lungs, what was that yell you made just before you threw Eddie out of the car back in Chicago? I've never heard anything like it. It wasn't human or animal. It was... I can't describe it. A banshee wail? A war cry? Whatever it was, it made the hairs on my arms stand up."

"It's a combination of all of those. Add a bobcat and rabbit scream, and you've got it."

"Did you make it up just then?"

"No. My Granddad Kane taught me. Back in the War Between the States, he was too young to sign up, so he lied about his age in order to serve with a Texas regiment. That's where he learned that yell. I've heard it called the Rebel Yell, Texas Yell, Comanche Scream, and the Scottish War Cry. Texas Rangers have their own version. I guess mine takes a little from each."

"Is it just for scaring the daylights out of everyone within earshot?"

Hagen chuckled again. "Well, it does that, but the real purpose is to control the soldier's—or warrior's—fear in battle through intimidation of the enemy and creating a sense of savagery in the soldier. There's a story General Jubal Early told his men who'd run out of ammunition and were afraid to charge. He said they should 'holler them across'. So, they did."

"That must have been a sight to behold and a terror to hear."

"Which was the point, and it was effective. My granddad and my brother and I go out from town now and again and howl just for the heck of it."

"I'd like to hear that in person someday."

His levity faded. Ceara instantly regretted saying the words and putting him on the spot. Embarrassed, she took a bite of her sandwich and kept her gaze lowered. She'd ruined a perfectly lighthearted interlude by not thinking of what she was saying. She knew better. There was no someday for them.

Why couldn't she keep her feelings for him in check? Why did she insist upon reading what she wanted into his care and concern for her welfare? He'd not denied she was just a job to him. He took his responsibility toward her seriously, plain and simple. When this ordeal was over and Hoover took possession of Eddie's books, they would go their separate ways. She had to remember that.

"I—I'm sorry. I didn't mean... I shouldn't have—"

"No. It's all right. You come to Amarillo any time. My family will give you a Texas welcome."

She could only nod. His family would welcome her, not him.

They ate in silence, and as the miles disappeared behind them, Ceara's interest and energy for conversation waned as exhaustion and the advancing evening settled in. Miles and many radiator refills along the highway later, they stopped at a motor-hotel with a Vacancy sign shining in neon letters.

"Maybe there's a payphone in the office."

Ceara hardly had time to notice he was gone before he returned. "That was quick."

"Telephone was at the desk. No privacy."

"Did you ask about a train?"

"Yes. Nearest passenger stop is in Mansfield."

"How far is that?"

Hagen tapped the fuel gauge. "About that far plus another fifty miles."

"Then we need a filling station. Is there one open at this time of night in this town?"

"No. I asked about that, too."

Ceara's shoulders slumped. "We won't make it. What will we do?"

"I installed a five-gallon auxiliary tank last week. It should get us that extra fifty miles. The toggle switch is right here under the steering wheel. The trick is to switch it just as the tank runs dry. When the engine coughs, rev-it, and flip the switch." He shrugged. "That's the theory, anyway. I didn't have a chance to test it to see if it works."

He grunted when she jabbed him in the ribs.

"You could have mentioned that earlier. I've more than enough to worry about without fretting over running out of fuel." She couldn't maintain her disapproving scowl against the sound of his laughter.

"Sorry. In the excitement of running for our lives and being chased down by gun-toting mobsters, it must have slipped my mind." Hagen pulled onto the street. "Will this make up for my bad memory? The motel owner gives out candy every Valentine's Day to anyone who stops in." He reached inside his coat and brought out a red, heart-shaped box with a paper rose attached to the top. "You mentioned you'd like a box of chocolates."

Ceara placed the candy on her lap. "I did say that, didn't I?" She blinked rapidly and turned her face so he wouldn't see how much this small gesture touched her. She felt utterly pathetic that receiving a gift of candy could bring her to tears.

Hagen touched her hand. "What's wrong?"

"Nothing's wrong. I'm just surprised you remembered my off-handed, flippant words this morning. I was scared. I didn't expect you to take me seriously. Thank you."

"You're welcome. Um... Are you going to just hold them?"

"Oh, I'm sorry." Ceara laughed. "Would you care for a piece?"

"Don't mind if I do."

"This is certainly a Valentine's Day I'll never forget."

"Neither will I, and it's not over yet."

She knew what he meant. They had to be ready for whatever came their way, but how could anyone predict what the madman she was married to might do?

Chapter Ten

Eddie Rocchelli's Sicilian blood ran hot. He was a man accustomed to people jumping at the snap of his fingers, yet here he was, walking along a highway on a windy winter night like some down-on-his-luck tramp. Every step chafed his pride with the same intensity as his fifty-dollar, slick-soled shoes rubbed blisters on the backs of his heels.

Damn that cowboy, and damn to hell my thieving, cheating wife.

Seething anger deepened with every car that didn't stop until rage and bloodlust-fueled-revenge fed his craving for vengeance that went beyond losing his ledgers. His fury, steeped in equal parts humiliation and fear that the foundation of his world, his empire-in-the-making, was crumbling under his feet, simmered on slow boil.

He descended into the dark dungeon of his mind that housed all of his plans and schemes. This private haven was his sanctuary where he knew who he was, what he wanted, and how to get it. No one crossed him or dared challenge his authority there, and the threat of imminent ruin didn't exist. He'd take care of his wife and her family and that damned mongrel dog Kane, whom Hoover had sicced on him.

Ceara would cough up his ledgers once he got his hands on her family. She wouldn't give them over to save herself, maybe not even to save Kane, but she'd do anything to protect her family. He fantasized about snaring them all at once, but he'd take them one at a time and be just as satisfied. If he had to, he'd hunt them all down on the street. Hound them. Follow them. Torture them when he caught them. She'd regret rebuffing his offer of a divorce and a hundred grand. If she thought for one minute she'd get another penny out of him so she and Kane could live the high life on his money, she was wrong. Dead wrong.

He likened his rise toward top dog status in Chicago's underworld to the way his grandparents had struggled to create the family fortune after they came to America from Sicily. It was a story he and his older brother had learned at their father's knee. Now, in his maniacal fervor, his father's voice came to him with the tale...

Your grandparents Edoardo and Clemenza Rocchelli worked for seven years as indentured servants at a shipping company in New York. The man who paid their way to America was a good man, a good friend to them. He treated them fairly and, in return, they worked hard every day of those seven years in gratitude.

Your grandfather was a sailor and a carpenter, and your grandmother could cook and bake as no one I've ever known. They saved their money, and, at the end of their service, their employer gave them a lump sum of money and told them to move to Chicago where there were more opportunities for men who understood the ways of the water.

To Chicago they went. They bought one tugboat, and it took almost all of their money, but within a year, their business was so good they bought a second boat. In five years, a dozen. Men worked for them now.

Do not forget what they did for this family. Never forget their sacrifices. After I am gone, it is up to you, Stefano, and to you, young Edoardo, to continue honoring their memory and their legacy when you inherit all they gave to our family. Spend wisely. Make good business decisions. You have a duty to build the family's fortune and to keep the name Rocchelli known and respected...

But his father died too soon, and Stefano followed two years later. Francesca Rocchelli inherited a business she was not equipped to handle. Eddie recalled the day she signed papers conveying to him the power to manage the Rocchelli holdings, interests, and finances in her name. He vowed to make his grandfather and father not only proud of him, but to double the Rocchelli fortune within five years. He'd done just that. He had the Feds and Prohibition to thank for his financial success. Transporting whiskey by tugboat from Canada to Chicago's thirsty patrons was his golden goose, and he was more than willing to collect the golden eggs. He'd ceased the risky business of transporting whiskey by tugboat two years ago, and turned his eye toward restaurants and speakeasies. His tugboats were strictly legit now.

Nothing, absolutely nothing, was going to destroy what the Rocchelli family had built. Not his double-crossing wife, not a lawman, and especially not J. Edgar Hoover. Once he retrieved his ledgers, he'd lay low for a while, then he'd hit Moran and Capone with everything he had. This time next year, Eddie Rocchelli would be sitting on the throne of the Crime King in Chicago.

Even if he ended up in court, the Feds couldn't pin anything on him, not with the lawyers and the judges he could buy or already had in his pocket. The ledgers held nothing but circumstantial evidence. Yeah. *Yeah. Circumstantial.* He'd beat whatever rap Hoover tried to pin on him.

His thoughts raced and jumped from one plan to the next then circled around again. His mind combined fantasy and reality. Kane became Moran's man, a hitman planted inside to kill him. Then, Ceara sold his ledgers to Capone for fifty grand— No. It was Hoover who paid her. Ceara and Kane lived off the profit in his house in Florida while he languished in prison.

These images and thoughts tormented him. He clamped his hands against his temples and screamed into the night.

"*Ceara*!" Too many thoughts, too many faces in his head, and all laughing at him, taunting him. He'd get even with her. He'd kill her before another man—

"Pops! Hey! Pops! Old man! Are you deaf? You wanna ride?"

Eddie stared at the Hudson Model O idling beside him. The passenger window was down, and the stupidly grinning, ruddy-complexioned faces of two teenaged rich kids gawked at him. They were clearly out for a joy-ride in grandpa's fancy car. Always quick on his feet, Eddie slammed the dungeon door in his mind closed, and forced a broad, friendly smile, choosing to ignore their *old man* reference for the sake of a ride.

"Yeah. Can you take me to a hotel in the next town?"

"Sure thing, Pops. Get in."

He squeezed onto the small seat like a sardine in a can, but he didn't care. Neither did he care that the boys reeked of cheap whiskey, or that the driver pushed speeds unsafe for his inebriated condition. He braced his feet on the floorboard with one hand against the dash, the other hand gripping the door's armrest, and held on.

The driver misjudged his speed and jumped the curb to park on the sidewalk in front of a two-story brick hotel. Eddie got out without a word or backwards glance.

One of the boys yelled at him, "Hey, Pops, you could at least thank us."

The bell over the hotel's door jingled, and a young male desk clerk greeted him.

"Hello. Welcome to the Blue Jay Hotel. My name is Bobby. How can I help you?"

"I need a room overnight."

"First or second floor?"

"Second with a street view."

"Sure thing." Bobby offered the register for Eddie to sign and told him the price. Eddie placed the money on the counter.

Bobby turned the register to read it. "Roger Vale." He looked Eddie over. "Mr. Vale. If you don't mind me saying so, you look like you're hurt. Can I do anything for you?"

He offered a dismissive wave. "I crashed my car outside of town. Knocked me around. Couple of boys gave me a ride here. I need to make a phone call for my brother to come get me."

"The telephone's in the booth." He pointed to the far end of the long, narrow lobby. "Local or long-distance call?"

"Long distance. Is that a problem?"

"No, but it's not a pay-phone. Local calls are free. You have to pay for long distance upfront." He shrugged apologetically. "It's an on-your-honor set-up. There's a pad and pencil by the phone to write down the charges."

Eddie placed a ten on the counter. "I may need to make several calls."

Bobby put the bill into the cash drawer. "Make as many as you need, Mr. Vale. You know, you seem familiar to me."

Not missing a beat, Eddie said, "I sell Baxter Brushes. I come through town every few months."

Bobby perked up. "I'll bet that's it. My grandma is a regular buyer."

"Where can I get something to eat?"

"There's a diner around the corner."

Eddie placed another bill on the counter. "You go there and get me a plate of the special and a pot of coffee and bring it up to my room, and you can keep the change."

"This time of evening, it might be busy. Could take thirty or forty minutes."

"I'm not going anywhere soon."

Bobby placed a triangular, stand-up notice on the counter that stated in bold letters— *Supper break - Will return soon*— then took his coat and hat from a hook by the door on his way out.

Eddie stepped inside the wooden, glass-fronted phone booth and closed the accordion door. He sat on the wooden bench across the narrow space from the walnut and brass candlestick phone perched on a wooden corner shelf. Grasping the phone's shaft, he lifted the receiver from the switch hook. In a few seconds, a female voice spoke.

"Operator."

"I need a person-to-person long distance connection to Chicago, Illinois at Klondike 5-4739 for Dave Vale."

The operator repeated his request, and he confirmed it was correct.

"Your name and number, please."

"Roger Vale." Eddie recited the number written on the paper tacked to the wall.

"Thank you. One moment, please, while I transfer your call."

He drummed his fingers while his call went through rate and route operators that ended with ringing at the number.

"Connecting. Please hold."

More waiting.

"Hello. Who's calling?"

Rocchelli recognized Paul's voice.

"Roger Vale calling long distance from Ft. Wayne, Indiana for Dave Vale," the operator announced.

Hesitation. "Dave's not here. Call back in ten minutes." He hung up.

Paul would go to a designated pay-phone and wait for him to call again. The operator told him the rate disconnected the call.

Eddie checked the time, then and moved to an upholstered lobby chair. Other than two couples passing through, he was alone. When the ten minutes were up, he went through the calling routine again with a different number.

When Paul answered, Rocchelli asked, "Can you talk?"

"We're clear."

"I'm stranded in a flea-trap hotel in Ft. Wayne without my car. The Blue Jay. It's on the east side."

"Where's your car and the two passengers?"

"We parted company."

"Dead?"

"No. On foot and on the lam. What happened to Big C and Little P? I saw them running away."

"Hiding out and waiting for orders."

"The Detroit Kid? He was loopy."

"Recovered and itching to get his knife back from the cowboy."

"You and Gramps? Both intact?" Eddie wasn't as concerned about their collective health as he needed a head count of who in his immediate crew were available.

"Not a scratch."

"All right. Put me wise."

"You're hot. Front page news hot. Cops talked to me and Gramps at the same time, and they showed up at your house and both restaurants with warrants. They've been to the docks and there's talk of a warrant to search your tugboats. The Kid was at headquarters when the cops searched without a warrant."

Rocchelli chuckled low in his throat. "Didn't find anything, did they?"

"No. But they're still watching. Patrol cars are cruising my neighborhood. Gramps's neighborhood, too."

"Let 'em snoop. Gives 'em something to do to earn their pay. Do you think Big C was in on it?"

"No. He called. He's sweating bullets that you think he was in on the hit when he let the brothers in. He was duped. He could have turned on us at any time."

"What do you know about the hit?"

"Word is Bugs and Scarface hit the warehouse at the same time for different reasons."

Eddie leaned forward with renewed grip on the earpiece. "Explain."

"Scarface intended to take Bugs out. Bugs was seen heading for the warehouse, but he doubled-back and went into a café."

So Scarface missed him. Too bad. "What about Bugs hitting the warehouse?"

"He never intended to be at the warehouse. The whiskey shipment was a ruse to get you there for a hit, and Scarface used the same scheme on Bugs."

Moran wanting him dead was a surprise. Capone sending a chopper squad to take out Moran wasn't. Maybe Ceara hadn't lied when she said she'd contacted both Moran and Capone about the ledgers, and they'd separately arranged to take him out at the warehouse.

"Are you there?" Paul asked.

"Yeah. Scarface could have been after me, too, since he knew I'd be there with Bugs."

"More like a coincidence, plain and simple—"

"I don't believe in coincidence. We've got a stoolie. Is it my wife?"

Paul's grunting scoff was loud and clear. "If there's a tattler, it wouldn't be her. Scarface and Bugs wouldn't give a woman, and especially a disloyal wife, the time of day."

Rocchelli saw the logic in his reasoning. "Then it's the cowboy."

"Doubtful. His business was legal not as a troublemaker between gangs."

Now that the idea of a turncoat was in his head, he couldn't let it go. Rocchelli dismissed the nobodies who worked for him. Mentally cataloguing his closest men, he pigeon-holed each as a likely or unlikely candidate. Jucca was too stupid to run a double-cross. Paul was rock-solid loyal. Phil and Cecil lacked the nerve to deal with the likes of Capone and Moran. That left Leo. Although steady and smart, he had a soft spot for Ceara. Eddie considered the strength of Leo's loyalty to him and decided he wouldn't jeopardize his job for a woman. At his age, Leo couldn't afford to lose his ample paycheck plus the lucrative side benefits. Of all his men, Leo adhered to a strong sense of right and wrong no one could budge, but he couldn't swear Leo was blindly loyal to him as were his other men.

Paul said, "We've also heard Capone or Moran put men on alert at places you might show up if you're trying to leave the country. You need to take a vacation to California or Florida. Hide out until this blows over."

"No. There's something I've got to do. It can't wait."

"Everything can wait until the heat dies down and—"

"Shut up and listen. Here's the deal. I want two cars with drivers who can follow orders and keep their traps shut. You know who else to bring along. Pack light. I need clothes, top to bottom. We're driving straight through. Bring along extra gas in case we don't find a place to fuel-up when we need it. And spare tires. Make sure we have extra tires. I want guns, ammo, and cash. Lots of cash. I need cotton dressing and tape with some sort of ointment."

"For what?"

"Does it matter? My shoes rubbed blisters, okay?" Did he hear a muffled chuckle?

"Where are we going?"

"New York. Five Points."

"Five Points? Isn't that Sebastian Lazzarano's territory? Muscling-in is suicide."

"Don't worry. We'll mind our Ps and Qs."

Paul didn't speak for some seconds. "What's in New York?"

"Important documents—"

"Put your lawyers on it."

"—and my runaway wife."

"You can get another wife."

Eddie barked, "Are you telling me how to do my business?"

"Boss, listen to me. You're asking for trouble we can't handle."

"No. *You* listen to me!" It was time to give Paul an allegiance reminder. "The names and locations in my books are coded, but in the wrong hands it won't look too good for some of the people who work for me." It was a lie to stir up Paul's imagination. He kept the legitimate books and the under-the-table payroll books separate, and he paid staff with legally earned money.

"All right. Understood. What do you need done?"

"Get us a hideout stocked with food and water for the weekend. I want a gumshoe watching my in-law's house. I need to know if my wife gets there before I do. I want to know if the cowboy's with her. I want them tailed if they leave the house, so I can find them. I want regular updates."

"That'll take a lot of men, which makes for suspicious activity in the neighborhood. Someone's bound to notice and call the cops."

"It's only for a few hours. We'll take over when we get there."

"Getting all this together here and arranging for a hideout four states away will take time and money."

"Pay what you have to."

Paul repeated in a low, cautioning tone, "It'll take time."

"You sound like you don't know what to do. It's business as usual."

"No, it's not."

"Sure, it is. Get on the blower. Call in favors."

"Things have changed, Eddie. No one here will stick their neck out for you now, not with Capone and Moran breathing down your back."

Eddie leaned back, stunned. This wasn't what he wanted to hear. What was wrong with him? "I pay people to do what I tell them. Do I need to find someone else to do your job?"

"No." Paul exhaled a heavy sigh. "I've got it. What's the hideout for?"

"A family reunion."

Silence.

"What's on your mind?"

Still silence.

"Spill it."

"What about her story about the baby?"

The question rankled. He wouldn't take that kind of accusatory comment from anyone but Paul, and Paul knew it, otherwise he wouldn't have had the guts to bring it up.

"If you have to ask, you've already made up your mind."

Silence lingered.

Eddie pushed him. "Are you with me on this?"

"Yeah. I'm with you."

Eddie wasn't convinced. "Then what's your problem? Are you stalling?"

"No problem. I'm thinking. My cousin Dino lives in the Bronx. He picks up a few extra bucks now and then doing leg-work for a shamus. I'll call him. Give me the details."

This was more to his liking. "The Galloways live in Five Points. They own a neighborhood grocery. Her father's name is Finn. Mother is Maureen. There are two younger sisters. Claire and Colleen."

"Address?"

"I don't know."

"You'll pay out the nose for this."

"I'll pay whatever it takes. We also need to swap out our Chicago license plates for New York plates."

"He'll want a legitimate reason to get involved."

Eddie thought for a few moments. "Divorce. I need evidence that my wife has run off with another man. Say there's a marriage contract, but she doesn't get a penny if I can prove adultery. But keep my name out of this."

Eddie laughed to himself. There was no marriage contract. The closest he had was a Last Will and Testament spelling everything out nice and legal-like. Other than bequeathing lump sums to the church and specific charities, he'd left everything to Ceara. He wasn't chancing the State of Illinois being able to take what he and his family had worked all their lives to acquire.

The beauty of this was Ceara didn't know a Will existed. He'd promised his mother if he ever married Ceara he'd provide for her in his Will just like his father had provided for his mother. That was well and good at the time, but things had changed. His wife had double-crossed him. He made a mental note to have his attorney rewrite his Will. Ceara wasn't going to get a red cent from him.

"How fast can you pull this together and get here?"

"I'll get Gramps and the Kid on the horn and have them contact Big C and Little P. They'll handle the leg work, while I get things rolling in New York. Let's say, three or four hours to get outfitted, then the drive to you... Call it seven hours."

"Make it six. Pull up in front on the street. I'll be watching."

"Will do. One more thing. The guys will ask questions. How much do I tell them? The last we saw, you were hanging off the side of your car beating the hell out of the cowboy."

"Tell them... Tell them the cowboy planned to turn me over to authorities, but I got away. Tell them he's heading for New York, and we're going to beat him there. Fill Leo in on the truth, but don't tell the others anything else. That's all they need to know until I say otherwise."

"Got it."

Eddie replaced the receiver onto the hook switch and stepped out of the booth as the clerk returned carrying a paper-board box.

"Here's your supper, Mr. Vale. Put everything back in the box when you're finished and set it outside your door. I'll take care of it."

Eddie tucked the box under his left arm to keep his gun hand free, then he remembered Kane probably had his .32, and he'd fired both rounds of his .22 Derringer into the car tire, and he didn't have cartridges to reload.

"Did you reach your brother?"

"My brother—? Oh, oh, yeah. He'll get here as soon as he can. Might be six or seven hours."

"Well, that's good. I hope you have a restful night."

Eddie took the stairs to the second floor. Once inside his room, he put the box on a table then pulled back the curtain and inspected the street. Nothing out of the ordinary. He draped his overcoat across a chair then dragged the chest of drawers in front of the locked door as an extra security measure and moved the bed out of direct line with the door and the window. He felt naked without a handgun, which was one more reason to get even with Kane for stealing his .32 while he was unconscious.

Satisfied no one could surprise him, he took off his shoes, which instantly alleviated the pain and pressure of his blisters, and he settled at the table with only two things on his mind—fill his belly with food and coffee, and then get a few hours sleep.

***

Two hours before daylight, Eddie left the hotel by the back stairs and met Paul on the street. He didn't recognize the four-door black Cadillac or the forest green, four-door sedan Model A parked at the curb, which meant the law wouldn't associate him with either car. Leo opened the back door passenger side on the Cadillac, nodded in greeting, and Eddie got inside. Paul followed him. Leo took the passenger front seat.

Eddie noted the driver was Gilbert Santino, the older of the two brothers he'd taken on as repayment for certain favors given to him by an associate, who was also their uncle. He assumed the driver of the other car was the younger brother, Lenny, and that Cecil, Phil, and Jucca were with him. He approved of Paul's shrewd choice to bring the young brothers in as drivers. They were as eager to please as they were to make names for themselves. He made it a habit to bring new young blood into his business, and Paul was a good judge of character.

"Gil, take the highway out of town going east. Push the speed limit, but not hard enough for coppers to notice. Mind your driving manners going through the towns."

"Yes, sir."

Eddie spoke to Paul. "Catch me up on New York."

"I haven't talked to Dino yet."

"What does that mean?"

"It means he's not home. I talked to his wife, Betty. Dino and my nephew Ronny have been pulling twelve-hour night shifts for two weeks. She said to call at seven."

Eddie checked his watch. "When it gets close, we'll find a restaurant with a phone and get some chow and coffee." He returned his watch to its vest pocket then focused his attention on the road ahead.

"What are you looking for?" Paul asked.

"My car. It quit me with a steaming radiator right about here. I remember that big, dead tree off in that field." He explained what happened from the time he regained consciousness to arriving at the hotel in Ft. Wayne.

"It's not here now," Leo said.

"That's because Kane has it."

Paul countered, "That's not reasonable or even probable. Kane had to backtrack to get it. He'd lose too much time. Plus with the radiator leaking, it wasn't drivable. That's why Kane shot at it—to slow you down and put you on foot the same as him. Some locals stole it during the night or a tow-truck hauled it off."

"No. His aim was deliberate. Kane's too good with cars. He knew what he was doing. He'll baby that car along for miles."

"If that's the case, then they've got a good lead on us. I agree with Paul. It's more likely the car gave out on them, and they ditched it somewhere up ahead," Leo said.

Paul added, "For all we know, they hid it in a town and thumbed a lift."

Eddie nodded to himself, only half-listening. If they got on a bus or train, they were well on their way to New York. His dismissed air travel, since finding an airport in one of these little towns wasn't likely during the daytime, and air travel wasn't available at night.

Leo pointed ahead. "We're coming up on the burned wreck."

"Slow down." Eddie rubbernecked as they drove past.

"Who do you think sent them after you? Capone or Moran?" Paul asked.

Eddie sat back against his seat. "Moran."

Paul nodded without comment, and that suited Eddie. He wasn't in the mood for anymore talk.

Fifteen minutes before time to call New York, they stopped for breakfast at a roadside restaurant, Jucca hurried from the other car to faun over Eddie as they gathered in a group outside the door.

"Good to see you, Boss. That was some gunfight at the warehouse, wasn't it? Did you get Kane? What happened to your car? Paul won't tell us diddly—"

"Later." Eddie cut him off.

Jucca persisted. "Are we going to D.C.? What's the plan?"

"He said he'd talk about it later." Leo tapped Jucca on the shoulder and received a dark scowl in return.

Cecil opened the restaurant door, and they filed in. The curious glances and out-right stares from patrons didn't surprise Eddie. Eight men in suits driving expensive cars branded them as mobsters, but it also kept people at a comfortable distance to mind their own business.

Eddie deliberately relegated Jucca to a table with the brothers and Phil to avoid listening to him bump his gums. He sat at the table nearest the semi-private telephone in the far corner with the others. They ordered and made neutral table-talk while they waited for Paul.

Eddie picked up an occasional word, but not enough to gauge the direction the conversation was going. He was on his second cup of coffee when the food arrived. Paul finished the call, came to the table, and made one nod, which told Eddie all he needed to know until they were in the privacy of the Cadillac.

Twenty minutes later outside the restaurant, Eddie instructed, "Jucca, Phil, take turns driving the Ford. Gilbert and Lenny need a break. Cecil, you're driving the Cadillac."

Once on the highway, Eddie asked Paul, "What's the scoop?"

"He wants a thousand for himself, five hundred for Ronny, plus reimbursement for stocking the hideout and another three hundred for plates."

"That's steep."

"He figured out you're desperate."

Eddie nodded, grudgingly admiring Dino's larceny.

"There's a complication."

"What?"

"He and Ronny can only watch the house for a few hours this afternoon."

Eddie's temper rose. "What the hell am I paying for? I need him there now." He slammed his fist on his thigh. "Get me someone else. Tell him to hire—"

"Eddie. Listen. There isn't anyone else. Not on short notice. I asked. The private dick he does part-time work for runs his own show. He won't take cases over the phone. You have to meet in person and put half the money up front, in cash. Dino's going out on a limb for me. He'll get us a place, then he's going to sleep for a couple of hours. I'll call his house around noon and tell him where we are. He'll tell us where to meet him."

"It's not good enough."

"If you have a better plan, I'm listening."

Eddie retreated into sulking silence. He didn't have a better plan. Doubt and second-guesses creeped into his mind, both threatening to sabotage his confident righteousness for revenge. He recognized those dangerous emotions for the traitors they were, and he banished them before they had a chance to take root in his mind and grow. Even if he missed Ceara and Kane in New York, they couldn't run or hide forever. He'd find them.

He'd find them.

CHAPTER ELEVEN

TOO TIRED TO SLEEP or talk, Ceara rested her head against the seat. Hagen seemed in no mood for conversation, either. It was just too much effort. Searching for and stopping at water hydrants and hand pumps broke up the monotony of staring at mile after mile of dark highway. The one outdoor pay-phone they found had a severed receiver cord.

Hagen toggled to the auxiliary tank thirty miles west of Mansfield. Even with the engine pinging and the temperature gauge hovering at the edge of *HOT* for the last hundred miles, the Rolls didn't falter. When they reached the city limits, Ceara rubbed a spot clear on the frosted passenger side window and peered into the snow-hazy night and the dim illumination provided by sparsely spaced street lights for a sign indicating the direction of the depot.

"There!" Ceara pointed. "Turn at the upcoming intersection."

Hagen drove slowly past the depot, eye-balling the area. "Now that we know where it is, we'll take to the alleys to find a place to conceal this car."

Ceara scoffed. "You're joking. Hide this car?"

Hagen smiled, made a left, and turned off the headlamps. A couple of minutes of cruising along the alleys brought them to a lean-to with a tin roof a few blocks from the depot. He backed in and cut the engine.

"If this is the end of the trail, we'll leave her with some life left in her. She kept going when I didn't think she could. She's got a big heart." He ran his hands around the steering wheel as if apologizing for the imminent abandonment. "I hate to leave her here like this."

"Maybe you can come back and claim her as spoils of war."

"Yeah, maybe so." There was a wistful tone in his voice.

"We need some luck. I hope we're ahead of the train."

Hagen pulled his fedora low and buttoned his coat. "This is ready to go." He situated the Browning sideways with the barrel pointed at the passenger side floorboard and the stock resting on the seat. "Grab it with both hands. Here and here. Hold it tight. It's got a helluva kick. When I get out, slide over here behind the wheel. Keep a sharp eye, and be ready to take out if I come running."

"What?" Ceara grabbed his coat sleeve. "*No no no no.* I'm not staying here alone."

"Ceara, this is a major train station not all that far from Chicago. We have to assume we'll find trouble waiting for us everywhere. A man and woman traveling together without luggage might tip them off. Me alone, no one will notice."

Dim light from a back porch was enough for her to see the resolve in his stern expression.

"If I'm not back in twenty minutes, you have to go to the police. This car won't get you to New York."

"No. No cops. We've been through this already."

He looked at her a long time. "Here. You take most of it." He dug out Eddie's wallet. "I'll keep a few bucks in reserve."

She shoved the money into an apron pocket.

"Drive her until she dies. Someone will give you a ride if you tell them a sad story. In the meantime, keep a hand on Cecil's gun and lock the doors."

The porch light went off. Ceara squinted and pressed her nose to the frosted window. "I can't see anything out there. How will I know when it's safe to unlock the door? Just telling me to unlock it isn't good enough. Someone might have a gun to your head."

"That wouldn't make me tell you to open the door."

"You know what I mean. I'm more than just a little scared."

"All right, I'll circle the block and come in from the other direction. I'll tap the driver's side window three times, pause, and repeat. Don't open—or shoot—until I repeat. Light a match so I can see the time."

Ceara rummaged around her coat pockets for the matchbook. She flipped open the cover, tore off a paper match, and flicked the tip across the friction strip. Hagen checked his watch with the dash clock.

"Close enough."

Ceara shook out the flame and tucked the matchbook into her left glove.

"Give me to the top of the hour, then leave."

"I'll consider it."

"Don't consider too long."

"Hurry every chance you get."

"I will."

Ceara swiped a clear spot on the windshield to watch Hagen. He put his right hand in the coat pocket where he kept Eddie's gun. She dropped her hand to the Browning. The feel of the cold, hard steel was a comforting thing. She wondered if it was the same for Hagen. When he reached the street, he looked back. It was a small gesture, but it bolstered her nerve.

There was no sound and nothing to see other than the occasional headlamps of a car passing on the snowy street at the end of the alley. In a moment of panic, she realized the back doors weren't locked, and she hastily took care of that. She tried to keep her mind busy by reciting her favorite poems rather than wasting matches every minute to check the time. When she finally gave into anxious curiosity, she was careful to shield the match flame.

His time was up five minutes ago.

She rehashed her options. He'd switched on the auxiliary fuel tank many miles back, which meant with or without him, the car needed gas, and there was probably no place to refuel until morning. Parked here until then meant wasting precious hours that should have been spent driving. An equally troublesome reality was driving this bullet-ridden Rolls-Royce with a bashed in driver's side and broken mirror in broad daylight was simply asking to get caught.

Her logical move was to go straight to Hoover by some other means and then retrieve the ledgers under his protection. But she couldn't sacrifice her family or Hagen to save herself. She rested her forehead on the steering wheel. She should go. Drive as far as she could before daylight, the fuel ran out, or the car quit. No. He'd be here any moment—

Tap, tap, tap.

She sucked in a gasp.

Tap, tap, tap.

Flicking up the lock, she scooted over. Hagen got in amid a swirl of snow.

"Miss me?"

His wisecrack did as much to calm her nerves as did his teasing chuckle.

"You're late."

"But you waited."

"You knew I would."

"Yeah. I did. I counted on it."

She almost stuck her tongue out. "Smart aleck. What did you find out?"

"When it's running on time, the eastbound train doesn't come through for another hour. Tonight, it's two hours behind schedule."

Disappointment steeped in exhausted desperation brought tears pushing their way to the surface. "So we wait?"

"Nope. I got us a ride to Cleveland. There are a couple of trains to New York that stop there between midnight and two, give or take."

"How far is it to Cleveland?"

"Ninety miles. But we can't dilly-dally. We'll cut it close if we leave now."

"How did you finagle a ride?"

"I showed my badge and a hundred-dollar bill. A janitor going off duty in ten minutes took my offer, no questions asked. I told her I'd pay another hundred if she could get us to Cleveland in under two hours."

"Were you able to call Amarillo?"

"Tried. No luck. The long-distance circuits are tied up. This time of night is the busiest for calling. We'll be in Cleveland late enough that the lines should be open."

"Did you see anyone suspicious?"

"Nobody I'd peg as a hired thug, but that doesn't mean there weren't any. I saw a lot of three-piece suits. Looks like a watering hole for rich criminals. Made me think Hoover needs to pay more attention to what goes on here." The B-A-R in one hand and his other hand on the door handle, he said, "Here we go."

Ceara glanced back at the Rolls-Royce with a little pang of regret that felt like she was leaving an old friend instead of an inanimate hunk of metal, wires, and rubber. On impulse, she ran to the car, patted the fender, whispered *thank you*, then hurried back to Hagen. He smiled and squeezed her hand.

***

Hagen came out of the Cleveland train station and approached the car idling in the parking lot. He opened the passenger side front door and offered his hand to Ceara, then he leaned inside after she got out.

He gave the driver the promised bonus for a speedy journey. "Thanks for the lift."

"Thanks for the cash."

When they reached the sprawling building, Hagen said, "The train we want is running late."

"Do all trains run late?"

"That's been my experience."

"How late is this one?"

"Thirty minutes to anybody's guess."

"Did you purchase tickets?"

"Yes, for a small compartment. There's a problem, though. I saw four torpedoes acting like paying passengers and not succeeding, extra security, too, and all of them eyeballing each other and everyone in the place. Probably competing to see who can catch us first and collect the reward money." Hagen guided Ceara through an open arch into the yellowish illumination of the covered walkway that spanned the perimeter of the station.

"Were you able to make the phone call?"

Hagen nodded. "I explained. My boss listened. We agreed there's no time for him to send reinforcements we can trust. He'll do what he can for your parents without compromising us—request a routine police check, send a telegram."

"Now what? Do we wait out here and hope no one notices us?"

"No. The thugs honed in on me right off and came snooping to hear what I said. I finally got to talk to someone who could make decisions. I said I was a bounty hunter with a bail jumper handcuffed out in a taxi. I asked for a private place to wait, because you like to make trouble in public. I hinted your language isn't ladylike, and I pointed out the women and children in the waiting area."

"I sound like a swell person."

"To drive home how dangerous you are, I explained you'd held up a New York bank with a submachine gun, wounded a teller, stole a car, drove halfway across the U. S., and finally got caught impersonating a nurse while trying to buy a baby in Texas with the money you'd stolen from the bank."

"Impersonating a nurse? What does that have to do with anything?"

"I had to have a plausible reason for your uniform. We should have bought new clothes for you."

"Ohhh... I'd forgotten that little detail." Ceara glanced down at her telltale uniform and shoes. "But what about buying a baby? That's outrageous. Did they actually fall for it?"

"They did. People like the sensational, and the more shocking the story, the better they like it, and the more apt they are to believe it. Those four heavies weren't interested in me after hearing the story, but it took a C-note to get a private waiting room. Money tends to make people feel important and cooperative. I suspect I'll shell out a few more bills to keep memories fresh and attitudes friendly until we get off the train."

Ceara returned the wad of bills. "Here. If you're going to throw money away, you'll need this."

Hagen took some of the money and gave the rest back.

"What's my name?"

"Crazy Connie Carmichael."

"Crazy Connie, huh? You just made this all up out of nowhere?"

"Actually, no. I thought about a cover for us on the drive from Mansfield. Crazy Connie was the first woman I ever arrested. She was a holy terror."

"Did she do all those dastardly deeds?"

"She did, and more, although dressed as a nun, and it all happened in Texas. I changed the bank robbery to New York, so no one would question why I was taking you there." He looked at her long and hard. “It’s in your hands now. You need to act the part of an unhappy prisoner, or those four tough guys will spot the charade.”

“That will be easy. I’ve been a prisoner for a long time. The eight-foot-high wrought iron fence around the premises and the guard dogs weren’t there when I met Eddie.”

The forced flippancy in her voice reminded him of what she’d endured to get this far from Rocchelli and that she still wasn’t free of him. He cast a quick look both ways then dodged through a gap in the line of people passing by and led Ceara to a partially secluded alcove out of the line of foot traffic and the direct breeze.

“Ceara… I understand living the way you did wasn’t easy. You deserve more. If things were different… If you weren’t… If I wasn’t…” He stepped closer, his chest pressing lightly against the front of her coat. She dropped her gaze. “Hey. We’ll make it.”

Lord, how he wished she wasn’t married to a crime boss, and he wasn’t a lawman. He wanted them to be just plain people who could love each other. He yearned to kiss her, but more than that, he wanted her to know forever love, his love.

She lifted her gaze, her eyes shining with regret—or was it longing for something neither of them could have? Either way, his heart responded. He slipped his hand along the back of her neck and pulled her nearer, dipping his head to feel her warm breath caress his face with the gentleness of a lover’s touch.

For a moment, one precious moment, Rocchelli didn't stand between them. It was just the two of them in the night.

She pulled back just enough to remind him to keep his professional distance, but in his heart, he wanted to believe she meant *I'm married, and not to you.* Reality was harsh, though. He couldn't tell her how he felt without compromising them both.

"It's time to go inside."

Ceara bobbed her head, while she tugged down her cloche hat. "All right, I'm ready."

"Shake out the handcuffs."

"Why?"

"To make this look real." Hagen closed the open ring around his left wrist.

"Now we're back where we were this morning."

"We'll manage."

"Wait a second." Ceara dug into her apron pockets and until she found the chewing gum and the cigarettes. She popped a piece of gum into her mouth then opened the cigarette case and removed a cigarette.

"You smoke? You don't seem the type."

"I never have. Help me light this."

Hagen struck the match cupped his hands to keep it from snuffing out in the breeze. Ceara put the cigarette between her lips and stuck the tip into the flame. Despite puffing superficially, she coughed as she waved smoke from her eyes.

"Ugh! I don't see how anyone does this."

"Me, either." The Browning in his free hand and a grin of we can do this on his face, Hagen stepped into the walkway. "Give 'em a good show, Crazy Connie. Make them wish we'd taken a different train."

Chapter Twelve

Back to the wall, eyes closed, Ceara trembled from the let-down of maintaining her act as Crazy Connie for the better part of an hour. Despite being hustled into an office, the door had a half window and anyone passing could see inside. Her ranting, swearing, kicking chairs, stomping feet tantrums would have put even the naughtiest two-year-old to shame.

Hagen requested coffee and food, and the money he slipped the porter ensured its timely delivery, then he locked the compartment door.

"Hey, what's wrong? You were great. I wanted a good commotion, and you delivered in spades."

Ceara opened her eyes. "I'm a little rattled from the waiting and worrying we'd be found out. I thought for sure those men would put it together. They were entirely too interested in passing by the door to look in."

"Your performance convinced them. I think the air actually turned blue."

"I was running out of colorful words, and my throat was getting sore."

Hagen chuckled. "Everyone was entertained, and it threw them off our scent."

"I'll be much better with food, coffee, and sleep. A bath or shower would be heaven right now."

"There's a shower at the end of the car, but we have to stay out of sight. We've got a private sink and toilet, though. There's probably bath towels and soap in there. Maybe you can make-do." He indicated the door with *Lavatory* engraved on the metal door plate.

Ceara lifted their joined arms. "What about this"

Dipping his fingers into his front blue-jeans pocket, Hagen brought his hand out with two bobby pins pinched between his thumb and forefinger. "Happy Valentine's Day a few hours late."

"Chocolates and now bobby pins. You really know how to treat a girl right," Ceara teased. "The candy was scrumptious, but these bobby pins are the best gift I've ever received."

"Well, they ought to be. I've never spent so much on anything except a gun."

"Where did you get them?"

"I bought them from Maddie when you were in the restroom."

"How much?"

"Twenty bucks."

"If I haven't mentioned how much I love spending Eddie's money— Well, I do. Let's sit over here on the sofa, and I'll get these off of us."

Hagen situated their joined arms across his knee and twisted the handcuff around to hold it with the keyhole at the angle Ceara could reach.

"Watch closely, Mr. Bounty Hunter, maybe you'll learn a new trick."

"I'm watching. I'm watching."

"First, you bend a rough *S* shape on the tip. Like this." Ceara spread the prongs of one of the bobby pins, inserted the tip of the straight side into a hole in the base of the handcuff, pressed it to the side, and pulled it out. She then inserted the bent tip back into the hole and pressed it the other way. She inspected the shape. "See?"

"Got it. Next step?"

"I assume you realize these are double-locking handcuffs."

"I do. I also know yours is double locked, but mine isn't."

"That's right, which makes yours easy to pick, since I only need to open the single lock." Inserting the bent end of the bobby pin into the single lock, Ceara probed one way then another until an inside lever clicked and the ratchet teeth released.

Hagen opened the swing-arm and rubbed where the metal had scraped his wrist bones. "Now we can take off our coats and work on yours."

Even with Hagen holding the handcuffs steady, after several minutes of concentrated work, Ceara gave up. "It's jammed just like Leo said. We need real tools. My dad will have what we need."

"Sorry about that."

"Oh, it's not so bad. I'm used to it now." Ceara surveyed the room. The lower bed was made down and an extra blanket and pillow lay on one end of the sofa. "I need something to sleep in." In a few steps, she was halfway up the ladder to the narrow upper bunk.

"I don't recommend sleeping up there. There's hardly breathing space for a small child."

"No. I mean I need something to wear. I feel so grimy. I'm going to clean up the best I can and at least wash out my stockings." With a few tugs, she removed the top sheet from the mattress. "This will do nicely." She took the sheet, smirking at the curiosity on Hagen's face, and went into the lavatory.

"That's exactly what I do every time I get on a train. I yank a sheet off the bed and take it to the restroom."

Ceara laughed. "Doesn't everyone?"

Some minutes later, she heard the porter arrive and the muffled conversation with Hagen. With her uniform spot-cleaned and her undergarments and torn-at-the knees thigh-high stockings washed, wrung out, and draped over the towel racks and spread out on the floor to catch the steam heat blowing from the sidewall heater encasement, she turned to the awkward task of washing her hair with the bar of soap in the small sink. After wiping her body down with a washcloth, taking special care to clean her scraped knees, she ran her fingers through her towel-damp hair, scrutinized her puffy cheeks and the cut, and the mottled coloring around her eyes, then gingerly pressed her fingers to Eddie's fingerprint bruises on her neck. All-in-all, she was a mess. Wrapping the sheet around her body in toga fashion, she returned to the compartment, refreshed, but exhausted.

"A washcloth bath never felt so good."

With his back to her, Hagen poured coffee. "Have some coffee while it's hot. There are dry sandwiches. Peanuts, chocolate." He turned, his hand outstretched to offer a cup, and did a double-take that sloshed coffee over his fingers.

"That's quite an outfit."

"What? This old thing?" Ceara feigned modesty. "It's just something I found lying around."

Hagen nodded approval, smiling. "Well, I like it. It looks good on you."

Ceara took the cup and held it to her face to feel the moist, comforting warmth on her face. "Thank you—for the compliment and the coffee."

"You're welcome."

She sensed he wanted to say more, and she certainly wanted to, but the awkward silence of not knowing what to say rose as a barrier to conversation. After enduring the ordeal at the warehouse followed by the tense hours of driving cross country together, why was it suddenly so difficult to talk? They'd had plenty to talk about up to now. Was it the intimacy of the private room, or because they were in a safe place and no longer functioning at the emotional level of fight-or-flight?

Hagen cleared his throat and stammered, "I'll...uh...I'll wash up now."

"My clothes are spread out drying. I hope you don't mind."

"They won't bother me. I have sisters." He closed the lavatory door.

Lifting her voice so he could hear her, she said, "You mentioned that you have a brother. How many siblings do you have?" Ceara sat on the sofa and curled her legs under her.

Hagen cracked the door open. "Two older sisters and a younger brother."

"Do they live in Amarillo?"

"Yes. Ian graduates high school this year. My married sister, Norah, is a school teacher and her husband works on our ranch. Sarah, my unmarried sister, owns a sewing shop."

"Are your parents and grandparents there, too?"

"Yep. All of them."

"That's nice. Tell me more about your adventurous life in the wild, wild west and about chasing bad guys all over the prairie."

Hagen peered around the edge of the door. "I don't chase bad guys. I catch them."

Ceara laughed. "My mistake. Then tell me more about your life and your family."

Hagen left the door ajar. "Not much to tell. I grew up on a quarter horse ranch outside of Amarillo. My great-granddad Kane raised horses for the military, then by 1880, the Kane family was making a living raising quarter horses for racing and for working cattle."

"What made you want to be a Texas Ranger?"

"I never thought of doing anything else. There's a long line of lawmen on my mom's side, so I went to college, earned a law degree, and got into the Rangers."

Twice, she started to ask the question that had been nagging her since she'd met Hagen, and twice, she clamped her mouth shut. She stared at the partially open lavatory door. Surely, it wouldn't offend him if she asked the right way. Taking a deep breath, and hoping her voice sounded casual, she tested the dangerous waters of disappointment.

"You didn't say anything about your personal life."

Hesitation. "What would you like to know?"

"Do you have a sweetheart...or wife and family?" There. She'd said it. Now, she'd know.

Silence.

Did that mean a woman waited for him back in Texas? Had she'd overstepped the curiosity line? Regret pinched her throat. She swallowed it down with a gulp of tepid coffee wishing she hadn't asked.

"No. There's no one. I...I haven't met the right woman, I guess."

Ceara smiled into her cup, satisfied with his response, but her moment of pleasure soon faded. Single or spoken for, it didn't matter. She shouldn't have pried into his personal life. The fact that she was married stood between them, and that wasn't going to change any time soon.

Hagen came from the lavatory in his stockinged feet, sleeveless undershirt, and jeans. She shouldn't have stared, but for several seconds, she unashamedly admired how the undershirt stretched across his broad chest and hugged his narrow, muscled torso. If he noticed her near-ogling, he politely concealed it when he refilled his coffee cup and joined her on the sofa to eat a sandwich.

"Anything else you'd like to know about me?" Hagen asked.

"No. I've been too much of a Nosey Parker already."

"I don't think you're nosey. I should have been more forthcoming, so you didn't have to ask."

Ceara caught herself casting a wistful glance toward the bed.

Hagen gestured with his cup. "Go ahead. You don't need to stay awake and keep me company."

Embarrassed, she asked, "You don't mind?"

"Not at all. You take the bed. I'll sleep here."

Hastily protesting her unintentional selfishness, she offered, "No, please. You need a good rest. This sofa is too small for you. I'll sleep here just fine."

"I'll manage. I can sleep most any place. Besides, I'm not ready to turn in yet."

"We both need to be clear-headed and rested when we reach New York. The bed is by no means large, but there's room for us both. I don't take up much space."

"That doesn't seem proper."

Ceara's eyebrows shot up. "Proper? After what we've been through, proper is the least of my concerns. If you'll recall, we've already spent one night together."

He chuckled. "Wrapped in a musty moth-eaten blanket, while trying to catch a few winks on cold concrete while handcuffed and chained to a truck bumper doesn't come close to my idea of sleeping in the same bed." He gave her a gentle nudge. "Go on."

Ceara laughed all the way to the bed. "All right, but I'll scoot over to the wall to give you room when you decide you've had enough of the sofa."

He said something, but she was already snug and warm under the covers and couldn't keep her eyes open. Her last thought was the irony of sharing a bed with him, and the only thing that was going to happen was sleep.

• ● •

Curled into a ball with her head burrowed under the blankets like a turtle in a shell, Ceara's coming awake brain vaguely registered the sound of a door closing. She poked her head out and squinted at Hagen as he pulled up a chair.

"Good morning. The porter just delivered a sorry excuse for breakfast, but the coffee's fresh and hot."

Mumbling around a whining groan, she managed a polite, "Good morning. How do you feel? I think a bus hit me."

"I've found a few sore places."

"Just a few?"

"Well, the tips of my fingers don't hurt. So that's a good thing." He tugged the blankets from around her face. "You've got a doozy of a shiner and a nice bruise where your face met the door frame."

"I'm not surprised." Sitting up, she sat cross-legged, propped her pillow at her back, then carefully arranged the blankets, partly for warmth and mostly for modesty.

"Here. I'll get this out of our way." Hagen folded-up the upper berth and latched it into place.

"Thank you. You've got a nice goose egg on your forehead." With a ginger touch, Ceara placed her fingertips on the bump. "And bruises on your arms and shoulders."

"We look like we lost a fight with Jack Dempsey. Can I get you a cup of coffee and a sweet roll?"

"Just coffee, please." Ceara accepted the cup, took a small sip to test the heat, then asked, "Where are we?"

"I don't know. The porter said we'll get in to New York late this afternoon. Trains make lots of stops in little towns, almost as often as a bus. We traded a little speed for anonymity. My grandma would say it's six of one, and half-a-dozen of another. So it doesn't matter, I guess."

"What time is it?"

"Just after nine."

"Short night."

"I think you were asleep before your head hit the pillow."

With the cup close to her lips, she stole a glance across the compartment to confirm her suspicion that he'd slept on the too-small sofa. For some reason, that disappointed her as much as she admired his integrity toward her.

"Did you rest at all?"

"Some. I've slept in worse places, and it kept me from sleeping too soundly. It served its purpose."

Ceara took another sip then rested her head against the wall.

"I did a lot of thinking about what you said about being a prisoner in your own home." He drew his gaze from toying with his coffee cup to look at her. "I'm going to be the Nosey Parker now and ask you something."

"All right."

"How did you hook up with a guy like Rocchelli? You don't seem his type."

"We are definitely mismatched." *Where to begin?* There wasn't an easy answer to his question. "It's one thing to admit to yourself you've made bad decisions. It's quite another to say them out loud to another person. That's when you have to face what you've done—really face it."

"There's not a person anywhere who doesn't have regrets. I won't judge. There's an old saying where I grew up about not judging a man until you've walked a few miles in his boots. I'm a good listener, too. But I'll warn you that I ask questions."

"I don't mind questions, but I'll have to go back to my childhood, so you'll understand how I ended up in Chicago."

"That's a reasonable place to begin."

Still, she stalled. "It's a long and involved story."

"We have plenty of time to spare right now."

She blew out a deep breath. "Hard work, frugal living, and education are important in my family."

"Those are important in my family, too. It's a good philosophy to live by."

She nodded. "But when you're poor Irish living in Five Points, there isn't much opportunity to get ahead, and getting ahead means being able to move someplace better and safer. Some place with more opportunities."

"Someplace safer, I understand. Someplace better is a matter of perspective—the greener grass on the other side of the fence. So what did better mean to you?"

"Better meant improved medical care, or at least, more available medical care. It meant less crowded classrooms in schools in nicer neighborhoods. Not being looked down on. That sort of better.

"I also dreamed of seeing what life was like in different cities, different states, even different countries. I was sure anywhere would be an improvement over where I lived, and I fantasized about my family moving and all of us starting over someplace together." She waved a hand toward that imaginary somewhere of her childhood. "Even when I was old enough to understand you make your happiness where you are, I saw Eddie's money as a fast route to a better life. Even after I married him, I still had this pie-in-the-sky fantasy that my family would leave New York and move to Chicago and we'd be together."

"By all of us, do you mean your parents and sisters?"

"Yes. In my younger years, it also meant my grandparents. Growing up, we all lived together above the grocery store, which is just on the uptown edge of Five Points."

"Why is it called Five Points?"

"Back in its early days, Five Points was a wretched slum that branched out from the intersection of Mulberry, Anthony, Cross, Orange, and Little Water Streets—the five points. It was a notoriously dangerous part of Manhattan's lower east side for decades. I grew up with stories of how dirty and poverty stricken it was in the 1850s to the turn of the century and even up through the Great War. It's still a rough neighborhood, although it's been cleaned up enough to be considered almost respectable—almost."

Hagen finished off his coffee and placed the cup on the floor. "What does cleaned up mean?"

"The houses and tenements have undergone restoration and modernization. Sanitation has improved. Through the efforts of women's committees and churches and donations, what was originally a poverty-ridden, criminal-infested place evolved to where good and decent hard-working people living on the fringes could make a living. It was an Irish culture in the beginning, but the Italians have moved in and pushed most of the Irish out."

"But your family's still there. Apparently, they can't be pushed."

"It was their home. They adapted by stocking food and goods that suited a variety of tastes and cultures, which has made them invaluable to the neighborhood. My parents are friendly to everyone, but that doesn't necessarily mean everyone they are friendly to are their friends, if you get what I mean."

"I do."

"If it weren't for a healthy strain of survival larceny that runs in my father's veins, the protection money he would have had to shell out to keep the store open would have ruined him."

"Survival larceny. I like that."

"He learned from his father to turn payoffs into reciprocal benefits. Strong-arm men like swapping favors almost as much as they like squeezing money out of business owners. My father gives them reduced prices on groceries, throws in an occasional carton of cigarettes in a grocery order, that sort of thing. He knows all the children by first name, and he always gives penny candy to them when they come in. It's those little considerations that people remember and appreciate. My parents know who's had a baby or when there's a death or a marriage, and they acknowledge it accordingly. They treat everyone with equal respect and consideration and, most of the time, they receive the same in return."

"What about the rest of your family?"

"My father's sister married and moved to Canada years ago. One of his brothers joined the Navy during the Great War and stayed in. His other brother died in a gang fight when I was a baby. My Galloway grandparents moved back to Ireland not long after I graduated from high school. They inherited what remained of the ancestral property. I haven't seen them since, but we write often.

"My Grandma and Grandpa Hayes—my mom's parents—died when I was too young to remember them. My mom's only sister married a soldier, and they live in Germany."

She was quiet for a few moments. "Much of what changed for the better in Five Points was due to my family's efforts to make it a safer place to raise their children and grandchildren. My great-grandparents and grandparents strived to improve the schools and build neighborhood churches and bring neighbors together to keep each other safe. My parents have worked diligently to keep that going, which is where much of the small profit from the store goes."

"Your parents swing a wide loop."

"Swing a wide loop? I don't understand."

"It means to carry a lot of influence."

"I hadn't thought of it that way, but, you're right. They do."

"We got sidetracked. Circle back with your story." He reminded her where she'd left off. "You were a kid who wanted to get out of Five Points."

That made her smile. He certainly was a good listener, which made him easy to talk to. Now that she'd formed the foundation of her story, it felt perfectly natural to explain to the man she loved why she married a man she didn't love.

Chapter Thirteen

Ceara drew her knees up, careful to keep the blankets tucked. "I was six years old when I discovered what I wanted to do when I grew up, but it was years before it occurred to me that what I wanted to be was the way I could get to that someplace else of my dreams.

"It happened on Christmas Eve. Someone pounded on the alley door of the store. My father and Grandpap Joe, both armed, went downstairs to see who it was. It wasn't unusual for someone to show up needing medical treatment. Our family was known for their skills and discretion when giving medical assistance. That night, five injured men showed up with broken noses, knife cuts, and bullet wounds, and who knows what else. Grandpap called for my gran and mom to come down. Mom told me to stay upstairs, but I didn't." Those memories brought a smile.

"I crouched at the top of the stairs with my face pressed between two bannisters. I didn't miss a thing. When the men had gone, and my family realized I'd not only watched, but that I was fascinated, they included me from then on. I can't tell you how many people over the years have come to my parents in the middle of the night for hush-hush treatment. In a strange turnabout, it was this close-mouthed kitchen table—well, countertop in the store that night—medicine that became our protection."

"Why didn't you become a doctor?"

"Once upon a time, I did have my heart set on becoming a doctor. My parents put-by what they could to help pay for college, and I ran errands, delivered messages, and walked dogs for rich ladies. I even dressed as a boy and hawked newspapers. In the end, college for a medical degree was too expensive, so I settled for nursing."

"Settled? That smacks of disappointment."

She shook her head. "Not at all. I'm content with what I do. It's satisfying work."

"But becoming a doctor is a wish that's still in the back of your mind, isn't it."

She shrugged. "Maybe. Someday." It was a wish never far from her thoughts, but she couldn't admit it for fear of jinxing the possibility.

"How did you pay for nursing school?"

"A women's clinic opened in my neighborhood. It quickly expanded to accidents and emergencies that people would have left untreated rather than go to a hospital and run up expenses they couldn't afford or be turned away because they couldn't pay. In exchange for three-quarters wages and committing to working there for three years, they paid for college. It was an attractive employment opportunity."

"Interesting idea. I can see the benefits on both sides. Tell me about your sisters."

"Claire is sixteen. She's our adventurer. She wants to see the world. No one is a stranger to her. She's so curious and full of questions, and such a daredevil. Colleen is fourteen and the complete opposite. She's not healthy, which I think is why she's so shy and quiet. She has asthma and allergies. She's learned to cope with her poor health by living other people's lives through all the books she reads and the stories she writes. Her imagination is her solace for not being able to live an active life."

Hagen cocked his head, surprise on his face. "I'm not making a crack about your age, but that's quite a span of years between you and your sisters."

Ceara smiled. "No offense taken. My mother had difficult pregnancies. There were three premature babies between me and Claire. Colleen wasn't born early, but she has always been sickly. A drier climate with cleaner air would do her a world of good. We all know that, but the store, and the expense of moving and starting over..." She made a *what-else-can-they-do* shrug.

"Five Points is home. It's difficult to leave that behind. No one else has the money to buy the store, and my parents saved for so many years to purchase their first house and not have a mortgage."

Ceara traded her empty cup for the extra pillow, put it across her lap, and absentmindedly smoothed out the divots and wrinkles. "I lived at home while I went to college and while I worked at the clinic. One day, a patient left a Chicago newspaper in one of the examination rooms. Out of curiosity, I browsed it. There was a notice in the advertisement section that Lakeshore General Hospital was hiring nurses for their newly created emergency and accident treatment and response facility. The hospital wanted full staff by the ribbon cutting ceremony for the small accident ward of twelve beds."

"That was a good fit for you."

"Yes, it was. The notice specifically stated only nurses with experience and training in traumatic injuries need apply. The facility was opening in four months, and the hiring process was underway. It was so tempting. The salary was many times more than I was making or was likely to make as long as I stayed where I was. My parents encouraged me to apply, so I packed my suitcase, and bought a bus ticket to Chicago. It was the farthest from home I'd ever been, and to go by myself was frightening and exhilarating all at once."

"Obviously, you were hired."

"Yes. Before my interview concluded."

“I have a feeling we’ve reached the point of Rocchelli’s entrance into your life.”

“We have. I’d worked at Lakeshore General about a year when Eddie’s Cicero restaurant caught on fire. The more seriously injured were brought to Lakeshore. Eddie showed up, throwing his weight around and carrying on with his wild arm-waving gestures and shouting in a combination of English and Italian and generally being an obnoxious nuisance which, I learned later, was his special gift.”

Hagen chuckled softly.

“I ordered him out using my rudimentary Italian vocabulary, which impressed him. He stayed until all of the injured people were released to go home or admitted for additional care. While I cleaned up and put the room back together, he made small talk that led to asking if I were married and, if not, would I have dinner with him.

“I refused to tell him my marital status, and I declined the dinner invitation on the sheer principle of his audacity. He came back five nights in a row. He’d snooped around and discovered I was single, where I lived, and he knew my work schedule. Each of those nights, he asked me out and, each night, I refused.”

“He’s like a bulldog carrying a bone around trying to find a place to bury it once he gets something in his head.”

“Yes, he is. He didn’t show up again for two weeks. By then, I’d put him out of my mind, although I’d done my own snooping to find out who he was. Instead of asking me out to dinner, he offered me a job in his home as his elderly mother's around-the-clock private nurse and companion. I would get room and board and a more than generous salary. He said I couldn't give him an answer until I'd met his mother." Recalling that meeting brought back bittersweet happiness.

"Mrs. Rocchelli was a darling little woman. Feisty and witty. Sharp-tempered at times, although never mean or petty. Eddie adored her, and it was that gentle, compassionate side of him that touched me. I loved her immediately, as Eddie knew I would. Everyone adored her. Sadly, her health was steadily deteriorating, and she died two years later. After her funeral, I moved back to the boarding house where I'd previously lived. I also went home for a long visit, which was my first trip back since I'd moved to Chicago. When I returned, I resumed the night shift at Lakeshore General."

"No contact with Rocchelli during your hiatus?"

"No. Not until a month later. I left at the end of my shift and there was Eddie waiting across the street with a bouquet of flowers to welcome me back. Things between us...happened. He took me to breakfast when I got off work and walked with me to the boarding house afterwards. Then breakfast became dinner twice a week at his restaurants. Three months later, he proposed on bended knee in front of his attorney, the mayor, and a judge, among other high-up political people whom he'd invited to witness the event." Ceara made a self-deprecating, eye-rolling headshake.

"He has a level of confident arrogance like no one I've ever known. Apparently, it didn't cross his mind that you'd say no. How could you live in his house all that time and be so close to his mother and not know what he was involved in? Or at least, suspect it?"

"Oh, I knew, but it's hard to put into words. On one hand, he has a public image of legitimate *restaurateur* and gentleman—a philanthropist. On the other, his name is associated with the likes of Al Capone and George Moran with the same level of awe and sense of something dangerous at the mere utterance of their names. Eddie sheltered me—most of the time—from that shady side of his life."

"His mother approved of what he did? She went along with it?"

"If she knew, she kept it to herself. She was a woman who kept her *place*, which meant she didn't cross the line into what she and Eddie considered men's business. It was so unlike my parents, who shared everything. But I reasoned a man who treated his mother with such tenderness and respect, and who was involved in charitable and benevolent activities, would naturally be the same toward me and my family." She shook her head. "I was so wrong," She picked at the pillow case for some moments.

"Eddie was the most charming, worldly man I'd ever known. It was easy to dismiss the rumors and stories about him, because it didn't affect my life. While I was never allowed in the back part of his restaurants, I knew they were among the most popular speakeasies in Chicago. It's difficult to admit how naïve and how willing to look the other way I was." Her shoulders rose and fell on a deep breath. "Ultimately, greed was my downfall." She couldn't meet Hagen's eyes.

"What do you mean?"

"I'd never had a male companion—boyfriend—just casual friendships with boys in my neighborhood. It was flattering to have a sophisticated, rich man like Eddie interested in me. When I accepted his proposal, I moved back into his house. I won't deny he treated me like a queen, and I liked it." Those words tasted like poison.

She clutched the pillow to her chest while her memories rolled back over the months. As if lowering her voice would make her next words—her confession—less incriminating, she whispered, "But I didn't love him. I've never loved him, and I thought it wouldn't matter. What I felt was nothing more than fleeting infatuation. A school girl's crush and idolization."

She mustered the courage to look at Hagen for his reaction, which was a slow, understanding nod with a flicker of a frown.

Ceara inhaled a deep breath, held it, then exhaled with a lamenting sigh. "Then I came up pregnant. There I was. Twenty-seven, unmarried, pregnant, *and* Catholic. It was a lot of guilt to carry. Even though, down deep in my heart, I knew I shouldn't marry him, I did. We had a private church wedding with Paul and Leo and their wives as our witnesses."

"Hold on. Hold on." Hagen lifted his hand, his left eye squinted in confusion. "You lost your baby in August." His eyebrows pinched in a hard frown. "That means you haven't been married a year yet."

"Tragic, isn't it, that a marriage could go so badly so quickly." A combination of disgust and humiliation colored her words. "In my head, I was too ashamed to tell my parents the truth. In my heart, I knew they'd not think less of me. Still, I couldn't bring myself to disappoint them. So, I wrote home and told them I'd married the man I'd been working for, but I wrote nothing about the pregnancy. Then I did just what I believe Eddie's mother did. I observed. I kept my mouth shut, but my ears open, and I looked the other way. I didn't ask, and he didn't tell.

"During the time I lived in his house when his mother was alive, I often played hostess to his cronies, and he was as free with the money he spent on me as he was with the money he gave me to spend on myself. I enjoyed those privileges. He put stars in my eyes, and I was willing to stay blind in his generous light. He promised so many things, but keeping those promises soon became inconvenient to him, as did I."

"So, just like that," Hagen snapped his fingers. "It all went south that night he beat you?"

"Oh, no, not at all. From the moment I met him, I chose to ignore what I didn't want to acknowledge, not the least of which was his temper."

Hagen's eyebrows dipped low again. "Are you saying he hurt you before that night?"

"He slapped me once. It was about two weeks after our wedding when I mentioned eventually I wanted to resume my nursing career. Since he'd never refused me anything, and he knew how devoted I was to the hospital, it never crossed my mind he'd say no." In her best Eddie voice, she mimicked, "No wife of mine is gonna work. No one's gonna say Eddie Rocchelli can't support his wife and kid."

Hagen chuckled. "Sounds like him."

"Anyway, we argued, and he slapped me for being mouthy. I'd witnessed his temper with his men, but he'd never directed it toward me, his mother, or any of our female staff."

Hagen snorted in disgust. "Swell guy."

"I should have left him then. Too bad I couldn't see what was coming in just a few more weeks."

"Unfortunately, experience is a harsh teacher. At least hindsight helps us remember those tough lessons."

"I paid dearly to learn my lesson with Eddie. I was too weak to leave the hospital for my baby girl's funeral." Ceara fixed her gaze on a place at the edge of the mattress, not seeing, but vividly remembering. For many moments, her thoughts remained where her heartache lived. "He named her after his mother, Francesca Louisa. She's buried between his parents—her grandparents." Her vision blurred with the pain of shattered dreams and empty arms. "I've found some comfort in that."

Hagen eased out of his chair to sit beside her.

"When Eddie came to see me after the funeral, he finished breaking what was left of my heart. He said it was time I learned why he'd married me. He said I was the most beautiful and decent woman he'd ever met and being a good Catholic girl from a poor family fit right into his idea of a wife—emphasis on poor.

"He'd been holding out for a young Italian girl with a clean reputation, but he was tired of waiting, and he wasn't getting any younger. He wanted children and grandchildren before he was too old to enjoy them, so he graciously disregarded my Irish blood. That I'd never been with another man was important to him. He said at his age, any wife was better than no wife."

"What the hell kind of man says—" Hagen caught himself. "Sorry. Go on."

She tried to smile, but failed miserably as tears pushed closer to the spilling point. Eddie's cutting reminder of this while Hagen changed the flat tire was now a raw wound opened wide.

"He said women like me should be grateful that men like him looked twice. He had money and social standing, while I'd come from nothing. He viewed himself as my savior, which, to him, meant I'd never give him any trouble. I'd be a perfect little submissive wife." She practically spat the words.

"I think the qualities he admired in me before we married—my independence, determination, strong-will, intelligence—were qualities he couldn't accept in a wife. He assumed those attributes would magically disappear once we were married, and I fully expected his compassion and kindness were truly who he was. At the hospital, he said he was going to send my father money—a reverse dowry, he called it—on our first anniversary to show him how well he could take care of me."

Hagen's mouth opened and closed on a wordless response. "Sounds to me like he was buying a clear conscience or buying-off your parents to keep them from interfering."

Ceara bobbed her head. "I've never told anyone a word of this. I don't have friends to confide in. Eddie made sure of that in a slow, insidious way I didn't see happening right under my nose. It began before we married.

"In early summer, I wrote home I was expecting. In September, I wrote that I'd been in an accident, and—" Her voice caught on a shudder that held the threat of turning into full-out sobbing beyond the tears she wiped from her cheeks with shaking hands.

"I hate him." It felt so good to say those words and to have someone who cared about her hear them. "I hate Eddie Rocchelli so much it's festering inside me. All of the good I once believed in is gone, destroyed. He ruined my hopes of ever finding love or happiness again. He killed my baby, and my heart died with her."

Hagen slipped an arm around her shoulders and drew her against him. "Hey, don't give up on love. Don't let a bastard like Rocchelli take it from you. He doesn't deserve that power."

"I paid an awful price." Burning anguish rose in her chest that gave way to hiccupping breaths of choking sobs. She pressed her face against Hagen's chest, clung to him, accepted the comfort of his arms. For so many months, hatred was all that prevented her from drowning in her ocean of anger and crippling sorrow. Hagen arrived just in time to throw out the lifeline that brought her from the dark depths of hopelessness and near-suicidal despair.

"Cry him out, Ceara. Cry Rocchelli out of your heart. There's always hope as long as one person believes, and I do. I'll help get back what you've lost. All you need to do is let me."

She wanted love—Hagen's love—but the grief and hate Eddie had put in her heart was so deep, so strong, she saw her life as nothing more than an empty, shattered dream of broken shards that could never be put back together. Giving herself over to anguish, she cried for her baby. She cried for herself. And she cried for what could have been a wonderful life if only she'd have met Hagen when she could have loved him.

Chapter Fourteen

"They're coming, Boss," Cecil said.

Eddie put his watch away, grousing under his breath about Ceara and time slipping through his fingers.

Paul and Leo walked along the sidewalk from the South Side Café toward the two parked cars. Leo got in on the rear passenger side of the Cadillac. Paul made a *follow us* wave to Len in the Model A before he opened the backdoor on the other side of the Cadillac. He handed two stolen license plates over the seat to Cecil and gave a folded paper to Eddie.

"Directions to the hideout. Top of the paper is north."

Eddie studied the hand-drawn directions.

Paul pointed as he explained. "This is where we are right now, between the hideout up here on the river and the house down here in a dead-end street near the intersections of Broome and Grand Streets. The Galloway Dry Goods and Grocery is farther south on Bowery Street."

"What gives?" Eddie looked at Paul. "I wanted a place close to the house."

"It's the best he could do in a pinch. We can take it or leave it. Makes no difference to Dino. He's been paid."

"I'll take it, but I'm not happy." Eddie passed the map over the seat to Cecil as he asked Paul, "What else?"

While conversation continued in the back seat, Gilbert and Cecil put their heads together, discussed the directions, then Gilbert pulled into traffic with Cecil guiding him.

"For all appearances, Dino says the Galloways' house was empty from mid-morning to one o'clock."

"How does he know that? You said he couldn't watch the house all day."

"While Dino and Ronny slept this morning, Betty went out door-to-door in the Galloways' neighborhood asking for donations to an orphanage."

"His wife? How much did that cost me?"

"Another hundred. He figured out you have a fat wallet. Can you blame him?"

Eddie waved it off. "Go on."

"Betty talked to Mrs. Galloway as she was leaving the house. Betty somehow got it out of her that she was going to the family store and wouldn't be home until after lunch. Dino was on the job when Mrs. Galloway returned. She hasn't left."

"How does he know that? Is someone watching the back of the house?"

"Ronny checked from the alley. There's a tall wooden and iron fence with a gate. The latch didn't budge."

"Locked?"

"No. Broken or jammed. It's unlikely anyone will come or go out the back, since they'll have to climb over the fence."

"Maybe she's not the only one in the house. Ceara and Kane might have snuck in before Dino got there."

"It's possible, sure, but not probable. Not for as fast as we got here. We'll know soon enough. When there's something to report, either Dino or Ronny will come to the café. Leo and me will alternate waiting for them, either inside or out in a car. We'll swap cars each time and park in a different place."

"Where's Dino watching the house from?"

"A dilapidated wood shed beside the vacant house on the right as you go in."

Paul gave Eddie another small piece of paper. "Directions to the house from here and from the hideout. The last contact we'll have with Dino is around five forty-five. After that, we're on our own."

"By the time a message gets to you and you report to me and we get to the house..." Eddie didn't like it. He didn't like it one bit. "That's a lot of time lost. She and Kane could be there and gone. It's a lousy plan."

Cecil caught the wadded-up paper when Eddie tossed it over the seat.

"You want we should drive down that dead-end street and park and hope nobody notices us, or drive back and forth where it opens onto the cross street? We'll have coppers breathing down our necks in no time flat."

Silently, Eddie conceded. Aloud, he said, "Since it's business as usual there, that means they don't know Ceara's showing up, which also means she hasn't alerted them. So..." Eddie didn't speak for some moments as an idea took shape. "...they probably don't have a telephone. Yeah. Yeah. That'll work."

"What will work?" Leo asked.

"We're gonna pay a familial visit to the Galloways just as soon as Ceara's father shows up, and I'll bet he'll be there in time for supper. Since we haven't met yet, it's only right I should drop in on my in-laws and my nieces since I'm in town."

"What do you mean, drop in?"

"We'll have a nice little tea party while we wait for Ceara. You know how hospitable and friendly I can be."

Leo cut a sidelong glimpse at Paul, who caught Leo's look and held it too long to suit Eddie. He cast a slow, suspicious glance between the two men.

"What's that look about? Spill it. You holding out on me? You know something I don't?"

Leo said, "No good can come of this, Eddie. Let me or Paul go in and do the talking. We'll negotiate for your ledgers. There's no need for violence."

"No need?" Eddie uttered a divisive scoff. "Violence is what makes people listen to reason."

"Kane's not a man who'll listen. Eddie, think about it. Over the years, you've dealt with city cops and beat cops, even a few Bureau agents, but not a single one could hold a candle to a Texas Ranger. I've heard their code of honor is to never back down or back off. They're the kind of lawmen who don't know when they're beaten. They keep coming when anyone else would be dead."

"Are you going soft on me?" Eddie's voice rose with his disgust. "You think I'm scared of Kane? You think I can't handle him?" He pinned Leo with a hard glower. "You've been with me a lot of years. You know how I operate."

"This time... It's different this time," Leo countered. "You're too close to the situation."

Eddie's temper flared. "It's not different." He punched the back of the front seat. "The only situation we have is my wife is a lying, thieving, unfaithful whore. But despite that, I put terms of a trade out on the table. She turned me down flat."

"When? What kind of trade?" Paul asked.

"Back on the highway just before Kane shot the hell out of my car. I offered her a divorce with property and cash in exchange for the ledgers. We'd call it square. But it's too late, now. I'm through playing games with her and her boyfriend. She won't turn over my ledgers to save herself, but she'll do anything to save her family." He shifted his gaze between Leo and Paul. "If you're not with me on this, your usefulness is over. We're done. You can get out right here. Aldo knows his place. He doesn't question me." He threw out the none-too-subtle threat to help them change their tunes.

Leo exhaled a slow, tired breath. “No need to bring Jucca in on this.”

Paul simply nodded.

“That’s better. No more talk. I need to think.”

At a weathered sign with CLAUNCY’S in faded lettering, Gilbert turned off the street and onto hard-packed gravel. He drove around to the back of the two-story abandoned building. Len pulled up beside them. Paul got out and held the door for Eddie.

Jucca and Leo went inside, while Phil and Cecil went around the outside perimeter. Paul oversaw the brothers while they swapped out the license plates. Eddie strode the few yards to the edge of the river, noting the rundown piers and dilapidated docks jutting from the bank in both directions. The current was quick, and the surface rough with the breeze. While he could swim, the look of the river was too treacherous for his taste. As he walked from the river toward the building, a dim glow of light shined through the broken window pane.

Jucca returned first. “We’re in a storeroom adjoining the kitchen. Inside’s all set up. The door is thick, solid oak. Two deadbolts on it. Walls look reinforced with extra layers of wood. No electricity, but there’s a kerosene lamp in the kitchen and three in the storeroom. There’s a fire stoked in the cook stove. Leo’s getting coffee and a meal going. Plenty of food and water. It’s not over-warm, but we won’t freeze.”

Eddie nodded approval. "Keep the lamps low so we're not night-blind when we go outside. Can anyone sneak up on us from a different part of the building?"

Cecil walked up and answered. "Not without making a lot of noise. All the windows are boarded up or have iron bars. Same with the front door. The inside rooms are blocked off, too. There's no access to us." Indicating the door and window a few feet to the side, he added, "That's the only way in or out that won't take a crowbar to open."

"Not good." Eddie noted the blackened window glass and the broken-out corner of the pane. "Makes us trapped. Make a way to escape on the other side of the building, but not an obvious one. The rest of you get our gear inside. When we're settled, Cecil will take the Ford and the brothers on a dry run to the Galloways' neighborhood. Locate the house, but don't get too close. I want to know how long it will take to get there. Don't come back until you're sure you won't get lost in the dark, but don't take too long."

"Right, Boss," Cecil said.

Paul added, "Len, Gil— It works like this. One car stays here all the time. We divvy-up watch. Two men outside. Both rotate inside every hour. That gives everyone time to eat, sleep, and warm up. The password is Manhattan."

Jucca and Phil remained outside. Paul opened the store-room door for Eddie. He surveyed the bare-bones accommodations. A moth-eaten sofa, a wooden box set on its end as a table with two wooden chairs beside it, mattresses on the floor, plank walls and ceiling, a short stack of newspapers, along with odds and ends of paper trash. It was adequate for no longer than he intended to stay. He'd had worse.

Eddie commented, "This has been used for other clandestine business."

"Dino said this place was a swanky restaurant in its day and then a short-lived speakeasy. He assured me no one, including cops, comes around this part of town any more. The kitchen and john are through that open door. All it lacks is a phone."

Eddie removed his hat, gloves, and overcoat then settled down on the sofa, his legs stretched out, head back, and eyes closed. He'd gone to the mattresses enough times in his life to know to sleep between hits, eat when the food was hot, and wait without complaining.

When Cecil and the brothers returned, Paul and Leo drove to the South Side Café. Paul brought back the first report.

"Dino and Ronny switch out coats and hats every so often and one of them takes a stroll past the house. Two teenaged girls arrived home from school, and Mrs. Galloway met them at the kitchen door. There's movement in the kitchen. Curtains are open. The drapes are drawn over the plate glass window in the front room. Nothing out of the ordinary."

Jucca asked, "Do you think they gave us the slip?"

Eddie shook his head. "No. It means they're not in town yet, or they're waiting until its good and dark. Either way, they'll go to the house. Ceara's family means more to her than her own life. She'll show up, and we'll be waiting."

"Want me to take a turn—"

"No," Paul cut Jucca off. "The fewer of us seen in public, the better."

Eddie eyed his right-hand-man curiously. Paul's icy expression meant he wasn't budging on Jucca staying out of his business with Dino. Eddie chalked it up to the conversation they'd had last night about a traitor in their midst, and he let it go with a slight nod.

Jucca bristled. "I was talking to the boss, not you. Want me to go with them?" He appealed to Eddie.

"No. I need you here to watch my back. Get something to eat and bring me a cup of coffee."

Jucca puffed up with the compliment. "Sure thing, Eddie."

Eddie threw on his coat and accompanied Paul outside. "What's up with you? You were abrupt with Aldo."

Paul continued to the Ford and opened the driver's side door before he answered. Looking over the roof, he said, "I'm not in the mood to listen to his prattle. He has trouble keeping his mouth shut when you're out of earshot. I'll send Leo back."

From his breast pocket, Eddie took out a gold and leather cigarette case and his Dunhill lighter. He couldn't argue with Paul when it came to putting up with Aldo's mouth. He wouldn't have Aldo on payroll except for his skills when he needed a nasty job done in a particularly nasty fashion. There was something else going on with Paul he couldn't put his finger on. He'd noticed it during their phone conversation last night. No matter. Paul was steady and dependable. Whatever was on his mind would show itself soon enough.

Dusk and the thin, misty fog rolling along the river darkened the already dreary sky. A cold, biting breeze caught his coat tail, and he ducked his head to shield the match flame at the end of his cigarette. He took a deep drag deeply into his lungs, held it, then blew a smoke ring and watched it disappear on the breeze. When it served him, he had the patience of a cat stalking a mouse and, right now, he was content things were going his way. The Galloways would make a nice, tidy hostage package guaranteed to get Ceara's full cooperation. He finished his cigarette and went back inside.

When Leo arrived, he stated the code word, and Lenny opened the door. Leo got right to the point.

"A man arrived at the house and entered through the front."

Eddie sat up straighter on the sofa. "How long ago?"

"By now, upwards of thirty minutes. Nothing unusual going on. There's movement in the kitchen, but that's to be expected at suppertime."

"Good." Eddie nodded. "Good. It'll be like taking candy from a baby when we waltz in to keep them company while we wait for Ceara. Kane's waiting for dark, and so are we, but we'll get there ahead of him as soon as Dino goes off watch. They don't need to know what happens. Relay that to Paul."

"I will. We'll probably only get one more report."

"Understood."

Leo swapped cars and left.

Sooner than expected, Eddie heard the Cadillac arrive. He put his coffee cup down.

"Manhattan."

When Len opened the door, Eddie knew it was time for the cat to pounce.

"What've you got?" Eddie donned his overcoat as he crossed the room.

Paul said, "Mr. and Mrs. Galloway and the two girls left the house and took a left at the end of the cul-de-sac. They were carrying things."

"Luggage?"

"No. Bowls and maybe a soup kettle. A picnic basket. They acted like any family going out for an evening visit. They weren't nervous-acting or in a hurry. The kitchen lights are on. The family left through the front room door. Mrs. Galloway and girls walked out first and waited at the street. Neighbors joined them. Finn Galloway stopped in the doorway and looked back inside like he'd forgotten something. Then he turned off the lights and closed the door."

"So you're telling me there's no sign of Ceara and Kane?" He was so sure Ceara would run straight to her family. For a few seconds, his cocksure confidence cracked around the edges to allow the dark paranoia in his mind slip out. Had she bamboozled him completely? Had she sent his ledgers to Washington like she said? Maybe Kane had contacted Bureau agents, and they'd gotten past Dino's notice and were laying in ambush for him at the house. She could be talking to Hoover right now. A shiver crawled down his back.

"There's more."

Eddie jerked out of his mental ramblings. "What?"

"Dino and Ronny called it a night when the Galloways left their house. They followed the whole bunch as they walked along as sociable as you please, laughing and talking, and other neighbors joined them. If it was food they were all carrying, Dino guesses they're meeting somewhere for pot-luck."

"That's normal? People carry food from one house to another?"

"Apparently they do in this neighborhood," Leo said.

"Hard way to get a meal." Eddie dismissed it as behavior of the poor, lower class with which he had no experience and no interest in finding out how they lived. "Why are you telling me this? I don't give a rat's ass about their neighborly get-togethers."

"There's a kicker," Paul interjected. "When Dino and Ronny left their hiding place to follow the Galloways, Ronny swears he saw movement inside the house."

"What kind of movement?"

"He's sure the drapes at the big window moved, like someone had been peeking and then let go. After following the Galloways a few blocks, they hot-footed it back to the alley. The gate's busted open."

"Now we're getting somewhere." Another thought came to him. "I wonder why she didn't leave with her family."

Leo shrugged. "Beats me. Dino sent Ronny running on the double to tell us."

"Too bad we missed the chance to wait inside the house for her. I was looking forward to some fun with those two girlies."

Jucca's sniveling chuckle rubbed Eddie the wrong way. "Keep your mind on business and your dick in your pants until I tell you otherwise."

Jucca ducked his head, his eyes narrowed to angry slits, and his small mouth set in a hard line like a kid enduring a scolding he felt he didn't deserve.

"They must have come in the back as the family went out the front. She'll stay until her family returns. That's when they'll go into hiding together. Too bad for her and Kane I outsmarted them." Eddie chuckled in satisfaction at his coup. In the end, Kane showing up to help Ceara get to Hoover had done her no good. He'd caught them both times. If Kane was the best Texas could send, Hoover should demand a refund.

He looked from Paul to Leo, his smile widening. "Let's go, boys! Get me to that house double-quick. The way this is going, we'll be back in Chicago before tomorrow night."

Chapter Fifteen

Ceara peered out the train compartment window. "I think we're coming into the terminal."

Hagen leaned over her shoulder for a better view. "Looks dismal out there."

"Welcome to New York's weather. This time of year, it could be foggy in one place and crystal clear just a few blocks away, or fog and freezing rain might settle in over half the city and stay that way for days."

Hagen tucked Rocchelli's gun into his waistband. "I don't like going in blind. Describe the station."

"I can't. I've never been inside. I've only seen it from a couple of blocks away. People say it's beautiful."

Skeptical, Hagen ducked his chin. "You grew up in New York, and you've never been inside Grand Central Terminal?"

"We didn't travel, and it's not in our part of town. Too rich."

"Is this the first time you've ridden a train?"

"Yes." Ceara gathered her few belongings. She peeked inside her Freedom Letter, where she'd tucked the flattened paper rose from the box of candy.

"Tell me what you do know. Anything will help."

"It's huge and open and teeming with travelers hurrying about, impatient to get to their destinations, especially when the trains are late."

"That's good. It'll be easier to lose ourselves in a chaotic crowd."

"Mind you, I've only heard of this. It's all electric with magnificent chandeliers and cathedral-height arched windows to let sunlight stream in. The floor is a wide-open concourse with a gentle slope all the way up to the marble stairs. The front doors open onto 42nd Street, which is as good as any street until we get away from the terminal. It's a busy street lined with businesses for people with money."

"Tell me how to find your parents' house in case we get separated."

Ceara considered for many moments. "Once you're on 42nd, just keep going across it, then it's pretty much straight down—

"As in south?"

"Yes. South."

"Name streets I could take."

"Park Avenue, Lexington, Madison, but the streets have a habit of merging and changing names along the way."

"What's your choice?"

Pursing her lips in a thinking expression, she said, "Park will have fewer turns, but I'd go over to Lexington to 3rd and down to Bowery."

"Which way is over?"

Again, she had to think. "Relative to 42nd... Left."

"How far south?"

"Fifty or sixty blocks."

"I'm a country boy. My mind works in miles. How long will it take to cover sixty blocks on foot?"

"I don't know. At a brisk step... I suppose an hour."

"An hour. Okay. Three miles. What are your parents' names, and what's the address?"

"Finn and Maureen Galloway. They bought the old O'Donnell house. That may or may not be useful depending upon how trustworthy you appear when you ask for directions and how close to the neighborhood you are."

"No street signs in New York?"

"In places, but you can't count on them at every corner."

"Then what streets are too far? I need a point of reference."

"Canal, Worth, Hester, Walker. You want the Grand and Broome area. My parents live on Caravan Court. I don't think any of the houses have a number. They're known by who lives in them now or used to live in them."

"Describe the neighborhood."

"Caravan Court is a cul-de-sac. An oasis amidst tenement buildings, you might say. There are fifteen, two-story brick houses of similar design arranged with five on each side. My parents' house is the one in the center at the dead end."

"At the bottom of the *U*?"

"Yes. Those particular five houses share the same wood and iron fence that runs the length of the alley. The property lines between all of the houses are marked by thick, gnarly hedges and huge old towering trees. Each front yard goes out to the wide cobblestone street. In the center of the street is a grassy strip with more trees. It's a pleasant area for picnics and such. When you drive into the court, you can circle up and out the other side in a continuous arc."

"Someone went to a lot of work to build a miniature community within the neighborhood."

"Some seventy or eighty years ago, a wealthy man donated the land to a charitable organization for building those fifteen houses for elderly folks. It was meant to be a quiet, safe place for them to live out their days in peace at little expense. This philanthropist left enough money for upkeep until ten or fifteen years ago. The houses have since sold privately. At least three are vacant." As an aside, she added, "I worry that as the little court falls more and more into disrepair the city will condemn it, and my parents will have to leave, which means they'll lose the money they saved to buy their house."

"All right. I've got a good picture of it in my mind. Now, we'll play this like Capone or Moran have men waiting for us just like in Cleveland, but they may have figured out they were duped. Keep the handcuff out of sight and your hand inside your pocket with a good grip on your gun and shoot through your pocket, but think twice before you pull the trigger. We'll be surrounded by people." He tugged up her fur collar, buttoned her coat to her chin, and situated her hat to better conceal her battered face. "We'll leave the train separately. Stay close, but not too close. Don't make eye contact with anyone, or they'll notice the bruises and cuts on your face. You don't need anyone remembering they saw you."

He tried out different ways to carry the Browning, none of which suited him. He decided his best concealment was inside his coat with the stock shoved up under his left armpit, his arm clamped at his side to pin the rifle against his body, and his hand in his coat pocket like a mitten to grasp and steady the barrel.

"What do you think?"

She squinted and shrugged, and shook her head apologetically. "It's not obvious-obvious, and I can't see it, but I can definitely tell you're concealing something."

"As long as we don't bump into anybody or stop and talk, it might be good enough."

As the train rolled to a rumbling halt, Hagen opened the compartment door to a hallway packed with shoulder-to-shoulder people inching toward the exit. Ceara went ahead, and Hagen followed at a reasonable distance. While he'd understood there would be a crowd, he wasn't prepared for the swarming buzz of people moving like cattle stampeding for a water hole from all directions.

There were more people in one place than he'd ever seen in his life, which didn't help the closed-in, suffocating sensation taking hold and urging him to get his back to the wall in an out-of-the-way place so he could breathe. It was beyond his comprehension how these big-city dwellers tolerated this jam-packed congestion and the pungent smells that went along with too many people gathered in one place. It was unnatural.

Keeping an eye on Ceara was like being a little bluegill caught in a school of bass swimming with the current in the Canadian River—constantly bobbing and ducking to keep from being run over. He lost sight of her several times, because of her ubiquitously inconspicuous attire. He was suitably unobtrusive in his hat and coat that pegged him as a typical business man, unless someone noticed the incongruity of his scuffed boots and worn jeans.

Hagen lengthened his stride to keep up with Ceara's near-trotting pace as she wove in and amongst the throng and crossed the center of the main concourse where he sensed the gentle rise in the floor's incline. Even if she didn't know where she was going, she wasn't wasting any time getting there.

Where the floor leveled off toward the doors and above the concourse floor, the crowd thinned as they dispersed toward the exits. He'd kept a sharp lookout, and it was here he spotted the two heavies near the doors, both wearing dark glasses and one holding up a newspaper as a cover for loitering. The nearer man was a head taller and considerably skinnier than the other, and both dapper in appearance and no doubt concealing weapons under their overcoats. There would be torpedoes just like them posted at all the exits. Capone or Moran was pulling out all the stops to catch Rocchelli.

Ceara cut a quick glance at Hagen when she spied the two men, and she slowed to let him come abreast. He nodded reassurance and mouthed, *Keep going*. Fifty feet to the doors. Thirty. Fifteen. Only a handful of people in the way, and the two heavies hadn't noticed them. A businessman cut between them, others followed, and the gap widened. Ceara threw a hasty glance over her shoulder seconds before a woman burst in from the street with the forward momentum of a woman on a mission to get where she was going in a hurry. Hagen saw the disaster coming and opened his mouth to yell a warning, but it was too late.

Ceara ran headlong into the woman, whose handbag went flying and landed at the feet of the thug standing a few feet away. She grabbed hold of Ceara to keep them both from falling. Hagen did his own fancy footwork to take himself out of the resulting bottleneck of bodies stacking up.

"Pardon me. I am so sorry. I know better than to be in hurry, but I got such a late start from home. Did I hurt you?" The woman's voice carried clearly over the murmuring hum of blended voices.

A security guard paused to assess the situation.

Ceara attempted to disentangle herself. "No. No. I'm fine. It was my fault. I wasn't looking where I was going. Excuse me." She stepped around the woman in her quest to reach the street.

"Ceara?" The woman clutched Ceara's coat sleeve. "Ceara Galloway? Imagine meeting you here."

"Gail Foley?" Ceara's head jerked up, but she caught herself and turned her face aside. "I—I—can't talk right now. I have to go."

Hagen's instincts urged him to hustle Ceara out of there before a problem actually developed, but caution counselled him not to draw more attention to them.

It was times like this when he wished he smoked, so he had a reason to stand idly while he lit a cigarette. As it was, he stretched out his arm from his coat sleeve, and made a production of checking his wristwatch against the grand, sentinel four-faced clock on the concourse floor. He did his best to appear nonchalant and bored, while keeping one ear tuned to Gail's nattering. The security guard continued on.

Gail embraced Ceara with the zeal of old friends reuniting. "We haven't visited since just before you moved to Chicago, and you've only written once. If it weren't for talking to your parents at the grocery and reading the society pages, I'd have lost track of you altogether."

Ceara kept her chin down.

"Ceara, why won't you look at me?"

"I'm sorry—"

"It's just so exciting to know someone important. You're practically a celebrity in the old neighborhood. We must catch up. Surely, you have a few minutes to spare for an old friend." Gail held her at arms' length, beaming her long-lost-friend smile.

"No— I mean, yes, yes, of course."

"I forget your last name. No. No. Don't tell me. It's Italian. Rodolfo. Ruffini. Rossi. I've got it!"

It was that moment the dark glasses-wearing thug handed Gail her errant handbag. "You dropped this."

"Rocchelli!" Gail cackled with satisfied delight. "Your husband is Eddie Rocchelli. He's always in the papers."

Ceara froze. Slowly, she lifted her gaze and looked right into the man's face. His vapid expression gave way to recognition and understanding.

"Oh, my Lord, Ceara! Your face. What happened?"

For an instant, the world slowed in a blur of simultaneous motion in Hagen's vision. The handbag went by the wayside when the man threw open his coat for his weapon. Ceara rocked her gaze left and right like a cornered cat desperate for way out whether it was over, under, or through.

Hagen lunged for Gail with a shove that sent her sprawling as he fired the B-A-R into the ceiling and yelled, "Get out of the way! Everybody down!"

The concussion echoed in the cavernous building. Whipping around to face the submachine gun leveling at him, Hagen fired point blank into the man's chest. In the ensuing screaming and wailing chaos, people scattered and scrambled, frantic to save themselves. Some braver passersby dragged others along in their own terror-stricken flight.

Lumbering on a run to intercept Ceara, the shorter, stout muscle-man made a wild grab at her coat tail as she dashed through the exit. He hit with a thumping bounce and slid belly down on the polished floor past the doorway, his arms outstretched without losing his Tommy gun. The man executed a roll and leap that put him in front of the exit.

From the corner of his eye, Hagen saw two more thugs closing in. With nowhere to go but through, Hagen ducked his head with the singlemindedness of a linebacker running for the goal line and drove into the man blocking the door.

"Give it up, Rocchelli!"

"You got it wrong. I'm not Rocchelli!"

His momentum propelled them through the door in a shower of shattering glass. The Thompson skittered one way and the two men the other.

Hagen scrambled up, wielding the Browning like a club. The man ducked and took Hagen's legs out from under him in a tackle. The Browning flew out of his hands and another hoodlum grabbed it. Hagen drew Rocchelli's .32, but he couldn't find his shot. People everywhere. *So many people.* Hagen scanned for Ceara.

"Drop your weapons! Hands up!"

He didn't stick around. Dead was dead whether by criminal or cop. Dodging through traffic, he narrowly avoided colliding with vehicles in his vie for the other side of the street. When his feet left pavement for the sidewalk, a barrage of gunfire that sounded an awful lot like it was fired from his Browning smashed into the building in front of him. Angry, biting shards of brick and shrapnel pelted him like buckshot from a scatter gun.

A snippet of conversation with Ceara popped into his head about having your own gun used against you. At least he now knew a cop wasn't hot on his heels. A triggerman wouldn't concern himself with the inadvertent death of a bystander. Trusting his instincts to point him in a general over and down direction, he ran for all he was worth, hoping like hell Ceara was making better time somewhere ahead of him.

By the fourth block from the terminal, a distant and gaining drubbing behind him caught his ear. Too late, he recognized the sound as running footfalls. The rat-a-tat from a submachine gun drowned out the city noises. Bullets zinged and pinged from cars on his left to buildings on his right. Something stung his left arm just off his shoulder an instant ahead of his right leg buckling under a wicked blow at his hip. He crashed into the gutter and rolled under the running board of a parked car.

He peered from his hiding place, expecting the hunter to creep along looking for him. If the eight bullets in Rocchelli's gun couldn't get the job done, he had eight more in the Colt strapped to his ankle. Seconds ticked off. He strained his ears to block out the hubbub of shouts and cries, the droning car tires-on-pavement hum, and the reverberation of trains beneath him for the sounds he needed to hear in order to stay alive. The barrage of gunfire rumbling down the street got him on the move.

Inching on his back, he cleared the car on the street side, braced an elbow on the running board, and dragged himself upright by the door handle. Back against the door, he glanced both directions, decided it was clear, and lurched forward in the stumbling, hop-skipping gait of a peg-legged man. Four intersections with no pursuit boosted his confidence that those five shots had taken care of whoever had wanted him dead.

A dozen blocks later, he cut through a park. His glance behind threw him off-stride and his boot heel missed the curb. He went down in a bone-jarring injured-shoulder-to-pavement crash with his hip taking a solid hit. An electric jolt of pain seared through his body. He eased out of the street and made it the few feet to a park bench. He sat with his head in his hands and eyes clamped shut while the worst of the pain subsided, and the sick feeling in his stomach let up. Cars zoomed by in a steady stream he was coming to realize was the way people lived east of the Mississippi—fast. They evidently lacked the ability to plan ahead to get where they were going on time.

"Hagan! Wait!"

He jerked his head up, twisting around to see Ceara sprinting across the park. *How did she find me?* Didn't matter. He was damn glad to see her.

"You're hurt." She dropped beside him, winded.

"Yeah."

"Broken leg?"

"No. Numb and bloody."

"Bullets?"

"Or shrapnel."

Nodding, her words came out in choppy, breathy chunks from running. "You move...pretty fast...for a man...dragging a leg."

"I told you I could run like a jack rabbit looking for a hole when someone was chasing me." It hurt too much to laugh.

"Yes, you did." She inhaled a deep breath, held it, and exhaled slowly. "And I said I'd like to see that."

He read a lot into her smile, mostly that she was relieved to see him alive. He returned the same smile with the same message. "You were supposed to be ahead of me."

"I was, until I heard the Tommy gun. I went back."

"To do what?" Then, her meaning hit him like a sledgehammer between the eyes.

"I didn't know what happened to you...if you were..." She swallowed hard. "I couldn't leave you there. If you were alive, I had to help you. There were two men working as a team. From their stalking manner and the way they checked under parked cars and in doorways, I knew if you weren't dead, they planned on finishing you off when they found you."

"No doubt they were looking for you, too. You took an awful chance."

Her veneer of calm cracked. "I wasn't scared for me." She studied the gun in her hand. "I...I need to reload." She reached into her coat pocket and fumbled the cartridges when she pulled her hand out. "I fired, but didn't hit them. A half-dozen or more policemen had better aim."

"Here, I'll do it." Hagen gathered the cartridges at his feet and reloaded.

"I confronted them and suggested they find a different street. One of them said, 'You must be The Roach's wife. We've been looking for you.' Then they burst out laughing, and one of them called me a stupid hussy for waving my little pea shooter in his face." Her eyebrows dipped in a deep frown. "I don't like being called stupid."

Hagen half-smiled.

"It wasn't the same as shooting into that car when they tried to run us off the highway. I could see it in his eyes, in his expression, daring me to shoot. He didn't think I would."

"For anyone with a conscience, it's never easy to pull the trigger."

"Everyone around was running, so that's what I did. I ran, but not the way I told you to go. I ran the long way around to throw off the cops."

Hagen returned her gun, and she put it into her coat pocket.

Ceara looked him over. "You lost your hat."

"Thanks for noticing."

"You're welcome. Can you walk?"

"Stand, maybe. Walk on my own...doubtful."

"I'll be your crutch." She draped his arm across her shoulders, and they stood as one. Helping him to the curb, her eye on a break in traffic, Ceara inched into the street.

"What the hell are you doing? I've made it this far without getting run over. Then you show up, and it's Katy, bar the door."

"You and your Texas sayings. You'll have to explain that one to me later. And, no, we won't get run over. I'm getting us a ride the same way you took Eddie's car from him, only minus the rifle."

Facing on-coming traffic and with one arm around Hagen's waist, she waved her free arm, standing her ground while cars swerved to miss them. A few pedestrians hurried by.

A dozen cars dodged them before a taxi driver, who didn't see them in time, slammed on his brakes and swerved to the curb to keep from running them over. Rolling his window down, he leaned out shaking his fist and shouting, "Are you drunk? Get outta the street you crazies!" He started to back up.

"Wait! We need a ride. Don't leave!"

"Geesh, lady. I'm off duty." A smartly liveried man peered at her.

"Get us to Allen and Delancey on the double."

Hagen cut her a sharp, questioning glance. Out of the side of his mouth, he said, "You didn't mention those streets."

"It'll get us close enough. We don't know him from Adam." She punctuated her words with a meaningful look.

Ceara opened the door and hustled Hagen in none too gently. "Don't try anything funny. I can walk these streets blindfolded. I'll know if you take a side trip, so don't."

The driver scrutinized Ceara, his gaze lingering on her face and then lowering to her hand where she held it inside her coat. His eyes registered what that meant.

"Take it easy. I'm not carrying much cash. It was a slow shift. You can have it. All of it. You can even take my car. Just let me go."

"I'm not robbing you. We need to get somewhere fast. Here." Ceara dropped money over the seat. "Does this change your mind?"

Cautiously, he picked up the bill. "Hey, I don't take funny money." He inspected both sides. "Whoa... Lady. Is this the real deal?"

"Yes. Now will you drive?"

He slowly dragged his gaze from the hundred-dollar bill to eyeball her again over his right shoulder. His frown changed to a grin. "Allen and Delancey?"

"That's right."

"Hang on." He cranked the steering wheel, took a quick look in traffic, found his opening, and floored the accelerator.

Hagen hadn't ridden in many taxis, but he recognized the drivers all possessed the uncanny skill of simultaneously watching their passengers in the mirror while keeping an eye on the road in all directions and while carrying on a conversation without getting lost or having a wreck.

"You look like you've run into some trouble. Do you need a hospital or police station—"

"No. Just drive. And no talking."

He groused something about uppity dames.

"I heard that," Ceara scolded.

Hagen's chuckle choked off when the car thumped in and out of a teeth-rattling pothole. The cramped backseat allowed no room to stretch out his injured leg, and fresh pain coursed to his fingertips when another rough dip jostled his injured arm against the door.

Ceara tapped the driver's shoulder. "Two more blocks—

He mumbled, "Women... All of them. Back-seat drivers." When he pulled over, Hagen got out, grateful to stand and relieve some of the pain gnawing at his hip.

"You never saw us." Ceara handed the driver another bill.

He drove away.

"Is your leg any better?"

"Have you ever hit your elbow so hard your hand goes numb, and you can't straighten your fingers?"

"Yes."

"It's like that, but worse. A whole helluva lot worse. I can't feel my toes. My brain sends signals to my leg and my foot, but they're not receiving a clear message."

"Lean on me. We're close." Casting around for signs of observers, she added, "Maybe anyone who sees us will just think you're drunk, or both of us are. For as much as I paid him, the taxi driver probably thought so. This way."

Their initial clumsy three-legged gait gained coordination and speed in a dozen steps. Ceara guided them down the first alley she came to then out to a street and over to the next alley and street in continuous zig-zagging progression. The few street lights cast eerie shadows in the freezing fog that rolled along like dingy, gossamer-shrouded apparitions.

"*Umm.*" Ceara inhaled deeply. "Do you smell that?"

"You mean the sewer stench, fishy-river tang and whatever that awful food smell is, and the smoldering wood smoke like someone's trying to burn a pile of wet leaves?"

"That's not how I would describe it, but yes. That awful food smell, as you called it, is not awful. It's from a Chinese restaurant. Chicago smells of industrial chemicals and vehicle exhaust. I don't like it."

"But you like sewer stench, stinky fish, and wet smoke?"

"How can I not? It smells like home."

"You need to come to Texas and breathe in something that's good for your health."

"What's that?"

"Sunshine."

"Sunshine doesn't have a scent."

"It does in Texas."

"This is the second time you've suggested I come to Texas."

They stopped at an intersection for a car to pass.

"Maybe if I ask a third time, you'll take me up on it." Hagen turned his gaze from the receding taillights. It was on his lips to say if he ever got her to Texas, he'd put a ring on her finger to convince her to stay.

Ceara nodded slowly. "Maybe I will."

"Then I'll be sure to ask again."

She averted her gaze. "We're almost there."

He kicked himself for pushing his luck right up against the too-personal line again and accomplishing nothing but embarrassing her. To get them back on neutral ground, he teased, "You said we were almost there five miles ago."

"Oh, stop your grousing. Five blocks, maybe."

"And that's been five too many."

Down more alleys and across a street to an alley that ran opposite of the others, Ceara stopped at an ornamental wrought iron gate in the center of six-foot-high wooden fence and grasped the latch handle, but it didn't budge. She lifted and jiggled, pushed and pulled.

"It must have rusted."

Hagen reached for the handle. "Let me—" He yanked his hand back an instant before the heel of her shoe landed at the junction where the latch bolt fit into the weathered wooden fence frame. The old wood splintered, and the heavy gate creaked open on stiff, sagging hinges. The bottom corner wedged between two bricks in the garden path.

"Not the most subtle move you've made. The whole neighborhood heard that."

"They'll think it was just a car backfiring. You have a bum leg and an injured shoulder. How were you going to climb over?"

Hagen shook his head in a combination of amusement and exasperation. “Thanks for thinking of my well-being.”

“You’re welcome.”

Ceara squeezed through the narrow opening. “It’s a tight fit. Make yourself tall and skinny. My parents don’t lock up until bedtime. I hope they haven’t changed their habits.”

Partway up the path, Hagen whispered, “Get your gun out. You don’t know who’s inside. Could be Moran’s men or Capone’s just as easily as Rocchelli waiting.”

Ceara stopped so abruptly that Hagen bumped into her, her eyes wide with the horror-stricken realization that she’d not considered the possibility.

“*Noooo*. Moran and Capone wouldn’t come here. My family is nobody to them.”

“Ceara, listen to me. Rocchelli is somebody, and you’re married to him. At the terminal, those thugs thought I was Rocchelli.” He held the .32 at chest level. “When you walk in— If you see something you don’t like... You’d just as well start shooting. Negotiations don’t work out in these situations. Surprise is your best bet.”

Ceara closed her eyes, her face screwed up in a pained grimace.

Hagen gripped her arm and gave her a shake. “Look at me.”

Ceara opened her eyes.

“I’m your backup. Just stay low and out of my line of fire.”

Easing the porch door open, she went in on tiptoes, and paused at the threshold of the kitchen, her attention locked on something, or someone.

"Claire! Have strangers come around? Are you safe?"

"Ceara! Oh, my gosh. You scared the dickens out of me. No. No one's been here. We're fine. Why? What's wrong?"

"Thank goodness we're ahead of him. You can put the knife away now."

Chapter Sixteen

Ceara stepped through the doorway and motioned for Hagen to follow.

Claire put the butcher knife in a drawer. "I heard noises outside. I couldn't tell if someone was tearing down our fence or if a car backfired."

Ceara deadpanned an *I-told-you-so smirk* at Hagen as he eased into a chair. He placed Rocchelli's gun on the table, and she put Cecil's gun beside it.

Claire's curiosity prompted a scrunched-up, freckled-nosed string of questions. "You look awful. What happened? Why is there a handcuff around your arm? Mister, are you hurt?"

"I'll explain later. Are Momma and Daddy here?" Ceara gave her sister a quick hug with silent thanks that no one was waiting for them.

"Just Momma."

"Go get her. Bring back clean cloth and towels, the medical bag, and the medicine box. See that the drapes are drawn in the front room."

"They are. Momma keeps them drawn in the winter."

Ceara shooed Claire from the kitchen, closed the kitchen curtains, took off her coat and hat, then followed the aroma of potato soup to the pot on the stove. Lifting the lid, she breathed in the simmering, creamy steam to which her empty stomach grumbled a reminder of how hungry she was. Another familiar aroma of fresh-from-the-oven yeast rolls prompted her to peek under the tea towel draped over a brown stoneware bowl. It was so good to be home. A rush of teary homesickness blindsided her. If only she were here under happier circumstances.

Pushing those thoughts aside, she filled another cooking pot with water, set it on a burner, and dialed up a strong flame under it. Turning to Hagen, she said, "Stand up. Let's take off your coat, so we can see how badly you're injured."

"Damn," Hagen muttered when he saw the dark patches of blood on his jeans and shirt sleeve.

"Shirt off." She inspected the wound on the outside of his right bicep. "There's a bullet just under the skin. It's not deep."

"It's deep enough to hurt like the devil, not as much as my hip hurts, but it's more than enough. At least I'm getting some tingling sensations back in my toes."

"Drop your pants."

Hagen grinned. "That's awfully personal."

"Don't be shy. I'm a nurse," Ceara teased. "And, we did sleep in the same room two nights in a row, and last night all I was wearing was a bedsheet." She wasn't normally coy, but it was fun to banter with him.

"And I've never seen anyone wear a bedsheet with such style and grace."

"I hope you're wearing a union suit or some such. My sisters are going to have giggling fits when they see you like this."

"I wouldn't want to cause an uproar with your sisters." Hagen unbuttoned and let his jeans drop.

"BVDs." Ceara wiggled her eyebrows.

"It's the latest fashion in Texas. All the real Rangers are wearing them nowadays."

"*Ooh*. Blue and white pinstripes. You strike me as a solid color sort of man."

"At least I'm wearing something under my jeans."

Giggling, she said, "And aren't I the lucky girl for that?"

She took pains to carefully loosen and fold back his bloody undershirt where it stuck to his skin. "Hold this out of the way, please."

Hagen's chuckle switched to a groan when she pressed her fingers around the edges of the abrasion and discoloration below his hip bone. "Hey! Watch out where you're poking."

"Does it hurt or tickle?"

"Yes."

"Don't be such a baby. It's a long way from your heart or other vital organs. You took a blunt blow that dug into your side and carved out a chunk of skin. It will be a few minutes before I can tend to your wounds." Ceara slipped her arm into his left coat sleeve and wiggled her fingers out of the hole. "See this rent and the wider gash here on the side. I've seen this many times. Ricochets—a bullet in your arm and shrapnel at your hip. Be thankful this coat is of a heavy, tightly woven material. It functioned much like silk deflects, or at least slows down, a bullet. Well, not always, but under certain circumstances it works."

Claire came into the kitchen carrying a box labeled medical supplies with folded towels and scraps of cloth on top and Colleen at her heels with the familiar leather Gladstone bag.

Colleen squealed in delight. "Ceara! I've missed you so much." She dropped the bag and threw her arms around Ceara's neck.

"Oh, sweetie, I've missed you, too. Both of you."

Her baby sister felt so frail and small in her arms. She had to find a doctor who could make her well. First things first, though. Until this ordeal with Eddie was over, everything else took second place.

"Do you want your surgical instruments in a bowl with carbolic acid?" Claire asked.

"Yes, and let me know when the water boils."

Maureen Galloway breezed into the kitchen. "Ceara? I was in the attic. Claire told me the most outrageous story. She said you came in through the porch and that you need help, because you have handcuffs on your arm, and there's a man...with...you..." Her words trailed off as her gaze moved from Ceara to Hagen and back. "Oh, my lands, child."

Ceara's breath hitched. "Oh...Momma..." Her voice failed.

"It's all right. It's all right," Maureen crooned, her arms open to embrace Ceara. "I don't care why you're here. I'm just so glad to see you. Now, who is this gentleman standing so politely, and I dare say, uncomfortably, with his trousers around his ankles?"

Ceara dabbed at her eyes as she left her mother's embrace. Colleen giggled, covered her mouth with one hand while nudging a snickering Claire. Maureen chastised them with a scowl that did little to stifle their snickering.

"Ma'am." Hagen dipped his head respectfully. "My name's Hagen Kane."

"I'm Ceara's mother, Maureen Galloway. Please. Sit down. These two silly girls, who should show more restraint with company, are Ceara's sisters, Colleen and Claire."

"Nice to meet you. Sorry for making a mess in your kitchen. The blood and all. The guns."

"Think nothing of it. It isn't the first time nor is it likely to be the last."

"Could I trouble one of you ladies for something to drink? Water? Coffee? Something wet will do."

"Certainly." Maureen filled a glass with water from a pitcher in the cupboard and gave it to him. "Please sit."

"Thank you, ma'am."

"Does this have anything to do with the two policemen who came by early this morning? They were reporting on a telephone call from Amarillo, Texas, of all places, with a request to send police to check on our safety."

Ceara looked at Hagen and back to Maureen. "Yes, that was us, from someone helping us. He might have sent a telegram, too."

"We haven't received a telegram, but I was gone a good share of the day at the store. Perhaps it's in the postal box."

"I'll check," Colleen offered.

"No!" Ceara held up her hands to stop her. "Don't show yourself at the door and stay back from the windows. The telegram doesn't matter now."

"I told Finn about the policemen. He was concerned enough that he sent a telegram to you."

Ceara's shoulders slumped. "Our telegram was to warn you."

"Warn us of what? Ceara. This makes no sense. What happened to you? Why are you here?"

"There's so much to explain. We don't have much time. Maybe no time at all."

"Time for what? Is someone following you or chasing you?"

"Yes. When will Daddy be home?"

"Any moment, now. He stopped at the church to help set up for the supper tonight."

"Supper?"

Maureen raised her eyebrows in gentle reproach. "It's the first Friday of Lent."

Ceara gasped, as embarrassed for forgetting what day it was as she was suddenly filled with fond memories. "Oh... Our community fellowship suppers every Friday until Easter. How I've missed them."

"When did you last eat?"

"A good many hours ago."

"Girls, put on fresh coffee. The soup is ready. No one goes hungry in this house."

The front door in the living room opened and closed. "I'm home. Where are my girls?"

"In the kitchen. We have a surprise." Maureen cast a sly grin at Ceara and mouthed *Shhh*! at Claire and Colleen.

"I like surprises. I'll be right there."

Ceara's need to see her father was stronger than the guilt of why she was here. There was so much to tell him and little enough of it to be proud of. The radio came on. She stared toward the living room, her heart full of expectation.

"Now, what is this surprise?"

Ceara met him on a run and threw herself into his arms. She was safe now. She was a little girl again, wrapped in the protection of her daddy's strong arms. Everything would be all right. He'd make it so. He always had.

"This is a surprise. A wonderful surprise."

She clung to him, her face buried in his shirt, and he rocked her for many long moments before he placed a kiss into her hair and eased her from his arms to look into her face. Unmasked concern flickered across his brow as he wiped her tears.

"Ceara Rose Galloway. What are you doing bringing men home unannounced? This is a fine way to introduce me to my son-in-law." The teasing lilt in his soft Irish brogue was a gift that made people comfortable, strangers and friends alike.

"Thank you for that, but you know he's not my husband." The words tumbled from her in a jumbled rush to say everything she needed in one breath. "I've brought a terrible mess upon this family. I don't know how much time before we're found here. We can't stay. None of us can. We all have to leave before—"

"Ceara, my girl, there's nothing so bad as can't be mended with love and help from your family. You just have to tell us what's going on. Why did police come here to see if we were safe? I sent a telegram to you for fear you were in trouble."

"Mom told me. I am in trouble. We all are."

"You keep saying that. What is going on?" Maureen insisted.

"Sir." Hagen, on his feet again, extended his hand to Finn from the other side of the table. Finn hesitated for the length of a startled blink at Hagen's lack of trousers before he grasped his hand.

"I'm Ceara's father, Finn."

"Hagen Kane, Texas Ranger. I'm on loan to the Bureau of Investigation. Special assignment. Sorry about my...uh... Standing here with my...I'll just sit down, if you don't mind."

Finn's eyebrows went up. "Well, now. What is my oldest daughter doing with a BOI agent? Why has someone been heavy-handed with her? Why is she wearing handcuffs? And where is her husband?"

Ceara bobbed her head in time with his questions. "Have you heard anything or read about the shooting in Chicago yesterday?"

"It's on the radio. I haven't looked at today's newspaper. It's beside my chair to read after supper."

"What did you hear about it?"

"Nothing I've not heard before, other than this one has a catchy name. St. Valentine's Day Massacre. I paid little enough attention. We have our own gang shootings to worry about."

"Water's boiling," Claire interrupted.

Maureen dipped out hot water into a smaller pan, set it on a trivet on the table beside Hagen, and dropped in a scrap of cloth. "I'll take care of your hip injury. I'll have you right as rain in no time."

"That'd be fine. Thank you, ma'am."

"And I'll get the newspaper. You've got my curiosity up now." Finn went to the living room.

With the medicine box at hand, Maureen said, "Claire, Colleen. Come close to watch what I do."

Finn returned, scanning the front page above the fold. He glanced at Ceara, then returned to the paper and read aloud in his deep, soft and resonant voice—a soothing voice that never failed to lull her with a bedtime story into a pleasant sleep.

"'Firing Squad Execution leaves Chicago Gangsters Dead. Chicago's cold and snowy Valentine's Day began with a bang in a warehouse on North Clark Street... '"

Ceara only half-listened. She didn't need to hear a newspaper's conjecture about the who, what, and why she'd experienced first-hand.

Finn paused, glanced at Ceara again, then started the sentence over.

"'Further investigation revealed a second, although possibly unrelated, gun battle occurred in the back part of the warehouse and spilled out into the alley at or about the same time as the executions.

"'According to witnesses, before they heard gunshots, a 1928 cream-colored Phantom 1 Rolls-Royce four-door sedan arrived in the alley and parked near the double-panel cargo doors. Witnesses further stated that several minutes later, half a dozen people ran from the warehouse into the alley amid an exchange of gunfire. Further investigation is needed to confirm that the Rolls-Royce is owned by Eddie "The Roach" Rocchelli, one of George "Bugs" Moran's lieutenants...'"

Finn lowered the newspaper, cast a frowning gaze between Ceara and Hagen, then resumed reading.

"'Witnesses reported the driver of the getaway car was a woman wearing white clothing described as a nurse's uniform or evening gown. She was accompanied by two gun-wielding men.

"'Rocchelli's whereabouts during and since the shooting remain unknown as does the location and identity of the three people in the getaway car. Mrs. Rocchelli, a nurse at Lakeshore General Hospital described as a five-foot-eight, slender, with strawberry blonde bobbed hair, did not return home at the end of her shift at 2 p.m. Her whereabouts are unknown.

"'Police contacted Rocchelli's key enforcers Paul Carta and Leo Passero at their homes. Aldo Jucca was questioned at Rocchelli's business office. These men were not forthcoming with information regarding the warehouse shootings or Rocchelli's whereabouts. Cecil Murra, one of Rocchelli's bodyguards, and Phil Bianco, a chauffeur, remain unavailable for questioning...'"

Finn lowered the paper and stared at an invisible point on the wall. "Is this accurate?"

Claire and Colleen put their heads close together over the paper and continued reading. Ceara inwardly cringed to see a small photograph of her with Eddie below the pictures of the massacre. At least it wasn't a quality photograph that made them easily recognizable.

Ceara said, "Yes."

"Where is the Rolls-Royce?"

"In an alley in Mansfield, Ohio."

"Where is your husband?"

"Undoubtedly on his way here, or nearby biding his time."

Finn looked at Ceara. "Biding his time until when?"

"Since he wasn't already here, my guess is until dark."

Finn slowly nodded. "And for what purpose is he waiting?"

She couldn't say the words.

"It's as serious as that?" Finn understood what her silence meant.

"Every minute we stay here is a minute closer to being caught. We have to leave. All of us. Gail Foley recognized me at Grand Central. If—when—the cops talk to her, they'll come here."

Finn lifted his hand. "We aren't going anywhere until your injuries are tended, and I understand what's going on. We don't have enough information to make a rational decision."

Ceara loved him for his solid-as-a-rock-not-to-be-pushed disposition, but she felt like a mouse trapped in a corner and Eddie was the cat preparing to pounce. Jittery, she went to the window for a look outside.

Hagen cautioned, "Careful. Stand at the side."

She peeked without disturbing the curtains.

"This may sting a bit," Maureen warned Hagen as she dipped the corner of a cloth in iodine.

"I'm ready." He sucked in a sharp breath at the bite of iodine on raw skin.

"There was talk at the church about gunshots fired at Grand Central this afternoon."

"A couple of hardcases tried to detain us."

Peripherally, she saw Finn draw his gaze from Hagen to her.

"Ceara Rose. What kind of life have you been living?"

If she looked at him, she'd cry, so she spoke to the curtains. "Not the right kind. Not one that would make you proud, which is why you haven't heard from me in such a long time."

Finn walked to the Hoosier cabinet, opened one half of the double top doors, and took out an opened whiskey bottle. "Ladies, I'd offer, but I know you'd turn me down."

He returned to the table with an opened whiskey bottle and two glasses. Maureen put the last touches on Hagen's hip. He thanked her, then pulled up and buttoned his jeans. Finn poured two fingers of whiskey into each glass, handed one to Hagen, then tilted his glass toward him and swirled the whiskey.

"The Eighteenth Amendment made the manufacture, sale, and transportation of hard liquor illegal, but not the drinking of what was already on hand or for medical purposes. So, as a foresighted man, I put aside a case or two. You have a legitimate medical need, and a man shouldn't drink alone."

Hagen studied the whiskey. "I was twenty-one when Prohibition went into effect. I haven't had a drop since." He threw it back in one grimacing gulp. "Never had much taste for hard liquor."

"A good philosophy it is when it comes to alcohol." Finn poured another for Hagen. "One more to take the edge off your pain. Ceara Rose, do your work on his arm. Then I want to hear your story. Every detail, no matter how insignificant or how difficult for you to tell...and no matter how long it takes."

"We haven't the time—"

"We'll take our chances. It's not full dark yet."

Ceara conceded to the gentle finality in his voice.

Hagen scrutinized the surgical tools on the towel arranged on the table. "Those are forceps, but what the hell is that— Pardon my language." He spoke the apology out of the side of his mouth. "If you're using that on me, I'll take my chances and leave the bullet right where it is." He pointed to the flat-ended scissor-like instrument with long, curved ends. "It looks like some sort of medieval torture tool."

Ceara explained, "It's a wound dilator. I don't probe blindly for bullets or shrapnel. Probing pushes whatever is inside deeper. I extracted my first bullet when I was thirteen, and it was against bone. I know what I'm doing."

Hagen winced when Maureen swabbed iodine on his arm.

"Yes or no?" Ceara dipped her chin and arched an eyebrow. "If you leave it in, it will hurt at the slightest touch. Your shirtsleeve will feel like pins stabbing your arm. Also, not removing it increases the likelihood of infection. I'm fast and steady-handed. If I can't grasp the bullet the first time, then I'll lance the skin, and remove it that way. It's under the skin like a splinter, I expect it to come out cleanly. All you have to do is not flinch."

Hagen eyed the girls, a grin lifting the corner of his mouth. "Don't move while she digs under my skin with sharp instruments. Easy."

"Want Dad to hold your hand?" Ceara teased.

"Nope. We Texas boys are tougher than boot leather. We rope and ride cyclones just for the fun of it."

"You tell tall tales just like Daddy." Colleen's grin was wide as the bright gleam in her eyes.

"Must be our Irish blood or—" A beat of silence followed then his low moan rose to a full-blown groaning, squinty-eyed complaint. "*Whoaaaaa damnnnn*! I didn't say yes."

"But you didn't say no." Ceara handed the bullet to him.

"I think lightning seared down my arm and exploded out the tips of my fingers." He blew out a long whistle. "But you're right. You are fast." He winked at Claire and Colleen. "And sneaky."

They giggled, and he smiled along with them. Maureen cleaned and bandaged his arm while the girls went about tidying up. Ceara washed her hands, her urgency to get her family out of the house and to a safe place battling with her longing to sit in this kitchen and pretend Eddie didn't exist.

Claire poured coffee all around. Hagen situated both the .32 and the Savage in his waistband, then took his cup to stand watch at the side of the window.

Maureen said, "Ceara. It's your turn. Let's tend to your injuries. Have a seat."

She started to say there was no need to fuss over her, then she caught Hagen's eye. His slight nod toward the table meant they'd risk staying a while longer.

"All right. Thank you."

With a warm, wet cloth, Maureen cleaned Ceara's face. Her mother's gentle touch and that she made no comment about the finger-bruises on her neck helped make the telling of her story easier.

Finn wrapped his big hands around his coffee cup. "I want to hear it. All of it. We'll listen, and ask questions after."

Ceara spoke to her father. He was her focus and his slow nods kept her going. She remained emotionally separated from recounting the events of her life since leaving New York on a bus bound for Chicago, until she told how she'd lost her baby.

"Oh, Ceara, if only I could have come to you then and brought you home."

"I wished for that every day I was in the hospital." Ceara's throat tightened around the words.

A change came over Finn. His easy-going, slow-to-anger countenance darkened and hardened. He leaned back in his chair, his gaze on her, yet his eyes looked beyond into some other realm of thought. She knew that expression for she carried it in her heart. It was utter and abject loathing for Eddie.

After a few moments, Finn said, "Go on. What happened after that?"

When she finished, Finn summed up, "So it was either Capone's or Moran's men who tried to run you off the highway and who waited in Cleveland and at Grand Central."

"Yes. One, or both, is after Rocchelli," Hagen said. "I think they're laying for him at all of the key train stations and airports in case he tries to skip out of the country."

"It's reasonable they'd think Eddie and I were trying to escape. They don't know I was leaving him, or that I have evidence that may incriminate them in illegal activities. Well, they didn't know at the time. They may now. Whoever wants Eddie wants him for their own reasons, which complicates this. When—if—Moran and Capone find out about the ledgers, they'll both come after me, because I know too much...or they'll think I do."

Maureen observed, "That is quite a coincidence that you took the ledgers just when your husband was targeted by the two most powerful men in Chicago."

"Incredibly coincidental."

"And that brings us to the police coming round this morning."

"Hagen made the phone call that got the police here, and maybe a telegram sent."

"Why didn't, or hasn't, your husband sent men to do his dirty work for him?"

"He won't involve anyone except his most trusted men. What happened is between us as husband and wife. His humiliation that I left with another man is worse than anything he's written in his books. Lawyers will handle whatever charges are brought against him in that respect, but only Eddie can deal with a runaway, disloyal wife." Ceara shuddered. "I've heard people say no one gets even like Eddie Rocchelli."

Hagen added, "Rocchelli probably can't call in favors in Chicago or New York, because no one will risk Moran or Capone getting the wrong idea about where loyalties lie."

"You've left out an important bit of information...or, should I say, avoided it."

Ceara nodded as he spoke. "The location of the ledgers."

"The location of the ledgers," Finn repeated.

Strengthened by her love for her family and her desperate need to protect them, she said, "If you don't know, you can't tell."

Chapter Seventeen

Her heart ached to refuse her father his request. "If Eddie gets his hands on you—any of you—he'll make you tell what you know. That's why we have to leave here. Soon. Now is better."

"We can do that easily enough." Finn said. "You'll get the ledgers?"

"Yes."

"And then what? Will you go into hiding?"

"We can stay where the ledgers are, at least for a few days, while we figure out how to get them to Hoover."

Finn cut a raised-eyebrow questioning glance at Hagen who shrugged. "Beats me. This is the first I've heard of it. She's been as tight-lipped as a teetotaler in a saloon."

Claire and Colleen snickered.

"Where do you suggest we hide for the long term?" Maureen asked.

Hagen said, “Texas. Get in your car—”

“We don’t own a car,” Finn said.

“Then take a train or a bus. Hell, hire a taxi cab if you have to, but get yourselves to Amarillo and the Texas Rangers’ headquarters. My boss, Wes Lansing, will take care of keeping you alive.”

Ceara emptied her apron pockets of money and dumped the bills on the table. “There’s enough to get you out of town with plenty left over.”

“What’s this?”

Hagen tossed the wallet onto the pile.

“Eddie’s money,” Ceara said.

Finn dismissed the offer out-of-hand. “We don’t need his dirty money. We’ve the means to pay our own way.”

“Do you mean we have to leave everything behind?” Colleen’s voice, tight and scared, tugged at Ceara’s heart.

Maureen gently assured her, “Colleen, dear, we’ve never let our possessions own us. All that matters is family. We have each other, and that is enough. If leaving is what we decide to do, we will make it work for us. Don’t fret. That’s mine and your father’s job to do the worrying for all of us.”

Colleen nodded, smiled, but her eyes shone bright with tears. Claire put an arm around her sister. “It’ll be an adventure. You’ll see. You can write a story about it when we’re settled again.”

Ceara said, “I’m so sorry that I brought this to you, but there’s no wishing it were otherwise. There’s only one way this can end happily, and that's when Eddie Rocchelli is dead. He's called *The Roach* for good reason. He's fast when he gets even. He's in and out. No trail. No witnesses. Nothing to pin on him. He's notorious for showing up when he isn't expected, and he always has an alibi.

"He's survived every attempt on is life with barely a scratch, and his retaliation was swift and devastating. He's been arrested several times since I met him, and not once was there enough evidence to hold him for more than a few hours, and he's never gone to trial." She moved her gaze from person to person. "He has to get to me before Moran or Capone get to him."

"We've been through hard times, and we've seen our share of danger. You remember the gang fights and the lootings and robberies."

"Yes, and the midnight medicine on the kitchen table. I also remember the payoffs you made to keep us safe—undoubtedly still make."

"Then you know we have survival running through our veins like blood."

"But what are you going to do? We can't just sit here and keep talking about it."

"Maureen and I need a few minutes alone."

Ceara was well acquainted with her parent's few moments alone discussions. They made their decisions together, and it was a rare situation in which they didn't see eye-to-eye. When they returned from their private talk in the next room, Maureen went straight to the porch, while Finn took a chair at the table. He motioned for Claire and Colleen to come closer.

"Girls, listen carefully. We'll walk to the church supper with our neighbors just as planned. To do otherwise will bring questions and people to the house to check on us, and we can't have that. You'll not breathe a word to anyone of what we're doing. Not a hint that anything is wrong. Not even to Bishop Morrissey.

"We'll take with us only what we can carry without seeming obvious that we'll be gone longer than this evening. We'll leave the kitchen light on, but we'll not be coming back tonight. We'll just make it look like we are. When the supper is over, we'll come this way at first in case anyone is watching or waiting for us along the way, then we'll double-back at Chessman Park, and go to the store." He paused to look at them individually. "Do you understand?"

"Yes," they responded.

"Why to your store?" Hagen asked.

"It's our safe harbor when seas get stormy. We can remain there for quite a while. We've got people to help us. We'll go on to family in Ireland just as soon as we can. Rocchelli won't find us there, especially when we take on the ancestral name."

Relief from bearing this heavy load of worry lifted from Ceara shoulders. "Thank you," she murmured.

"Now, you're not leaving here wearing handcuffs. Let's get them off. Sit here beside me. Girls. Gather close. I want you to see this." He inspected the handcuffs from all angles. "These are poor quality. See the rust on the hinge pin? This bend in the ratchet just above the teeth is creating the bind. And here," He indicated a dent. "This has been smashed against the swing arm. Ceara, fold that towel and rest your arm on it, then tuck an end between your skin and the metal."

Maureen returned to the kitchen. "I found the handcuff key in our catch-all box."

Finn offered a wink and a smile. "Never throw out what you might need, no matter how obscure or insignificant it may be."

Hagen chuckled. "I've heard that since I was born."

Finn went to the porch and returned with tools. He handed a screwdriver to Hagen. "You'll pry at the dent, while I work the pliers. Maureen, you're in charge of inserting and turning the key." Pliers in hand, Finn warned Ceara, "This will hurt."

"Only for a little bit."

"Always my pragmatic girl." He grasped the ratchet bar with the pliers, held Ceara's arm with his other hand for leverage, and pulled and twisted while Maureen worked the key.

Ceara set her teeth against the pressure and pinching, while Finn twisted and turned the pliers until the teeth gave way, and the metal arm released.

Ceara rubbed her raw, bruised wrist. "Thank you."

Maureen placed her hand on Ceara's shoulder. "Now. We'll leave this alone. Worrying won't change a thing. We've been given an unexpected gift in your return home, and we're going to treasure it." She looked to the girls. "Colleen, ladle a bowl of soup for Ceara and Mr. Kane and bring the rolls and butter.

Claire, put the handcuffs and the tools out on the porch. I'll pour coffee."

"Please, ma'am. Call me Hagen."

"Only if you'll call us Maureen and Finn."

"Agreed."

"Momma," Ceara protested. "Eddie is—"

"Not here right now, is he?"

Fear urged her to argue, but in her heart of hearts, love told her to embrace these precious moments. How could she refuse? Come what may, if these were their last moments together, then the warm memory of her family together would be her solace. She looked to Hagen, and he nodded. He understood. If she hadn't already fallen in love with him weeks ago, she would have right then.

Talk around the table turned to the happenings since her one visit home, and she pushed her worries aside as she soaked up every word, every gesture, every bit of laughter. It was as if she'd never left home at all.

As she listened to Hagen and Finn swapping stories and discovering a common ancestor back in the Old Country, it came to her that had she not married Eddie, she'd have never met Hagen. Even now, knowing there was no future for them together, she'd not change a thing. A comfortable peace found its way into her heart. The two men she loved more than anything else in the world were right here with her, talking as friends, as family.

Life held promise again, even if only for a little while longer. Eddie Rocchelli could never take that from her.

• ● •

Ceara helped her sisters and mother collect the few treasures, keepsakes, and necessities they could carry in their pockets and pack into a picnic basket and extra bowls—Maureen's recipe book, family photograph and letters, heirloom jewelry, family Bible, Colleen's medicine. Ceara's sisters packed their favorite books, writing paper and pens, and other items they couldn't bear to leave behind. Ceara teased her sisters that with everything they were taking, they'd waddle like fat geese under the weight. Finn emptied their cash savings from the Mason jar buried in the back yard under a path stone.

At the front door, they gathered for teary goodbye hugs. Maureen and the girls went out to greet two families waiting at the street to join them. Finn lingered. He looked long and hard at Hagen.

"Take care of my Ceara Rose."

"I will, but she's done a damn fine job of taking care of herself. She'll be all right."

Finn lifted his Mackinaw from the rack beside the door and tossed it to Hagen. "You'll have more freedom of movement. You may need it."

"Thanks. I'll do my best to return it without holes."

Finn smiled. "You do that."

With one last look at Ceara, Finn turned off the light, heft-ed the lidded soup kettle, and closed the door. Ceara peeked through the narrow gap in the drapes where they met at the center of the wide window and watched her parents and sisters walk away in the company of neighbors and friends. Even after they reached the edge of the light cast out from the last porch on the block and the foggy night drew in around them, Ceara remained at the window. There was small comfort that the casual observer wouldn't suspect these four people were leaving their home and their life's possessions with only a few cherished keepsakes. What she wouldn't give for a second chance to correct the wrong decisions she'd made. An icy finger of foreboding touched the back of her neck, and she shivered. Would this be the last time they'd see each other?

Shaking off her cloak of dread, she looked around the darkened living room. She'd not grown up in this house, but she'd been here countless times to visit Mr. and Mrs. O'Donnell and to run errands for them. There was love in this house. It felt as much like the home she'd grown up in above the grocery, because her family had made it so.

She exhaled a slow sigh of relief. "I'm so thankful they're going to Ireland. Maybe I'll be able to join them someday."

"That sounds hopeless. How about later? You'll join them later."

"I like that." The draperies gently swayed when she turned from the window. "I'm going to change clothes. Momma and I are the same size, and she's a practical dresser. I'll only be a minute."

Swapping her uniform for a long woolen skirt, long sleeve blouse, and loose-knit, button-up sweater, Ceara returned to the living room sofa carrying a pair of flat Oxfords and knee-high argyle socks.

"The irony in this is that Eddie should thank us. If we hadn't been caught at Union Station and taken to the warehouse, Eddie would have been one of the casualties in the hit."

"Next time I see him I'll mention it. I'm sure he'll thank us." Hagen stood at the side of the window where he could see the front yard in the sliver of space between the edge of the drape and the window frame.

Ceara giggled. "No doubt. He has such a keen sense of humor."

"Listen." Hagen cocked an ear toward the radio. "Bessie Smith."

"I like this song."

Hagen held out his hands. "Dance with me."

Before she had time to think, she was in his arms, her cheek resting against his chest, and her body pressed to his, swaying with his slow, shuffling steps while he hummed a few measures then picked up the song just a few beats behind Bessie.

...after you've gone and left me crying, after you've gone there's no denying, you'll feel blue, you'll feel sad, you'll miss the bestest pal you've ever had... You are, you know."

"What?"

"My bestest pal."

Her breath hitched; her heart thumped out of rhythm. Softly, she replied, “I will feel sad and blue when you’re gone.”

His arms tightened around her. Tilting her head up, she saw in his eyes what had always been there, but she’d denied acknowledging, because she’d wanted it too much.

“Let me leave you with a special memory so you won’t forget me.

“I’ll never forget you.”

His lips touched hers. She’d dreamed of being kissed by a man who loved her, and she knew in every part of her being that Hagen was that man. There was nothing else, only this moment and this man holding her. She stole this memory from Time, and locked it forever inside her heart.

He drew back, his hands cradling her face. Her desire, her wanting, her need for him responded to the warm love in his eyes. They had such a short time to make a memory that would last them forever. If they were to have more, it had to happen now, and he’d be hers as no man had ever been. One more kiss, and she would cross the line of *gone too far*.

But, she couldn’t. He dipped his head to kiss her again, and she pulled away. One kiss was as far as she could go. She clamped her eyes shut to keep her tears from betraying her heart. With the strength that comes from doing what’s right, she opened her eyes and said the words that would part their hearts forever.

"I'm married. I made a vow to be faithful. If we give in to what we both want... We'll have nothing more than a love affair—a mob affair. I've had that. I want more."

"You deserve more." Hagen took her into his arms again, gently swaying to the music until the song faded and ended. With a kiss to her hair, he whispered, "We'd better get out of here."

Her head said he was right, but her heart wouldn't let her move. "Another moment, please. Just hold me."

He nodded against her head. "Ceara. I want to tell you... I have to tell you... I need to say how much I—"

She put her fingers on his lips to shush him, her gaze searching his. "Don't. I know what you want to say, because I want to say it, too. But it's not ours to do with as we'd like."

"Maybe not right now, but it will be. That's a promise, and I've never welched on a promise in my life."

"I'll hold you to that." She stepped out of his embrace.

Hagen turned off the radio, donned Finn's Mackinaw, and adjusted his hat, while Ceara buttoned up her coat and tugged on the cloche hat. He checked their handguns again, and handed Cecil's to her.

"Ready?" Hagen asked.

"Yes."

"All right, lady with a plan, lead the way to the ledgers. I'm right behind you."

"We'll go out the back. We need to take our time, though. The ledgers are in a place where I'm sure I'll be recognized. We need to wait. Please don't ask."

Hagen's exhale was the sound of resigned frustration.

"Once we have the ledgers, it's up to you to get us to Hoover."

"We can take a cab out of town and find a likely place to board a train. That worked pretty well for us. Or we can contact Hoover and just lay low until agents can give us protection to Washington."

"Whatever you decide—"

Headlamp lights from two vehicles crisscrossed the window like flood lights sweeping in a prison yard. Hagen snaked an arm around Ceara's waist and dragged her to the floor with him. He crawled to the window, the .32 in his hand, and peeked between the drapes. Ceara crouched beside him, peering under his arm, Cecil's gun clutched in her hand.

"Rocchelli and his goons. Damn."

"How did he know to arrive at just this moment?" Ceara's mind refused to accept what her eyes beheld as fact.

"He must have had someone watching the house."

"At least he doesn't have my parents and sisters." The tentacles of terror squeezing her heart eased. "I don't recognize two of the men."

"They were our nurse-maids overnight at the warehouse. Couple of youngsters. You were asleep when they checked on us."

"I remember now. Leo called them Gilbert and Lenny. They're brothers. They're too young to waste their lives working for Eddie."

"Age doesn't matter when money talks."

"Ceara! I know you're inside." Eddie's thundering voice carried clearly into the house. "I know your family left here not long ago." He pulled out his timepiece. "Maybe you're waiting for them to come back. Maybe they're on the run. Doesn't matter. I've got men out looking for them right now. I've got eyes on the store, too. We'll find them. They can't get away. Come out unarmed, and I won't kill them on sight." Eddie checked his watch again. "I'm feeling generous. You've got two minutes before I decide whether to torch the house with or without your family inside. The clock's ticking." Ceara hissed, "Scram! Hagen, go! He's crazy. There's no reasoning with him."

"He's bluffing. He only has seven men, and he knows if he kills you or your family, he doesn't get his books. For all he knows, Hoover already has them."

"Don't you see? This isn't about his books anymore. Maybe it was never about his books. It's about me running off with you. I've lost, and he's won. It doesn't matter if his ledgers make it to Hoover or if I give them to him or if they never surface. It all ends the same way. I have to surrender. I was foolish to think it would end any other way." She left Cecil's gun on the floor and scrambled for the door.

"No, Ceara— *Shit*!"

Cracking the door open, she called, "I'm coming out. Alone. Give me a second to write a goodbye note to my family." She looked at Hagen, her heart screaming not to leave him like this. "Down that hallway— The bedroom at the end. Go out the window. You can jump over the hedge into the next yard. You have to help my parents and sisters get out of the country. Promise me. The store is on Bowery. Keep going south. You'll find it."

"Where are the ledgers?"

"Without the ledgers or me, there is nothing keeping you here." She shook her head in utter defeat. With her hand on the doorknob, she looked at him many long seconds. "But don't get caught. Please, don't get caught."

"You can't go back to him. I love you. Don't say you don't love me. I won't believe you."

She rested her forehead on the doorjamb, her eyes closed. *Any words. Any words but those three.*

"Time's up!"

"St. Brendan's." She turned. "They're at...our church..." The words fell upon the silence in the empty room. Wasted words for a wasted life.

Why? Why hadn't she just told him when he'd asked? Agony, gut-wrenching, soul-shattering agony, tore through her heart as she stared at that empty hallway. Yet, within that emptiness a tiny glimmer shined. Hagen would stay nearby until Eddie took her away, of that she was certain. Somehow, she'd give him hints.

"Aldo— The gasoline."

Ceara opened the door. Fog rolled in thick waves across the car lights like wraiths set loose from the Underworld. She hardened her heart to the scene before her—Eddie flanked by Cecil, Gilbert, and Lenny, gasoline cans at Jucca's feet, Paul and Phil coming toward her, and Leo going around to the back yard with a flashlight.

She abandoned her short-lived freedom as she descended the three steps of off the stoop to the brick walkway. She harbored no regret. Her love for Hagen and her family and the knowledge they were free would sustain her no matter what dark fate awaited her at Eddie's hands.

She passed between Paul and Phil without acknowledging them. Cecil, Gilbert, and Lenny moved aside when she reached Eddie.

His smarmy smile sickened her.

"I knew you'd give in to me, babe."

She slapped him.

Chapter Eighteen

Hagen crouched on the far side of the hedge, burning poker-like pain seared his side and along his arm from the clumsy, headlong dive off the narrow window ledge after awkwardly closing the window to cover his departure. Watching the woman he loved return to the bastard Rocchelli while he hid in the bushes like a scared rabbit sent shame knifing through his heart. He pulled Rocchelli's gun from his waistband. Peering through the dead spaces amongst tangled branches, he watched for his shot to put Rocchelli down. Leo circled around back. Paul and Phil went inside. Lights went on room by room.

Cagey like a coyote, Rocchelli stayed between the broadsides of the cars as protection. With his poor field of vision combined with Ceara moving into his direct line of fire, Hagen couldn't risk a shot for fear of hitting her or a neighbor. Neither did he have enough cover or fire-power for an all-out gun fight. He cussed his bad luck for losing the Browning.

Rocchelli said, “I knew you’d give in to me, babe.”

Ceara slapped him.

“Ah... That’s my girl. Subtlety isn’t one of her attributes.”

Finn’s low, raspy whisper at Hagen’s ear sent a rush of goosebumps scuttling along his arms.

“*Shit*! How long have you been lurking? And what the hell are you doing here?” He hiss-whispered through clenched teeth.

Finn shook his head and crouched lower beside Hagen to see through the spaces in the hedge.

“Not your best move.” Rocchelli removed his white leather gloves.

“I guess I’m a slow learner.”

Jucca finished patting her down. “She’s clean.” He gave her another grope. “I’ll bet you liked that, didn’t you?”

Hagen wished she’d punch the sniveling little prick in the nose.

“Where’s your family?” Rocchelli demanded.

“Not here.”

“I’ve warned you your smart mouth is gonna get you hurt. Where’s Kane?”

“Not here, either.”

Rocchelli struck her across the mouth with the gloves.

“We did this song and dance yesterday. Try again.”

"He dumped me at a bus stop and went back to Texas. He said he didn't get paid enough to risk his life for me."

"You think I'm some sort of maroon? I want the truth, and I want my ledgers."

"Truth. That's a laugh coming from you. He stuck to me like glue, but when you showed up, I sent him to get your ledgers. At least I have the satisfaction that Hoover will get your books, and that Moran or Capone will eventually kill you. My only hope is that I'll live long enough to see it."

"You're lying, and you're not that lucky."

"You're fooling yourself if you think you can go back to Chicago. You're a dead man, Eddie."

"Capone and Moran are nothing to me." Rocchelli's scoffing laughter didn't ring true. "I'm bigger than both of them. They're gonna find out real soon just how big I am. I'm taking over all the Chicago territories by the end of the year."

"You're not only wrong, you're delusional. You're finished. I told our priest how our baby died. He knows, Eddie. He knows your guilt. You're going to the deepest, darkest bowels of Hell for what you did. For as long as you live, there is no penance you can do to absolve yourself of the death of an innocent. You have a lot of blood on your hands, Eddie, but the blood of a baby can never be washed off. You'll find no sanctuary in any church, no peace from any confession. Even St. Brendan can't save you—not even if you make a pilgrimage in his name or leave all of your money to the church."

"No. That's where you're wrong, babe. I've confessed my sins and bought absolution." Eddie tapped his gloves in a rhythmic beat against his palm. "You're my wife, and you're coming home like a good little girl, and you're bringing my books with you. As long as you remember how to be Mrs. Eddie Rocchelli and give me sons, your parents and sisters will remain alive and well taken care of. In fact, I'll move them to Chicago, just like you've wanted, where I can keep a close eye on them. I'll buy the best doctors in town for your sickly little sister. As long as you mind your wifely duties, they'll stay healthy, but for each time you give me any guff, someone in your family will suffer."

"*The Roach* fits you." Disgust dripped from the words.

The front room went dark as Paul and Phil came out of the house.

Paul talked as he approached Rocchelli. "Nothing out of place. Looks like they went out for the evening."

"You weren't in there long. They might have snuck back while we were gone. Did you check the attic? Crawl spaces under the floor? Secret panels—"

"Eddie, take it easy. Don't jump the tracks," Paul cautioned. "Why would they hide in their own house? They were there, and now they're not. There's no reason to think they won't be back. There is one thing. Phil found bloody towels stashed on the porch along with a doctor's bag and a box of medical supplies."

Rocchelli cocked his head at Ceara. "Want to tell me about that?"

"No."

"You're not injured. I doubt it's any of your family. That leaves Kane. What happened?"

"Skinned his elbow."

Leo interrupted Rocchelli's response. "There's a wood shed in the back. No sign anyone's been in it, but the fence gate is wedged open."

"Did you check the neighboring yards?"

"I'm not keen about poking my nose where I can't see what might poke back. But, yes, I shined my light all along and through gaps in the hedges."

Hagen perked up. Leo hadn't shined his light on this line of hedge. Why would he tell Rocchelli he did?

"Then we're done here—for now. Get in the car. We'll wait down the street."

"Wait for what? Where are we going?" Ceara resisted.

"What's it to ya?" Then a nasty smirk spread over his face. "Ah. I get it." He swept a piercing look about the yard. "Kane! I know you can hear me. This just got simple. You bring my books here at ten o'clock. We'll talk about a trade. We end this tonight."

"Hey, Boss. Want me to tear the place apart? If your books are in there, I'll find 'em." Jucca's sniveling whine set Hagen's teeth on edge.

Rocchelli put on his gloves. “No. Kane will do the work for us.”

“*Hehehe*. Let me torch it.”

“No! Eddie—”

“Shut up!” Eddie snapped at Ceara.

Finn tensed, leaned forward, but Hagen put a hand on his shoulder with a cautioning head shake.

“I’ll let it stand if I get what I want, when I want it.” Rocchelli grasped the front of Ceara’s coat and yanked her to him. “I think you’ve stashed my books where you can’t get to them, or Hoover’s boys would have been here and gone, and so would you and Kane.”

He shoved Ceara into the backseat and got in beside her. “Time to go, fellas.”

Hagen and Finn remained where they were until the cars were out of sight.

“Give it a few minutes to see if Rocchelli circles back or sends in a snooper.” Hagen swiveled on his knees to look behind them. “How long have you been here?”

“Since Rocchelli arrived. You landed ten feet from me when you jumped the hedge.”

“Then you heard it all.”

“Did Ceara tell you where the ledgers are?”

“Maybe. She said something as I took out for the back of the house. It wasn’t clear. It could have been the location.”

“What did it sound like?”

"Snake blended churn. Same breaded chicken. Sane braid ed...something." Hagen shook his head, trying to recreate the muffled words from ear-memory. He shrugged. "Not much to work with."

"You're right. That's not much help. Follow me."

"Where?"

Finn moved along the hedge toward the backyard. "Legal documents I should have taken when we left earlier."

Branches scraped and tugged their clothing as they crawled through a narrow gap where the hedge was mostly dead.

"For leaving the country?"

"No. We're not leaving without Ceara."

"That's not what you told her."

"We'd never abandon her. It was a ruse to ease her worry."

"You mean a bold-faced lie."

"Call it what you will. I'll not have her waste the rest of her life with Rocchelli, and we're not living in fear of him for the rest of our lives. If we need help, I know someone who owes me for certain courtesies I've shown him over the years."

"Who?"

"Sebastian Lazzarano."

"I've read about him in newspapers. Where I'm from, Sebastian Lazzarano is what we call a bad man to tangle with."

"That he is. Maureen and I gave generously to the wedding dinners of his two daughters and three sons, and we've sent christening gifts for his grandchildren. We've also removed bullets and fixed-up the knife wounds and broken bones when a son or nephew or one of his men showed up on our back step needing medical assistance, and we developed amnesia as soon as they left."

"Rocchelli might kill Ceara out of sheer cussedness."

"Then he'll follow her to the grave, but he'll know why before he dies. I'm not bound by an oath to uphold the law as you are. You've the law on your side, and I'm depending upon you to use it as far as it will go, but if the law fails... Well, I only have to make peace with my conscience, and I've already done that." Finn stopped and faced Hagen.

"Galloways don't run with their tails tucked between their legs. Rocchelli doesn't know us. He has no idea what we stand for and what we'll fight for. I'll put a scrappy Five Points Irishman and an Irish Texan against an Italian gangster any day of the week."

Hagen waited outside, while Finn went inside and took care of his business in the dark. When he came out, he took to the alley at a jog-trot. Hagen fell in beside him, a decided gimp to his stride. The freezing mist hung heavy and thick, sticking to clothing, and chilling faces and fingers.

"Tell me what Ceara has told you about the location of the ledgers."

"She sent them to New York. She called it a sanctuary. She has absolute faith in the person who has them. She sent them to a building I've recently become reacquainted with—whatever the hell that means—and this building is within easy walking distance of where she grew up and even closer to where you live now."

"How does one become reacquainted with a building?"

"I don't know. I'm a country boy. My job doesn't keep me inside much, other than when I stop in at headquarters." He grabbed Finn's arm. "Hold on."

"What is it?" Finn moved them into the shadows of a building.

"Is it odd to you that she carried on to Rocchelli about church and penance and going to hell? She said sanctuary. Why would she use those particular words unless she was trying to convey a message to me?"

"Was she alluding to a connection you have with a church?"

Hagen shifted his weight off his sore leg. "Hell, until I took over driving her and Rocchelli to church on Sunday mornings, I hadn't been in a church...in...years." There it was, clear as the summer sunrise on the Texas plains.

"*Ahh*...clever girl." Finn understood it, too. "Reacquainted with a building. Our church is St. Brendan, the Navigator. Nearly a hundred years ago, it was constructed as a place of sanctuary for the Irish who arrived destitute and hungry from the Old Country. Of all the people she can trust, or have absolute faith in, is Bishop Morrissey." A broad smile worked its way over his face. "St. Brendan's is that way." He pointed to the right, but continued on the original course he'd set.

"Wait. Where are you going? We need the ledgers." Hagen hustled to catch up.

"That we do, but until the supper is over, we won't be able to talk with Bishop Morrissey."

"Maureen and your girls, aren't they expecting you to return to the church?"

"No. Maureen and I decided that after I got our papers from the house, I'd go to the store and wait for them there. They'll be along. Maureen can take care of herself and twenty others. She knows what to do, and how to do it. I don't worry about her. There's nothing she won't tackle head on."

Hagen kept up with Finn's steady ground-eating pace, but barely. For a man of his age, Finn was in exceptional shape, and Hagen was thankful he was fit enough to match him. Trusting to Finn's lead, Hagen followed him along dark streets and alleys and dodged around corners and across empty lots to avoid cops walking their beats. Finn made his way between two buildings and stopped at the other end to look both ways before he motioned Hagen to follow. Finn took the rickety wooden steps two at a time to a roof-covered wooden loading dock at the front of one of the buildings. With a skeleton key, he unlocked half of the double cargo doors, made another check both ways, and pulled the door open just enough for them to slip inside.

"Move to the right."

When his eyes adjusted to the dim surroundings, Hagen made out the shapes of large, wooden barrels

Finn closed and locked the door. "This way. Stay close."

"I smell pickles." Hagen bent down and sniffed a barrel. "And sauerkraut." Every few feet brought a new aroma.

"You have a good nose." Finn wended his way through the maze of barrels and boxes like he'd done it a million times. "The barrels are empty. Most of them are broken or their usefulness is long past. They're from a forgotten time."

"Is this place yours?"

"No, but I'm good friends with the owner."

"Now I smell tar and turpentine."

"That you do." Finn laughed lightly. "We're here. Stand to the right again."

Another door opened on silent hinges and a tendril of old, cold air rose from below.

"Where are we?"

"One street over from my store."

Hagen recognized the metallic sounds of Finn handling a lantern then he struck a match. The light cast a dull glow on the crumbling rock and cement stairway at their feet. Hagen could make out a crawl-sized door at the bottom of the steps. His heart made a quick double-thump, and his mouth went dry.

"Where does that door lead to?" He knew the answer when he asked. He just hoped he was wrong.

"A tunnel."

Tunnel. Damn. "How big is it?" Hagen's memories ignored the fact that it was too cold to be sweating.

"You mean, how small? You have to crouch or crawl. It's wide enough for pulling along a narrow sled or skid."

"You use it often?" Hagen dragged his gaze up from the bottom of the pit.

"I come through every week or so to check the rat traps and sweep to clean out spiders. Normally, I carry a flash-light. We'll have to go by feel. The lantern stays here for Maureen and the girls."

"Rats and spiders." A shiver shook Hagen to his socks. This was deteriorating quickly. "What's at the other end?"

"Our safe place."

"Is this the only way in or out?"

"No. There are two other ways. One is a trapdoor in the ceiling with a pull-down ladder that opens into a closet in the back the grocery. The other way is another tunnel of some twenty feet. I've been through it a handful of times with a shovel for just-in-case. The last time was a good ten years ago. It's a desperate route of elbow and belly crawling. I'd be hard-pressed to try it now."

That went nowhere in easing his anxiety. "What about air?"

"The room is ventilated much like you'd find in a mine, and the tunnel doors aren't tight. Take it slow and easy, and you won't get light-headed." Finn held the lantern up in Hagen's face. "Do you want to tell me what happened?"

"A sand cave collapsed on me when I was a kid. I wasn't conscious when they dug me out. It's— It's stayed with me."

"The ceiling and sides are shored-up. It's never collapsed."

"That's all well and good, but I'd be more than happy to take the long way around."

Finn nodded that he understood, but there was no give in his expression. "The store is visible from all directions. It's impossible to enter or leave by the front or back doors without being seen."

Damn. It was Hagen's turn to nod as he eyed the crumbling stairs. "So you go through that tunnel blind as a mole and hope nobody's waiting at the other end?"

The lantern light cast a murky light into the yawning hole. "There's a piece of stick about half the size of a kitchen match wedged above the upper hinges at both doors. If the sticks aren't in place, then someone who shouldn't be down there has gone in or come out."

"Has that ever happened?"

Finn shook his head. "Not in my lifetime."

"How do you reset the stick on the outside once you're in the tunnel?"

"The gap over the hinges is big enough to slide the stick in from either side of the doors."

"Once we're at the other end, how will we know if someone's coming in behind us?"

"On the left as we go in, a wire runs the length of the tunnel along the edge where the wall and ceiling meet. The tiny bell on each end of the wire rings when either door opens."

Peering at the sorry excuse for stairs, he said, "It's a near-vertical descent. That doesn't bother you?"

"Checking this tunnel gives me chills. Every time. And I've been doing this since I was ten years old. I just don't think about it. I put one foot in front of the other."

Hagen muttered, "In other words, don't be a pansy." He inched his way down the decaying concrete steps, some barely wide enough for his entire foot, others accommodating only his heel with his shoulders brushing the sides until he reached hard-packed dirt at the bottom of the stairway.

"Is the stick in place?"

"Yes." Hagen faced the four-foot-tall door like it was an enemy to defeat. He swore the door taunted him, mocked him for his reluctance, laughed at his cowardice— *Coward.* Shame surged through him. Ceara had returned to a life of hell with Rocchelli, and here he was, scared of a tunnel. Enough. It was time to take this beast head-on and slay it. "How long is it?"

"One hundred man-sized steps—give or take. Stay crouched, or you'll hit your head. It's wider and taller at this end and gradually narrows as the ceiling slopes down. Since we're going through without light, keep one hand on the ceiling and one on the wall to stay oriented."

Hagen grasped the door handle, but his hand didn't respond to his brain's instructions to open the door.

"Coming down." Finn hung the lantern bail on a hook and doused the light.

The sudden darkness sent another shiver racing along Hagen's arms and a sense of suffocating rising in his chest. He wiped a hand across his brow. Finn's sure steps brought him to the bottom without a misstep.

"You're not alone this time. Count your steps aloud. The sound of your voice and counting off the steps will help you stay oriented."

"Easy. Sure. Count." Hagen inhaled a deep breath and exhaled slowly as he turned the handle. The bell tinkled with his too-hard shove, which slammed the door off the tunnel wall and back in his face. This time when he eased the door open, he was conscious of the dank, earthy aromas of dirt and damp wood. Crouching, his left hand on the ceiling and his right hand against the wall, he forced himself to take a step into the abyss of his nightmares. Five steps into the tunnel, Finn closed the door. Tar-black nothingness engulfed him. His eyes bulged to catch a glimmer of light.

"Count," Finn reminded.

"Ten, eleven, twelve..."

The sides and ceiling pressed him. His hand over his head caught a cobweb before it stuck to his face. Shivers went down his back; his heart thumped a few quick beats.

"Twenty-one, twenty-two..."

All sense of direction vanished. The sound of his shuffling steps blended with Finn's. His mind played tricks. Was it Finn or some creature following him? Was there something lurking ahead? He stopped. Finn ran into him.

"Keep counting. Keep moving," Finn ordered. "Forty-five, forty-six—"

"Forty-seven," Hagen said. Finn's voice, a reminder that he wasn't alone, gave him direction in a directionless void.

Sixty steps. Seventy-five. His shoulders ached from holding his arms up, while shuffling in a progressively stooping crouch. A scratching, scurrying sound came toward him and continued on past. *Shit. Rats.* Another shiver of dread prickled along his arms. Two more steps and he bumped his head on the ceiling.

Instantly, the image of a coffin lid lowering flashed in his mind. Panic welled; his throat constricted. A death shroud of darkness wrapped around him and pressed him to the ground under the weight of sand burying him alive. Sweat trickled down his chest.

A hand gripped his shoulder. Finn's disembodied voice said, "One step. Take just one step. Don't think about anything but that step and then the next. We're almost there."

Hagen meant to take a step, wanted to, but his feet didn't budge. He fell to all fours, breathing ragged, head hanging. The sensation of hard-packed ground against his palms cleared his head. Dirt. Not sand. Dirt. He could move on dirt. He crawled with Finn's droning words driving him forward.

"Ninety-one, ninety-two, ninety-three, ninety-four—"

Hagen's forehead met the door. "*Ow*! Damn. Found it."

Chapter Nineteen

Finn chuckled. "The door opens toward you. You can stand full height once you go through. The string pull for the light is along the door frame to your right. There's a bucket beside the door with candles and matches if the light doesn't come on."

Hagen crawled into the room and collapsed onto his back. He sucked in a deep lungful of refreshingly stale air. Dank aromas that lingered in abandoned places—dust, old wood, mold, a hint of the people who once lived there—bombarded his nose and a bout of sneezing ensued.

The rattle and click of the light chain when Finn pulled it was a welcomed sound. Although the bulb gave off a dull yellow glow, Hagen squinted as he removed his hat to wipe his brow. The air wasn't as close here as in the tunnel, but it was still none too fresh.

Finn closed the door then offered Hagen a hand up. "You're done with it. Your fears don't own you anymore."

Hagen half-grinned. "I haven't made it back out, yet."

"You will." Finn removed his coat and hat, placed them on the wooden table in the middle of the room, and Hagen did likewise. He'd worked up a good sweat in those couple of minutes.

"I'm going above for a check. If I'm not back right away, don't waste any time leaving."

Finn stood in the narrow space between the two sets of bunks, grasped the short piece of dangling rope, and pulled. A trap-door came down with a hinged ladder attached to the top side. He unfolded the ladder extension and settled the legs on the floor. He went up and through the narrow hole in the ceiling with the ease and agility of familiarity.

Hagen stood at the ladder, breathing in the fresher air while he inspected the room. He estimated it at twenty feet square with a ceiling so low he could place the palms of his hands flat and keep his elbows bent. He wondered if noise—footsteps, voices, and the like—in the store was loud down here or if there was a noise-retarding space between this ceiling and the store's floor to keep sound from coming down or, conversely, filtering up.

The tunnel door opened in the middle of a wall with backless benches on either side. Bunks enough for six people took up the opposite wall. The remaining wall space was covered with floor-to-ceiling shelves crammed to overflowing with crates and boxes.

Each box and crate bore a label of the contents, some easier to read than others—canned food, shoes, shirts, trousers, water, whiskey, candles, kerosene. Crates labeled *Medical* in faded red lettering filled the shelves over one bench and bedding took up the shelves over the other bench. Jugs of water, bleach, and little brown bottles of Halazone tablets for purifying water had their places under each bench. An empty cracker barrel with the lid propped against the side sat in a corner. Although Spartan, the room had everything a person needed for an extended stay.

Finn returned, and closed the drop-down ladder. "No sign of visitors."

"Good. I figured Rocchelli was bluffing." Hagen gestured in a general way. "This isn't just a storage room. It's outfitted for people to live in."

"It was once a safe place along the Underground Railroad. With the store above, it was convenient to provide food and clothing for escaped slaves on their way north. No one ever suspected what was going on right under their feet."

"Ceara told me your store has been in your family for generations. Helping runaway slaves was risky. Noble, though. I admire the people who took the risk."

"As do I, but then, my great-grandparents on both sides were of sturdy stock. They came to America from the County Kerry parish of Kenmare, where they'd long been suffering the rising oppression of the aristocracy. At the first sign of what history would name as the Great Potato Famine, they knew the time for leaving couldn't be put off. When they got off the ship in New York Harbor, they joined other Irish families who had come with them and before them. My great-grandparents had money in their pockets and hope for a future in their hearts."

"I grew up with similar stories."

"These first families weren't poverty-ridden like the ones who followed years later. They believed in absolute freedom for all peoples, and they were good for their word. They set up businesses. The Galloways began a grocery then added dry goods. Everyone helped their neighbor for the good of all."

"Ceara said you pay the local strong-arms to leave you alone. That's not what I'd call freedom."

"True enough, except for an important difference. The men who demanded protection money became dependent upon what my family could, and did, provide for them. It eventually became a mutually satisfying arrangement."

Drawn to the shelf with long wooden boxes butted end to end, Hagen said, "These are the right size for rifles."

Finn joined him. "Open them."

Hagen removed a latch pin and lifted the lid on its stiff hinges. "There's a small arsenal here, and this is just one box."

"We Galloways know how to fend for ourselves."

"Who knows of this place?"

"Maureen and the girls. A few old and trusted friends who shared the hard times."

"These aren't hard times now?"

"No. The worst is behind us. People are tiring of the killings and robberies and the graft. I predict the days of Alphonse Capone, Lucky Luciano, and their ilk will come to an end soon enough. The government has paid a costly price for Prohibition, and it can't be sustained when the criminals are becoming wealthy while the government is going broke.

"Give it a few years. Prohibition will be repealed. It's in the works, but the wheels of the government's decision-making machine turn slowly. When that day comes, the men who have profited from it will fall. I also see trouble coming for the plain Joe who's been spending beyond his means and the convenience of easy credit and instead of saving and purchasing with cash.

"I've preached to my girls that credit will get a person in trouble unless it's managed well. Dabbling in the stock market will, too. Both are gambles, and you'd better have the money to spare if you play that game. If the money you're putting on the table should be buying food for your family, you're asking for trouble."

"My family preaches from the same pulpit." In a smaller wooden crate, a blued-steel handgun with a checkered walnut grip caught Hagen's eye. "Well, I'll be damned. A LeMat revolver." He hefted the heavy weapon. "Just under three thousand were made for the Confederacy. Cap and ball black powder. Two barrels. This one's a .42 caliber on top and 20-gauge under. There were some .36 calibers made, too. None of them are accurate at any distance, but they're damn deadly at close range."

"You know your guns."

Hagen put the LeMat back with some reluctance. "It's an interest I have my folks say borders on obsession. I collect rare guns and restore old ones. I've got an 1873 Winchester—a One of One Thousand 1st Model—with documentation of authenticity and ownership. Cost me a pretty penny."

"Then you'll want to handle this old gal." Lifting the lid on a long narrow crate tucked in behind a larger wooden box, Finn removed a musket.

Hagen's eyebrows shot up, and he whistled through his teeth. "A Long Land Pattern Brown Bess." The reverence in his voice didn't do justice to the awe of actually holding this gun in his hands. He sighted down the barrel. "I wonder how many battles she's seen and what stories she could tell." As with the LeMat, he returned the musket to its resting place with respect for its history. "Wish she could talk."

"I've kept many of these old guns with an eye to their eventual value as vintage relics. When cash gets tight, it pays to have items for barter."

"When you're feeling money-tight, talk to me before you sell to anyone else." Hagen opened another box and picked out a rusted bayonet from the menagerie. "You mentioned the stock market. It's a big topic around my family's supper table. Too many people are buying stocks with money they don't have.

The bottom's bound to fall out. When it does, this country's in for some bad times."

"I believe you're right. I've seen it coming, which is why my money isn't setting in a bank, and why Maureen and I saved to buy our house and not have a mortgage."

Hagen chuckled. "Are you sure our families aren't closely related? My parents and grandparents keep their savings sealed in glass jars and buried in the back yard just like the one you dug up."

Finn grinned with him. "Must be our frugal and wary Irish blood."

"Must be."

"Which is one of the reasons we're here." Finn tilted the cracker barrel and rolled it aside. Dropping to his knees, he brushed at the thick layer of dust inside the circular imprint left by the iron ring around the bottom of the barrel and uncovered a metal plate that he lifted to reveal a hole beneath. Reaching down the length of his arm, he brought up a metal box. The tight hinges grated when he opened the lid. From inside his coat, he withdrew two envelopes.

"Last Will and Testament. Deeds to our house and the store. They'll be safe here, even in a fire."

"That's why you came back to your house."

"Yes. I didn't think of taking them when we left for church." Finn put the envelopes into the box, closed the lid, and returned it into the hole. Then he replaced the metal plate and rolled the barrel back to its original position after which he brushed out telltale signs of disturbance. "Maureen and the girls know to look here. And now, you know."

Finn took two cans of peaches from a box, cut the lids half way open with a claw-end can opener, and bent the lids back. He offered a can to Hagen along with a tarnished butter knife.

"Thanks." Hagen fished out a slice of peach. "Do you expect Maureen and the girls soon?"

Finn nodded, thinking. "No. They'll take their time so they don't raise the curiosity of our friends. I'll go out in a bit and wait on the loading dock to give them a hand coming through the tunnel." He cut a mischievous side-eyed grin at Hagen. "Unless you want to accompany them."

"Oh, hell no." Hagen nearly swallowed a peach slice whole. "I'll hold down the fort right here. Next time I go through that black void is when I leave this room, and I'm not planning on coming back this way anytime soon."

Finn laughed just a little too much in Hagen's estimation, but he chuckled along with him.

After a few quiet moments, Finn said, "Rocchelli won't trade the ledgers for Ceara. Once she gives up the location of the ledgers, he'll either kill her, or she'll be stuck with him for the rest of her life, which is the same thing as dead."

Hagen had come to that conclusion long ago. "If I hand over the ledgers, I'm dead for sure." His gaze drifted to the shelves of weapons and ammunition and then over to the boxes and crates of bedding. "We could hide and watch to see what Rocchelli does if we don't show." He ate the last peach, drank the juice, and set the can and knife on the floor.

"We could." There was no confidence in Finn's voice, and the idea died in the silence that followed.

"We could lay in ambush and kill him." Countless times since meeting Ceara, Hagen had wanted to do just that. "But how would we find Ceara?"

"I don't know." Finn put his empty peach can beside Hagen's. "We're not going anywhere for a while. Something will come to us. We'll figure it out."

Hagen checked his watch. With every passing minute, it felt like the walls of the windowless room were creeping toward him at the same rate the ceiling seemed closer overhead. "Time is getting away."

Finn's shrug could have meant *that's true* or *don't be so impatient*. "Get your mind on something else."

"Like what?"

"Ceara's explanation of the circumstances that brought her home left me with more questions than answers. I want to know more about how you two ended up in that warehouse, and how you met. I'm interested in your perspective as a lawman. You might also tell me how a Texas Ranger became mixed up with J. Edgar Hoover."

Hagen drew his thoughts in, quickly rolling back over the weeks. So much had happened in such a short time. He started with the day his boss offered him the Rocchelli assignment and went from there.

"Hiring me as his mechanic got me inside, but it didn't gain me access to Ceara. She was never alone. It was clear she was prisoner under armed guard in her own house. I spoke to her in passing. Not every day, but most days. She was cordial and polite, but that was it. Never an extra word. She rarely looked me in the eye. By the end of the second week, when Rocchelli invited me in for supper with them, I was as nervous as a long-tailed cat in a room full of rocking chairs that I'd be fingered as a lawman before Ceara and I could talk privately.

"I played around with kidnapping her and taking her out at gunpoint, but Rocchelli had too many men. One thing I made sure of was to make friends with the guard dogs in case I needed to prowl at night. Dogs naturally take to me, so that was easy.

"I buckled down and worked daylight to dark, either on the vehicles or around the grounds without being asked. I had to convince them I wasn't a slackster, and I was willing to pull more than my own weight. I didn't take my days off."

"Good way to build trust," Finn observed.

"Not only that, but I didn't want to miss anything. I observed and learned the routines. When I realized Rocchelli and Ceara went to church together on Sunday mornings, I saw the possibility of getting a message to her if I could wheedle my way in as their driver. I buttered-up Rocchelli's chauffeur, who still held a grudge for the way I made him look incompetent when the Rolls wouldn't start. I offered to take his Sunday morning duties as a good faith apology.

"While Rocchelli liked my eagerness to make inroads with the other men, he wasn't sold until I told him how happy it would make my mother if I wrote home that I was going to church regularly with my boss. He said it was important to take care of your eternal soul and please your mother."

"I hate to admit agreeing with him on both points."

Hagen grinned. "I know. It chafes like a saddle sore on a high-withered horse." He waved-off the question in Finn's expression to explain another time. "I made the first contact with Ceara on Sunday, January twentieth. For the next four Sundays, we passed notes like kids in a classroom, and Rocchelli never caught on."

Hagen stared at nothing in particular as he recalled those Sundays and the notes. He'd slipped the first one along with a stub of pencil to her as he helped her out of the car on the opposite side from Rocchelli.

Have the package at hand. Prepare for midnight house raid with warrant to remove you next time R's out of town. Will take you out under police protection.

She excused herself after the service to use the restroom, while Rocchelli stood at the door shaking hands and mingling. When she returned, she slipped the same paper back to him. Later, in his apartment adjoining the garage, he read her response.

No!!! Can't trust cops and judges. They're on his payroll. His influence runs far and deep. He has eyes watching everywhere all the time. OK with leaving next time he's gone. How?

Looking back, he should have taken the word everywhere with the bold underline more seriously.

The next week, he slipped her a note the same way.

Understand your concerns, but will chance it. Will take day off this week to make pertinent phone calls. Plan stands as is for armed escort. Have yourself and package ready to go.

As before, she visited the restroom to read the message and write her response. This time, though, Rocchelli hurried her to the car before she could give it back. At the car, she dropped her purse and palmed the note to him when he picked up her purse and handed it to her.

Show up with police and I'll deny everything. I have to in order to survive. Even denial may not save me from his anger. Can we leave separately and meet somewhere? I may be able to sneak away from the hospital.

Ceara risking an out-and-out run without police protection hadn't made his list of viable options, but running out of time had a way of altering plans. For the rest of the week, he dismissed every idea he came up with as either too complicated or too chancy. That Friday, two of Rocchelli's men invited him for a night on the town. He suspected Rocchelli put them up to it to find out more about him, since they'd not shown interest in buddying-up with him until now. He took the bait.

On the way to a favorite speakeasy, they drove past Union Station, and the solution hit him right between the eyes. He offered to pay for their drinks in exchange for a look inside. By the time he delivered his drunken comrades to their respective houses hours later, he knew what he was going to do.

The next morning when they arrived at church, Rocchelli instructed him to accompany Ceara to their pew, while he talked to a man waiting beside a car on the far side of the parking lot. Careful to sit a respectable distance from Ceara, but close enough that she didn't have to make an obvious reach for the note when he slid it to her, Hagen watched from the corner of his eye as she read.

I concede to no police and meeting separately. We'll make our run the next time R's gone. Meet me at Union Station in the Great Hall on the east wall between the sculptures of the rooster and the owl. We'll take any train leaving in any direction. I can see your front door and the big bay windows from my apartment and the garage. On the day you can leave, set up the same amount of objects as the time you can meet in one window. Space them so I can clearly count them from a distance. In the other window, put a flower vase for a.m. or a framed picture for p.m. Can you do this?

She'd folded the note and tucked it into the palm of her left glove. Looking straight ahead, she'd whispered one word.

Yes.

She'd turned to him then. To his dying day, he'd never forget the spark of hot, raw hatred blazing in her eyes. How much longer would she last before she killed Rocchelli?

Then the real waiting began.

The next Sunday came and went without exchanging a note. But the following Sunday, Ceara had brushed past him on the way up the church steps with Rocchelli right beside her when she slipped a note into his coat pocket. Lagging behind, he dawdled to read it.

Moran called last night. He's sending Eddie to St. Louis this week. Cecil and Phil will go along. He'll leave right after daylight Mass on Ash Wednesday. I'll send the package to a safe place—too heavy to take with us, will slow us down. I'll arrange the items in the windows as instructed.

Hagen came back from his private journey with the realization that Finn patiently waited for him to continue his story. He sat up straighter and cleared his throat. "Sorry. I got bogged down in some memories. Where did I leave off?"

"You made contact on Sundays."

"Well, those details don't matter. We exchanged notes with a plan to meet at the train station. We got caught there when a security guard on Rocchelli's payroll recognized Ceara. That's how we ended up in the back of that warehouse and—"

Jing-a-ling

Hagen's gaze locked with Finn's. "It's too soon for Maureen and your daughters."

Chapter Twenty

FINN LEFT THE BENCH an instant before Hagen made a bounding leap to the middle of the room and tipped the table over as a barricade. Behind it, and down on one knee, he leveled Rocchelli's .32 at the door. Finn stood at the hinge side of the door, his back pressed to the wall.

"Catch!" Hagen tossed Cecil's gun.

"Finn! Finn! Don't shoot! It's Maureen. Colleen is with me." Maureen's voice, distant and stifled through the thick barricade of the wooden door, carried clearly enough to hear her urgency as she neared.

Hagen whispered, "Could be a trap."

"No. She'd have used my given names to warn me—Finnegan Noah. We've done this a time or two." Finn pushed the door open. "I'm here, Maureen."

Colleen stumbled in first. Finn caught her before she fell. "Jesus, Mary, and Joseph. You're soaked to the bone. Are you hurt?" He put a free arm around Maureen and held both of them tightly to his chest.

Maureen said, "Look to Colleen. She's chilled, and she can't catch her breath. I'll be fine. I've only a knot on my head, and a bloody nose. I don't think it's broken. No doubt I'll have black eyes tomorrow."

Hagen righted the table, as Finn guided Maureen and Colleen to the chairs. He placed Cecil's gun on the table and knelt in front of them, his attention bouncing from one to the other. Maureen accepted his handkerchief and dabbed at her nose.

Hagen made a quick look into the tunnel then closed the door. His skin crawled with the unpleasant thought of how quickly Maureen and Colleen had made it through the tunnel. He and Finn hardly had time to react. If he owned a tunnel, he'd do something to remedy that— Hell, what was he thinking? He wouldn't own a tunnel.

"Colleen, sweetheart, are you hurt?"

She shook her head, but her rapid shallow breathing, ashen color, and chattering teeth weren't convincing. Finn crooned calming words while drawing the blanket closer around her body. He smoothed her wet hair from her face. "Look at me, Colleen. You're safe now. Take it slowly. Breathe with me." In a few seconds, color returned to her cheeks. "Better now?"

She offered a weak smile and nod on a shuddering breath, her tears right on the surface.

"That's my girl." Finn pulled up a chair. "Where is Claire?"

"Captured."

"Rocchelli?" Hagen handed a wool blanket to Finn for Colleen, draped another blanket around Maureen, then put Cecil's gun back in his waistband.

"Thank you. Yes." She winced with the nodding movement and clutched the blanket tightly to her body.

"Tell me everything," Finn encouraged.

"At the church... We sat down to the meal with everyone. Then, one-by-one, we excused ourselves for different reasons and met in the kitchen. I was afraid that carrying everything we'd brought from home all the way to the store would slow us down, so we put it into a cupboard. I was so glad we did.

"We were hardly away from the church when we met two cars. They went on past. We'd just made it to where we were going to double-back to come here when out of nowhere, men came from the darkness. They had guns. They told us to be quiet if we wanted to see Ceara alive.

"I didn't think. I just reacted, hoping someone would hear me. I screamed for you. A man slapped me. The two cars came around, and we were rough-handed inside. They put the girls in one car and me in with Ceara in the other. He's got them. Finn, that crazy man has our girls." Her voice cracked in a half-sob. Finn put his arms around her, and held her as he met Hagen's hard gaze.

Colleen reached for Maureen's hand and squeezed. "Momma—"

"Oh, Colleen, I'm sorry. You know I'm not usually like this." She exhaled a hard breath. "He threatened to hurt the girls to make me tell where you were, but Ceara didn't give me a chance to say more. She told him you'd gone out to make arrangements for us to leave the country, and it would be hours before you returned. She said we'd agreed earlier the girls and I would go home to pack to be ready when you got there."

"Did he believe her?" Hagen asked.

"Yes. He said it worked into his plans. When he caught Finn, he'd have you both. That made no sense to me. Oh, how that awful man gloated. He said Ceara had betrayed us. He saw it in her eyes when they'd driven past us. I didn't—I don't—understand. All I could gather is she must have said something about St. Brenden's, and that they'd been driving the neighborhood for quite some time looking for us. He figured out we must be at the church because of the activity and people coming and going. They made us put our coats over our heads. We drove in circles for some time."

"No doubt to confuse you so you wouldn't know where they were taking you."

Maureen nodded. "At first, I knew where we were. We bumped over the rut on Grand three times and always when turning left. On the third pass, we turned right then drove mostly straight-on for what I counted to be five minutes, then we turned again. After that, I lost count and couldn't keep our changes in direction straight in my head.

"When we finally stopped, I immediately smelled fishy water. We were on the docks, but I didn't know where. Our hands weren't tied, but a man threatened us to be quiet and leave our coats over our heads. They dragged me out of the car and pushed me along. I heard a scuffle ahead of me and a man swearing. Ceara screamed for us to run. I threw off my coat. I—I didn't know where I was going. I just ran. I felt so guilty leaving the girls, but I could do nothing to help them if I stayed."

"And right you were to run," Finn assured her.

"A man tackled me not ten feet on. I kicked until I broke free. Before I could get to my feet, he grabbed my ankle and got on top of me. He hit me...punching and punching. Then someone pulled him off." She smiled at Colleen.

"Claire helped me. She knocked him off of you, then he hit her. I jumped on his back and wrapped my arms around his neck." Colleen sat straighter, her chin jutted. "And I bit his ear."

Finn looked at his youngest daughter. "You... You bit his ear?"

Colleen's face screwed up in distaste. "I gagged."

Hagen laughed at her ugly expression. "Aldo Jucca. As nasty on the outside as he is on the inside."

A spark of pride glinted in Colleen's eyes. "I would have vomited down his neck if he hadn't thrown me off."

Hagen chuckled at her spunk.

Maureen said, "I grabbed Colleen's hand, and we ran toward the river. Ceara was still screaming for us to run. Someone cursed and told her to shut up—maybe slapped her—I'm not certain. When I looked back, I saw that man Jucca dragging Claire toward the building, and Colleen and I tripped over each other. I don't know if I hit my head when I fell or if something hit me and then I fell. I have a vague recollection that Jucca threw something at me—a piece of pipe or a chunk of wood." She ducked her chin for Finn to inspect where she pressed her fingers on her head. "Here."

"You've a good-sized lump, but it didn't break the skin."

Hagen said, "Jucca has a sap he uses as a club. It makes him feel big and mean. I've got a knot on my head thanks to him."

"It could have been that. Everything went topsy-turvy, and I blacked out. I don't remember falling into the river. I'd surely have drowned had Colleen lost hold of me."

Colleen took up the story. "I turned Momma onto her back, while we floated in the shadows of the old docks with the current carrying us right along. By the time they shined lights into the water, we were too far away for them to see. I could hear them yelling and cursing. I took to land when I thought it was safe. That's when Momma came-to. We had to rest often because of me, or we'd have been here sooner."

Her downcast gaze tugged at Hagen's heart.

"Look at me, Colleen." Finn cradled her face in his hands. "We'll have none of that kind of talk. You're so much stronger than you realize, and this proves it. You saved your mother's life. You went beyond what you thought you could do, and you didn't give up."

Tears shone in her eyes, but she smiled and nodded.

"Did you recognize where they took you?" Finn asked.

Maureen said, "Clauncy's abandoned speakeasy. The windows are blacked-out, but I saw a faint glow inside through the corner of a broken window pane on the ground level. There were at least a half-dozen men."

"Clauncy's? That's up on East River near the tunnels. How did you get here?"

"Finn—" Maureen's shoulders rose and fell on a shaky breath. "We came on foot. I lost my purse when they kidnapped us."

"On...foot..." Finn leaned back, a combination of awe and amazement in his voice. A grave darkness settled over his features like storm clouds building in the sky—ominous and foreboding. "That is a good long ways under the best of circumstances."

"Daddy, we did what you always tell us to do—put one foot in front of the other and keep going until you can't go anymore."

Finn offered a slight smile to Colleen.

Softly, Maureen said, "Those ledgers are all that are keeping Ceara and Claire alive—or at least, unharmed."

Hagen said, "Yesterday, I would have agreed with you, but he's had time to think, and so have I. He's sure his lawyer can handle whatever Hoover throws at him in court. He's not particularly concerned about Capone or Moran, either. Taking turns trying to kill each other is standard business amongst those crooks.

"He wants Ceara more than he wants his books. She's his possession he bought and paid for with a piece of paper called a marriage license. In his twisted mind, I've taken her from him and his pride is cut to the bone. There's no satisfaction in killing her, only in punishing her every day for the rest of her life." Hagen's gaze wandered again to the shelves of guns and ammunition, this time with a glimmer of an idea.

"Rocchelli wants this business finished tonight. His confidence is also his weakness. He's sure I'll show up. But he doesn't know where you are, and he presumes Maureen and Colleen are dead." Hagen looked at Finn. "This is the plan. You'll go to your house and let him catch you packing a couple of suitcases like Ceara said. I'm gambling that Rocchelli will take both of us to the hideout."

"They'll search us for weapons."

"Armed or not, we have to get to where Ceara and Claire are. But understand this," Hagen cautioned. "The minute we get there, we take control, or we've already lost. No negotiating. No bargaining. No waiting. We make our stand right then and there. You have to be ready for whatever I might do."

"Are all Texas Rangers this single-minded and confident?"

Hagen chuckled. "Some say we're too dumb to know when we're whipped. I call it a gift of determination." He sobered.

"People are going to die tonight." He looked at Maureen and Colleen then at Finn. "And it might not be the ones you want."

"A mad man has threatened our family, and he's holding two of our daughters hostage. We won't stand for that." Finn dropped his gaze to meet Maureen's. "We'll do whatever it takes to be free of Eddie Rocchelli."

Hagen saw the same silent understanding pass between them that he'd witnessed in their kitchen earlier. No words spoken, but everything understood in that look. Finn gave Maureen's hand a final squeeze as if a deal had been struck between them. He assessed Hagen for some moments before speaking.

"You know where the ledgers are. Why haven't you taken them to Hoover?"

"My job as a lawman was only to deliver Ceara and those ledgers into the keeping of Hoover's agents." Hagen met Finn's steady gaze. "I haven't been a lawman since the night I met Ceara, but I didn't know it until she walked back to Rocchelli tonight. I don't give a rat's ass about those ledgers. I never did."

"How much do you care for her?"

"When Rocchelli's out of her life, I'm going to marry her...if she'll have me."

"That's what I thought." Finn punctuated his words with a smile and approving nod.

"What do we do now?" Maureen asked.

Finn stood. "First, we get both of you settled upstairs and changed into dry clothes." He helped Maureen and Colleen to their feet.

"And then what?"

He shifted his gaze to Hagen. "We don't know. Rocchelli expects Hagen to meet him at our house with the ledgers at ten o'clock."

"I've been thinking about that. Here's what we'll do. You go to your house like you're packing a couple of bags to leave town in a hurry. Rocchelli will find you there. I'll show up. He'll have both of us, just like he wants."

Finn nodded thoughtfully as he and Maureen looked at each other. "I need you and Colleen to stay here where I know you're safe. Once you're warm and dry, come down here to wait. Rocchelli won't find you."

"How long do we wait?"

Hagen answered. "Give us a couple of hours, then get to a telephone and call my boss. Tell him everything. He'll take care of you. Get me something to write his name and telephone number on."

Finn followed Maureen and Colleen to the ceiling ladder. Maureen went up first.

Finn said, "I'm right behind you." To Hagen, he asked, "What will you do with the ledgers?"

Hagen lied. The less they knew, the better for their well-being. "Stash them. I'll take one as proof that I have them." Truthfully, he was leaving all but one at the church. They were as safe there as any place he could think of. "Is there a place near your house where I can see what's going on in the neighborhood?"

Finn said, "There is a vacant house with an old wood shed on the right as you come into our cul-de-sac. Trees block some of the view, but it might do."

"Could be where Rocchelli planted a spy."

Finn nodded, thinking. "Any of the houses in our neighborhood can be approached from the back, and we wouldn't be the wiser." He put a foot on the bottom rung. "I won't be long."

Hagen used the time alone to prepare. On his mother's side, he was cousins to a courier who died defending the Alamo. The Kane side also reached back to a defender. Those connections ran strong and proud in both families. If tonight was to be his Alamo so Ceara could be free from Rocchelli's tyrannical rule, he couldn't think of a worthier reason to die.

Rummaging through boxes, he found a military rucksack that had seen a skirmish or two from the looks of its scars. He put it on the table then continued his search for the other items he needed. He'd heard the old timers talk about making body armor, but stories were all he had to go on. He grunted a mirthless laugh. A story was a hell of a thing to hang your life on.

With a bolt of silk cloth, cotton batting, a wool blanket, the suturing needles and a tin of catgut sutures from one of the boxes of medical supplies, he sent a silent thank you to his Grandma Hayes for teaching him how to sew up holes in his trousers and socks. Satisfied with his menagerie, he opened Jucca's knife and went to work.

Hagen mumbled, "Broken ribs are a given. Bullet penetration likely. Sure as hell hope they aim for my chest and not my head."

Chapter Twenty-one

Ceara huddled with Claire on a filthy mattress. It was better than sitting on the frigid floor, which was an uncomfortable reminder of being in a similar plight a day ago. She tried not to think about the insects and rodents living inside the three-inch-thick cotton batting or the residue they'd left on the striped ticking. Shadows wavered on the floor and walls from the low-wick light of kerosene lamps.

Claire wore the welt on her cheek from Jucca's backhand with pride. She favored her side where he'd planted a hard kick, but she hadn't uttered a whimper. Only now that Jucca had left with Eddie and Cecil, had she relinquished the vigilant glare she'd pinned on Jucca. The room was eerily—and pleasantly—quiet without the little man's inane chatter.

Lenny and Gilbert covered outside watch. Phil snored. Leo sat in the chair beside the door nursing a cup of coffee, pointedly avoiding looking toward the mattress. Ceara wished Phil wasn't there so she could talk to Leo. A little part of her heart broke that Leo had chosen loyalty to Eddie over his affection for her, even though it didn't surprise her.

She regretted waiting too long to tell Hagen where she'd sent the ledgers. She had no doubt he'd watched and listened to her confrontation with Eddie. She hoped he'd put together the hints she'd dropped. For all his sharp-shooting at the Rolls-Royce's radiator, Hagen couldn't win in a stand-off against armed men with only shrubbery as his protection, but she didn't believe for a second he knew that. Positioning herself so he couldn't get a clear shot at Eddie was her way of keeping him alive.

She clung fiercely to the hope Hagen and her father were together and concocting a plan, and her mother and sister had survived the fall into the river. Her mother was a strong swimmer, but Colleen was so fragile. Her heart hurt for not telling Hagen she loved him. If they somehow managed to live through this— No! *When*. When this ordeal was over, not a day would pass that he wouldn't know how much she loved him.

Exhaustion undermined her determination to remain alert for an opportunity to escape, and she closed her eyes. Her drowsy thoughts drifted back to those Sunday mornings Hagen had taken over driving them to church. A glass panel between the seats separated them, but it just as well have been a brick wall. Still, the brush of Hagen's shoulder against hers, the touch of his fingers when they exchanged the notes, her hand in his when he helped her from the car— Small, but cherished treasures.

Tears burned hot behind her eyelids. Gentle fingertips wiped her cheeks, and she opened her eyes to see Claire, her eyes shimmering with her own held-back tears. Ceara squeezed Claire's hand to reassure her. Her fingers were like ice.

Reaching into her pocket for the gloves, Ceara felt the matchbook tucked inside the left glove. For a few moments, she held her breath. An idea flashed in her mind. Slowly, she dropped her gaze to the worn and frayed mattress and over to the kerosene lamp a few feet away. It was a dangerous move. She might kill them all, but it might also get them outside, which was one step closer to freedom.

Claire mouthed, "What is it?"

Ceara shook her head slightly. She left the matches in her pocket and gave the gloves to Claire. As her father said, Eddie Rocchelli didn't know the Galloways.

***

Hagen crept to the rickety back porch of the vacant house, peered around the corner, then quickly crossed the twenty feet to the clapboard wood shed and eased inside to keep the sagging door from falling off its hanging hinges. A ragged piece of canvas nailed over the small window beside the door flapped with the sporadic breeze.

As his eyes adjusted to the dark interior, he picked out the shapes and outlines of an empty coal bucket and a chair with broken seat. Wadded-up, light-colored paper caught his eye. Squatting on his heels, he picked up the crumpled paper and felt the waxy coating at the same time catching a whiff of liverwurst and rye. Inspecting the ground at his feet, he counted a dozen cigarette butts. This answered his question of how Rocchelli knew the goings-on at the Galloways' house. Most likely, there had been two people here taking turns running reports to Rocchelli.

A missing slat in the door provided a clear enough view toward the Galloways' house despite the island of trees in between. Rucksack strap slung diagonally over his chest and shoulder, he hunkered down to wait.

City noises hummed at a distance but, in the Galloways' neighborhood, it was quiet. No one and nothing stirred as house and porch lights blinked out as people turned-in. A light came on in the Galloways' house—Finn's signal.

Hagen hit the alley at a run in the opposite direction from the way he'd come in. He continued several blocks before circling back. Blending into the shadows across the street from the entrance to the cul-de-sac, he waited for Rocchelli to arrive. He tilted his watch toward the street light half-a-block away. Two minutes to ten. At ten on the dot, a car coming his way slowed then made a right turn into the cul-de-sac. It was Rocchelli's Cadillac. Another car passed right then. In the glare of the headlamps, Hagen saw Cecil was driving, but he couldn't see who else was with him.

Hagen counted to a hundred then stepped out in an unhurried pace, partly to give Rocchelli time to apprehend Finn, but mostly to take stock of the situation he was walking into. Halfway into the cul-de-sac, he saw Finn leave the house, his hands behind his head, and Jucca following him at gunpoint. Finn went up Rocchelli where he waited near the open door of the Cadillac. Jucca checked Finn's coat for weapons then made a cursory pat of Finn's trousers, found nothing, and didn't check further. Hagen expected just that to happen, which is why he risked Finn wedging Jucca's flick-knife in his shoe. One of them had to have a weapon. He deliberately left his Colt in his boot for Jucca to find. Rocchelli would expect him to have a hideout gun and would be suspicious if a pat-down didn't find it.

A few words drifted his way—*daughters, river, drowned*. Finn lunged at Rocchelli.

"You heartless bastard—"

Rocchelli backhanded him. Jucca shoved a gun into Finn's ribs.

"Boss." Cecil gestured toward Hagen.

Hagen kept his hands away from his body as he approached.

Rocchelli looked him over. "That bag's too small for all of my ledgers."

"But it's just the right size for one."

"Where are the others?"

"In a safe place as insurance to keep me alive and to find out where you've taken Ceara."

"You don't need to know where my wife is, and insurance won't help you. She'll tell me where they are."

"I moved them. Only two people besides me know where they are now, and she's not one of them. Until I know she's alive, and I'm satisfied she's unharmed, negotiations are closed."

Rocchelli's expression went hard. "I don't strike bargains. I have the power here. You'll do as I say."

Hagen snorted a disparaging grunt. "Keep telling yourself that, and maybe someday you'll believe it."

"Oh, I believe it, Cowboy. I've got you, Ceara's father—and don't give me a song and dance that you don't know each other." A smirk curled the corners of his mouth. "More importantly, I've got one of the little sisters."

Hagen dodged the trap of knowing too much. "What happened to the other one?"

Jucca piped up. "She jumped in the river with her mama. Double suicide. Someone's gonna find their bloated bodies down current, but there won't be nobody left alive in the family to identify them. Ain't that a kick in the head."

Jucca's sniveling laughter pushed at every ounce of Hagen's self-control not to kill him right there.

Steeling his voice, Hagen said, "My job is to get Ceara and your ledgers to Hoover. I don't care who dies in order for that to happen."

"So, it's Ceara, not Mrs. Rocchelli. I thought so." Rocchelli shifted his gaze from Hagen to Finn and back. "You expect me to believe you two didn't plan to be here at the same time? That you're not in collusion to run a double-cross on me?"

"Believe whatever in the hell you want. I don't give a shit. I won't deny why I'm here. I want Ceara." Hagen threw an indifferent glance at Finn. "All I know about his plan is he and his family had a church meeting and he was coming back sometime tonight for suitcases and money, so they could leave the country."

Surprise flashed in Rocchelli's eyes. "You're abandoning your oldest daughter?"

Finn's expression went granite-hard. "She made her bed when she married a dago." He cut a narrow-eyed glare toward Hagen. "When she ran off with another man instead of honoring her marriage vows—" He set his shoulders and looked back at Rocchelli. "That's not how she was raised. You two can kill each other over her for all I care. I'll have no more of her shaming the family."

Rocchelli considered his words. "All right. Maybe you are done with her. We'll see." He drew his gaze to Hagen. "Turn over all the ledgers, and I'll cut a deal for her."

Hagen stood his ground. "Take me to her, and I'll consider letting you live."

Rocchelli almost smiled. "I think my books are in the house."

"I wouldn't bet the ranch on it," Hagen drawled.

"Enough talk. Jucca. Take the bag and search him."

When Jucca reached for the rucksack, Hagen batted his hand like he'd swat a mosquito. He slipped the strap off his shoulder, held it at arm's length, and dropped it right when Jucca reached again.

Jucca lunged. Hagen sidestepped. Jucca stumbled past, wheeled, and came at Hagen. Rocchelli grabbed Jucca's arm, spinning him to a stop.

"You can have at him later! Frisk him."

Jucca ordered, "Open your coat."

Hagen took his time unbuttoning his coat.

When Jucca saw the dark bloody stain on Hagen's shirt and jeans, his mealy-mouthed grin widened. "Well, well, lookee here." None too gently, Jucca retrieved the two handguns from Hagen's waistband. He made sure to jab Hagen's hip. "These don't belong to you."

Hagen gritted his teeth against the renewed pain in his hip. Jucca wasn't getting the satisfaction of knowing he could hurt him.

Jucca tossed Cecil's gun to him then handed the .32 to Rocchelli, who slipped it into his empty shoulder holster. Jucca then made a quick feel along the outside and inside of Hagen's legs with extra attention at his boot tops. He found Hagen's Colt and took great delight in relieving him of it. He stuck the Colt into his waistband.

"Where's my knife?"

"I tossed that piece of tin three states ago." Hagen added a wide grin to get under Jucca's skin. "Take care of my Colt. I'll be taking it back from your dead body before the night's over."

"You ain't man—"

"Cut the chatter!" Rocchelli snapped his fingers for the bag, interrupting whatever Jucca might have said or done. Rocchelli lifted the satchel flap, looked inside, then gave the bag to Paul. "Don't lose this. Let's find out if the others are in the house. Aldo! Get the gasoline."

Finn stiffened, his gaze locked hard on Rocchelli. The corners of Rocchelli's lips curled in a smile of heartless satisfaction.

"No protest?" He looked at Finn.

"Burn it and be damned."

"Cowboy?"

"It's nothing to me."

Rocchelli slowly nodded. "All right, I believe you. It's time we go for a drive. Cecil, Jucca, get 'em in the car."

Hagen tensed. That was too easy. Something was up. It wasn't like Rocchelli, and it struck him odd that Paul hadn't spoken, and he'd stayed off to the side as if separating himself from the situation.

Cecil shoved Finn forward. "In the back—slide to the middle. You! Kane. Down on the floor. It's gonna be a tight fit. Heads down. Coats over your heads. Try to see where we're going, and I'll bust you a good one."

Paul got in on the passenger side backseat. Cecil squeezed in on the right. Hunkered down, cramped, and blind with his coat over his head, Hagen still smiled. His hands weren't tied, and Finn had Jucca's flick-knife. It wasn't a lot, but it might just make the difference between being dead or getting out of this with their hide intact.

Then Rocchelli said, "Aldo. Torch it."

***

"Daddy!" Claire ran to Finn and clawed his coat from over his head. "Momma and Colleen—They fell into the river." Sobs cut off her words.

Finn embraced her, crooning, "I know, sweetheart. I know. We can't do anything about that right now. We have to take care of ourselves."

Cecil followed Finn inside. He positioned himself beside the door, his gun covering Finn. Ceara stood, as relieved to see her father as she was crestfallen he was here.

"How did you get caught?" She came up short when he deliberately turned away without answering. Something was wrong. He'd never been brusque with her. This wasn't like him. Was it a warning? She cut a quick glance toward the door at the moment Hagen stumbled in ahead of Jucca prodding him with a handgun.

"How's this feel, Cowboy? Does it hurt?" Laughing, Jucca poked again at the bloody stain on Hagen's side.

Hagen jerked from the prod, pulled his coat off his head, and took stock of the room. When his gaze found her, she read the same message he'd conveyed the night they'd met—confidence and reassurance wrapped up with a cocky grin and topped off with a devil-take-the-hindmost gleam in his eyes. She understood. He had a plan. Was her father in on it?

Eddie talked as he sauntered to Ceara. "Kane. Take a good look at my wife and her sister. Hardly a scratch on them. It's up to you to keep them that way. Kane brought one ledger to prove he has them. He says he moved the others, and you don't know where they are. I think he's lying. Let's find out."

His gaze drifted from Ceara to Claire. Wiping her tears, Claire met his gaze with a bold glare that dared him to touch her.

Eddie chuckled at her overt defiance. "You've got your older sister's spunk. Little good it'll do you." He jerked his head. "Aldo!"

Jucca set his dark, piggy-eyed gaze on Ceara. She sensed his grab, but he feinted and snaked an arm around Claire's waist. Twirling her, he trapped her backwards against his chest, and rubbed the barrel of his gun against her cheek. He taunted her. "I wanted the sickly sister first, but you'll do fine in her place. After we're done dancing, I'll put you out of your misery, but not right away. I want to see how long you can last." Jucca flashed an ugly grin toward Finn. "I especially like 'em young."

"When I kill you, it won't be slowly." Finn's expression was as hard as his words

"I ain't a-skeered of a grocery store man."

"You should be. I have a few skills other than stocking shelves."

Jucca's cackle sent shivers scuttling along Ceara's arms. She looked to Leo, appealing with her eyes for help. He'd stopped Jucca at the warehouse, surely he'd intervene now. If he noticed her silent plea, he didn't let on—or refused to. Her terror skyrocketed with the sinking realization he'd forsaken her, washed his hands to her fate and the inevitable torture and death of her family. How could she have misjudged him so? How could he—and Paul—leave here and live with themselves knowing they were part of Eddie's torture and murdering schemes?

"Last chance, babe. Where are my ledgers?"

Ceara tore her gaze away from Leo and looked at Hagen. "I...told Hagen where they were. Then you showed up, and I went with you. I don't know what he did with them, if he did anything at all."

Hagen's face revealed nothing.

"I'll ask a different way. Where *were* my ledgers? We'll start there and go forward."

The truth balanced on her tongue, but she caught herself. The truth would gain her nothing but trouble, or worse, death, for Bishop Morrissey, who was an innocent participant in a plan gone terribly wrong.

Smooth as butter melting over hotcakes, she said, "I mailed them home. They were right under your nose. If you'd taken the time to thoroughly search the house, you'd have found them."

Eddie didn't speak for some seconds. "Then it's too bad Kane took my ledgers."

Ceara didn't like the glint in his eyes or the nasty tone in his voice.

"What do you mean?"

"If he'd left them at the house, this little husband and wife misunderstanding could have ended right now."

"What are you talking about?"

Finn said, "He burned our house."

Ceara sucked in a sharp breath; her stomach flipped over. Claire uttered a choked cry.

Hagen stepped closer. "Let them leave, Rocchelli. Once they're safely away, I'll take you to your ledgers. Just you and me."

Rocchelli looked at Hagen a long time. "I like that. Just you and me." He feigned apology. "But I promised Aldo the little sisters. I don't renege on my promises. Since there's only one little sister now, he'll have to make her last."

Finn went through Cecil like he wasn't there, knocking him out of the way as he made a driving tackle that took him to the floor on top of Jucca. Claire spun backwards into Ceara, and they hit the mattress in a heap. As fast as he went down, Finn was on his feet, his attention focused on Jucca.

"I learned to fight on the streets with a knife before you were out of short pants."

Jucca leaped up, eyes bulging, and mouth opening and closing, but only guttural noises came out. He looked down at his belly then up to Finn. Confusion clouded his eyes. The revolver slipped from his fingers and clattered to the floor, bouncing to rest at Finn's feet. Jucca grasped the handle of his flick-knife where it protruded from his midsection, blade buried up and under his sternum. He yanked downward and stood there for the count of three before his legs gave out. He collapsed face down.

"Bad move, Dad. Bad move."

Eddie's voice shook Ceara from her transfixed daze. She tore her gaze from Jucca to look at Hagen. He had eyes for one person—Eddie Rocchelli. In that instant, she knew Hagen was going to kill Eddie. She also knew he'd likely die doing it.

Chapter Twenty-two

"You took my wife and youngest child. I killed your boy in return. That's the way it works here in Five Points. If you were any kind of a man—*son-in-law*—you'd let Ceara and Claire go. You can have me."

Eddie shook his head with menacing slowness. "No. I'm saving you for later. Much later to remind Ceara how to behave. Kick the gun to me, or Cecil will shoot Claire."

Finn barely nudged the gun with the toe of his shoe.

Suspicion darkened Eddie's eyes. "What are you up to? You think you can get away from me? You thinking about picking it up? I said kick it to me."

Ceara pleaded, "Eddie! Stop! You win. Hagen will give you the ledgers. Let my sister and father leave."

"Too late, doll." Eddie's laugh, a deep, rumbling noise that built to a high-pitched chortle, ignited a fiery gleam in his eyes. Eddie was beyond reason. There was no penance she could do to bring him back from his precipice of insanity. One more step and he'd take them with him over the edge into the black abyss of death.

The sound of cars pulling up outside turned all heads toward the door. Paul crouched at the window and peered through the broken pane.

"Two cars. One's between us and the car Gil and Lenny are supposed to be watching from."

"Coppers?" Eddie asked.

"Can't tell. Too dark. Three, maybe four people moving around."

Eddie ordered, "Phil. Go out the other way and see what's going on out there. If they're not friendly, dispose of them. The river's running fast."

"Right, Boss." Phil took off through the kitchen

Ceara strained her ears. More car doors closing. Muffled voices.

"Rocchelli! Eddie Rocchelli! I have your two boys. Send out the Galloway women."

"Who the fuck is that? How does he know I'm here or that—?"

Eddie turned a dark and accusing glare on Hagen, but Hagen didn't notice. He was fixed on Finn.

"I visited a friend on my way to my house tonight." Finn shifted his gaze from Hagen to Eddie. "Sebastian Lazzarano is paying back all the favors I've done for him since we were kids growing up in the same neighborhood."

Phil yelled. Gunfire followed and abruptly stopped, sending men to the floor. Ceara shoved Claire to the mattress. Eddie scuttled to the window, bobbing and ducking his head to peer out the broken pane.

Lazzarano's voice boomed in the aftermath silence of the gunfire. "You just lost your man. Release the women."

Eddie stood and put his back to the wall. His eyes clouded with a bright sheen of insanity.

"Paul, stay here. Cecil, remind Dad and Cowboy who's in charge. Leo, drag my wife over here. She's gonna tell Lazzarano everything is swell. It's just a little marital spat."

Ceara stood, keeping Claire protectively behind her. "I'm not telling him anything. You want me? Then come and get me." Ceara slipped her left hand into her coat pocket and clamped her fingers around the book of matches.

Pounding like a battering ram on a door and glass breaking brought Eddie up short in his single-minded stride across the room to Ceara. He whipped around toward the sound of the break-in.

"Cecil. Do a better job at stopping them than Phil did."

"Rocchelli!" Hagen yelled.

Eddie only half-turned. "What—?"

Hagen's fist caught the side of Eddie's face, sending him reeling backward and stumbling to keep his feet under him. He went to one knee, rose slowly, and faced Hagen.

"All right, Kane. You want to go a few rounds with me? Okay. I'm gonna beat you within an inch of your life. Then I'm gonna keep you alive so you can watch me kill Ceara's father and sister, whether I get my ledgers or not."

"You're finished, Rocchelli. If I don't kill you, Lazzarano will. Then you know what I'm going to do after you're dead? I'm going to marry Ceara."

Any pleasure she could have taken from those words was crushed with Eddie's bellowing roar that sent a shudder of horror through her. Eddie lunged for Hagen, swinging his meaty arms, hammering with his fists, but Hagen staved off the blows, dancing around Eddie on cat feet, which fueled Eddie's anger that he couldn't land a killing hit.

Eddie ducked his head and charged into Hagen with the force of a battering ram. Hagen deflected Eddie's charge, but Eddie caught his arm and pulled him around into a bear hug from behind. Hagen thrust out his elbows, reached across his chest and grabbed one of Eddie's hands, then Hagen threw his own weight forward, and ducked his head as he dropped. Eddie catapulted over Hagen's shoulders and landed flat on his back.

Eddie writhed, gasping and clutching his chest for air. Hagen stood over him.

"We'll call it a draw. I was a university state boxing champion four years running, and I did some wrestling, too. You're just a street brawler—no skill, just brawn. You hit me with everything you have, and I'm still standing. You're not. You're under arrest." Hagen cast a side-eye toward Jucca's discarded gun.

Gunfire erupted from the direction Cecil had gone.

"You hear that, Rocchelli? You're down another man." Lazzarano called out. "I'm counting to ten. The women come out or my men go in."

"*Dad*!" Ceara screamed as she pushed Claire forward.

Finn caught Claire's hand and ran with her toward the door Paul had thrown open.

Finn yelled, "Don't shoot! Girl coming out!"

Ceara didn't have time to ponder why Paul had opened the door, or why Leo's attention was pinned on Hagen and Eddie. She snatched up a kerosene lamp and heaved it against the wall. The glass bowl shattered, splattering kerosene over two mattresses.

Ceara struck the matches, held the flame to the other matches then dropped the matchbook onto the mattress where she'd plucked at the batting. The fire caught and spread to the splattered kerosene. She whirled and ran toward Finn, his arm outstretched and urging her on.

Eddie came off the floor as Hagen dived for the gun. Eddie took Hagen broadside, to the floor. Eddie wrapped his hands around Hagen's injured arm and squeezed. Hagen yelled with pain, but got one knee between them and heaved Eddie off. Eddie slid into Jucca's gun, sending it spiraling into Ceara's path. Changing her stride to grab the gun threw her off-step, and she missed the gun.

"Watch out—!"

Finn's warning cut off when Hagen and Eddie slammed into Ceara from behind and took her feet out from under her. In a blur of motion, she saw Paul shove her father outside, then slam the door and lock deadbolts. Finn pounded on the door, yelling for Paul to open it.

Ceara scrambled on hands and knees to reach the gun. Eddie sat astraddle Hagen. He got in two punches to Hagen's head, the rubies on his ring drawing blood, before Hagen reared up and tossed Eddie off. Both men scrambled to their feet; Eddie's hand dipped inside his coat.

"You're finished, Cowboy. Say goodbye."

"Ceara! Texas! Run!"

Hagen charged. His voice rumbled from down low in his belly and lifted to a spine-crawling *yee-aay-woo-yah* squalling howl.

Ceara screamed.

Five shots blended into one deafening roar. Her ears rang; smoke from the spreading fire stung her eyes. Hagen slammed backward into the wall and slid down, his head lolling over his chest. Ceara screamed again as she scooped up the gun. Eddie turned on her, his gaze locked on the gun pointed at him. Confident and smug, he relaxed his gun arm.

"You don't have it in you to shoot me, doll, or you'd have done it yesterday when you had the chance."

"You hadn't killed Hagen yesterday."

Eddie's arm came up. Ceara squeezed the trigger.

A shot boomed from behind her. Ceara flinched. Eddie's body jerked, and a dark hole appeared in the center of his fore-head. He remained standing for several seconds, an expression of disbelief frozen on his face, then his legs crumpled. His gun clattered to the floor, and he fell.

"It's over, Sis." Leo put his hand on Ceara's gun hand.

Paul walked up, holstering a handgun. "This has been a long time coming." He stepped around Eddie, picked up a lamp, and tossed it at the edge of the fire. Kerosene spilled in a widening puddle toward the slow-spreading flames.

"Why didn't you let me kill him?" Ceara relinquished her gun to Leo's gentle insistence.

"You don't need his death on your conscience." Leo looked at Hagen's slumped over body. "He wouldn't want you to bear that guilt, either."

"You— You and Paul planned to kill Eddie?"

Paul opened the door and yelled, "We're coming out. Rocchelli's dead."

Finn burst in. "Ceara—?"

He took it all in with a sweeping glance, his gaze lingering on Hagen.

"Dad...Help me. I can't leave without him." She whirled and stopped in her tracks.

Hagen was standing, not quite upright, but he was on his feet with his back to the wall.

"Eddie shot you point blank. I—I thought you were dead."

Hagen groaned. "I thought I was dead, too. Damn. Knocked the wind out of me." He pressed a fist against his chest, still not able to stand straight. Coughing from the increasing smoke, he muttered, "Shit. My chest hurts like holy hell." His words came out on a rough, breathy rasp. His words came out on a rough, breathy rasp. "Busted ribs— Blood seeping. Let's...get out before we burn up."

Ceara caught him when his knees buckled.

"So that's what you were doing while I was upstairs with Maureen and Colleen." Finn draped Hagen's right arm across his shoulders and the three of them headed for the door.

Hagen mustered a grinning grimace. "You could have warned me you called in the cavalry."

"Since when did a Texas Ranger need the cavalry? My hope was to give you an advantage to get Ceara and Claire out alive."

"I was hoping to stay alive long enough to get my hands on a gun to do the same thing."

They followed Paul and Leo outside, smoke funneling from the building with the draft created by the open door. Claire ran to meet them. Headlamps from four cars backlit Lazzarano's men gathered around Paul and Leo who were talking with Lazzarano.

"...his two men will burn with him. The police will determine they all died as a result of disagreement among themselves." Lazzarano raised an eyebrow and nodded once to make his point. "I have the means to discourage any doubt that may arise as to the truth of that."

Paul said, "Good enough. Thank you."

Lazzarano sized Hagen up. "You're the BOI man?"

Hagen shook Lazzarano's hand. "Hagen Kane, Texas Ranger. I appreciate your help."

Lazzarano's stern expression slowly eased into a slight smile. "As a citizen of this fine city, it is my duty to assist lawmen in their efforts to clear our streets of criminals and hooligans. However, it will be my pleasure for us never to meet again."

Hagen grinned. "Mine, too."

Finn offered his hand to Lazzarano, who grasped and held it. "We'll take care of our business this week."

Lazzarano inclined his head in respect. "You and your family are always welcome at my house in friendship and in business." He signaled his men it was time to leave.

Leo handed Hagen the gun he'd taken from Ceara. "You warned Jucca you'd get your gun back from his dead body."

Grinning, Hagen stuffed his Colt into his waistband. "I'm a man of my word."

Paul gave Ceara the satchel. "We'll give you a lift."

"Wait—"

"For what?" Hagen asked.

"I have to know he's dead. That he won't come through the door."

"You deserve that. We can afford a few minutes."

"Gil, Len," Leo said, "If you haven't realized it, you're lucky to be alive. Why Lazzarano didn't kill both of you is nothing short of a miracle. Take it as a sign to change your ways. You saw nothing here. You heard nothing. If you want to live long and happy lives, you'll forget you ever worked for Eddie Rocchelli. If Capone and Moran hear you blabbing a word of this, you'll be sleeping with the fishes. Now, get the cars started."

Leo turned to Ceara. "I'm sorry we let Eddie go so long. We've known he wasn't right in the head for some time. It was getting worse. When Eddie called from Fort Wayne with his crazy plan, Paul called me, and we agreed we had to stop him."

Paul added, "But Eddie alluded that our names were in his books and not in a good way. We needed his books to find out how we were implicated in his illegal business. We were going to destroy the ledgers, so Hoover wouldn't have anything on us."

Her resentment toward them dissolved. "The only place your names are written in the ledgers is on his legitimate payroll. You're clean and clear."

Paul took a deep breath and exhaled with relief. "Well, since we're apologizing, I'm sorry we let Eddie go so far with his irrational scheme to make you return the ledgers. By the time he kidnapped your mother and sisters, the ledgers weren't the driving force behind his plans." He looked at Hagen. "It was you."

Leo said, "You were too good for him, Sis. Don't you ever regret he's dead."

"I won't." Ceara hugged Leo. "Thank you for looking after me. I know you risked a lot when you stood up to Eddie at the warehouse, so I could tell the truth of what happened the night our baby died."

Leo held her for many moments. "Don't forget me when this is all behind you." His voice held the husky tone of held-back emotion.

Tears came to her eyes. "I won't. I promise."

Leo held his hand out to Hagen. "I said it before. You're a good egg. Don't do her wrong."

"Thanks. I won't."

Paul asked Hagen, "How does this end?"

"I get to a telephone and make two calls—the first to an attorney for Ceara. I know a good one in Amarillo. If he can't represent her, he'll recommend someone she can trust. The second call is to my supervisor. He'll contact Hoover. Hoover will clean up what happened here." He looked at Ceara. "You've got decisions to make about Rocchelli's books before you talk to Hoover."

Paul said, "What you do with the ledgers is your business, but my advice is to keep the books that implicate Capone and Moran as insurance against retaliation." He lifted his gaze to the burning building. "It's a shame those particular books were lost in the fire—this one or the house." He dropped a knowing wink. "Give Hoover the books that show Eddie's illegal business dealings, excluding Moran and Capone. Hand over the legitimate accounting ledgers."

Paul paused as if considering whether he should stop talking or say what else was on his mind. "Two weeks after your marriage, I signed as a witness on Eddie's Last Will and Testament. Unless he changed it, you're set to inherit everything. With a good lawyer, you'll breeze through probate. He told me he didn't trust it out of his hands, so he stashed it in the wall safe in his den."

The ramifications of his words hit her, and she muttered, "*Ohhh*... I didn't expect that."

"He probably took the combination with him to his grave, though. You'll have to find a safecracker who can keep his mouth shut."

Ceara glanced at Hagen, a little smirk on her lips. "Oh, I'm sure I'll find a way to open it."

Hagen smiled back.

Leo said, "We'll talk to Moran and Capone. We'll make sure they understand as long as they leave you, your family, and anyone else you care about alone, the ledgers with their names will never see the light of day. In exchange, you promise not to give those ledgers to the Internal Revenue Service or Hoover. If you do, they'll kill you to get even. It's an agreement none of you can refuse."

Ceara smiled at the simplicity of his suggestion. "Thank you."

"It's about time to leave." Leo nodded for Paul to go with him to the cars.

Ceara leaned against Hagen, and he put an arm around her. "So, Texas Rangers always get their man?"

"No, that's the Pinkertons, but I'd say we did pretty well taking care of a Chicago mobster."

"He ended up taking care of himself." Ceara wondered when it would be real to her that she was free of Eddie, free to be happy, free to love Hagen.

"Amarillo's nice this time of year. You should consider a visit. A permanent visit."

"That's the third time you've invited me."

"Really? I wasn't counting," he teased.

"You wouldn't happen to know a priest who would perform a certain *permanent* ceremony, would you?" Ceara tilted her head to look at up him.

"Are you proposing?"

"I am. Are you accepting?"

"With bells on."

Finn interjected, "On the condition that I get to give my oldest daughter away to a real man, to an Irishman."

"I wouldn't want it any other way," Hagen said.

"I love you, Hagen Kane."

"Took you long enough to tell me, Ceara Rose Rocchelli."

"Galloway. It's Galloway. I'm taking my maiden name back. It'll be an old-fashioned Irish girl who walks down the aisle to marry you, not a Chicago mobster's widow." She recalled those minutes with Hagen as they waited in the warehouse, chained to a bumper, and his efforts to ease her fear.

"What's that look mean?"

"I suppose we should go on a date before we get married. You did promise me dinner and coffee."

Hagen chuckled. "That's right. I did. I've never welched on a promise, and I'm not starting now."

Flames flickered at the second story windows.

"Let's go home," Finn said.

"Dad— We lost our home." Claire's voice trembled.

Finn pulled her close to console her. "No. Our house burned. Our home is where our family is."

"But without Momma and Colleen—"

"Sweetheart... Your mother and sister are safe and mostly unharmed. They're waiting in the hideout room under the store. I'm sorry I couldn't tell you earlier."

Claire uttered a startled yelp, and threw her arms around his neck, laughing and crying at the same time. Ceara closed her eyes for a moment, relief flowing through her like a warm breeze on a spring day. Somehow, she'd known they hadn't drowned. She cut a side-eye glance at Hagen.

"You knew?"

He nodded.

Finn squeezed Ceara's hand. "And I'm sorry I gave you the cold shoulder. Rocchelli believed I'd disowned you. I had to keep up the charade."

"At least we're not completely homeless. We can move in above the store," Claire added.

Finn grimaced. "That's not quite true..."

"Dad... What happened to the store?" Ceara's heart skipped a few beats.

"Nothing happened. Sebastian has badgered me for twenty years to sell to him. He's wanted the store for the land that goes with it. I reminded him of the favors I've done for him over the years, and we came to an agreement. He'd take care of Rocchelli and any backlash that resulted, and he'd help rescue you and Claire, if I'd throw in the deed to the store for a nominal price."

"Then we really don't have any place to live," Claire lamented.

"Yes, you do. You're coming to Chicago to live with me, while I get my life in order and we can make a permanent move to a new home." She looked at Hagen, and he nodded.

"Let's go," Hagen said.

Paul held the backdoor of the Ford for Finn and Claire. He got into the front and the car backed up and pulled onto the street. Leo waited in the Cadillac. When Ceara reached the car, she looked back at the burning building one more time. The sound of sirens grew nearer.

Maybe in the light of day she'd believe Eddie would never hurt her or her family again. Maybe she'd never really believe it. What she did know was difficulties lay before her to settle Eddie's business affairs—legal and otherwise. Had Paul not killed Eddie, she was sure Eddie would have made a stand against Lazzarano, which would have killed them all. She owed Leo and Paul so much. Simple words of thanks weren't enough.

She recalled a comment Leo made during one of their driving sessions. He wanted to live out his old age on a Florida beach and play with his grandchildren. She had no idea what hopes and dreams Paul had. What she did know was they both had families, their boss was dead, and their employment in question. A gift of two legitimate restaurants seemed a decent way to convey just how much she appreciated what they'd done for her.

Hagen opened the back door. "I promise. He's not coming out."

Ceara got into the car. A new life in a legendary land called Texas awaited her.

She couldn't wait to get there.

About Kaye Spencer

Native Coloradoan Kaye Spencer grew up on a cattle ranch in northeastern Colorado. Since 1990, she's lived in a small, rural town located in the heart of the Dust Bowl area of the 1930s in southeastern Colorado. Kaye writes mostly western romances.

Louis L'Amour's western novels, Marty Robbins' gunfighter ballads, and western movies and tv shows inspired her love of the American Old West. Kaye's favorite movie line is from 'Quigley Down Under'. "I said I never had much use for one. Never said I didn't know how to use it." (This is exactly her relationship with her kitchen.)

During Kaye's younger years, she followed the amateur rodeo circuit and experienced life on the thoroughbred racetrack. She even did a stint as a cleaner of sugar beet storage silos (after beets are processed into sugar) to keep down the sugar dust and minimize static electricity in order to avoid an explosion. She soon realized a college education to earn a teaching degree was a safer way to support herself and her three young children.

She earned a B.A. in elementary education which landed her a position as librarian for a 90,000-volume children's library and then as a teacher of students with special needs. Later, she returned to college for her M. A. with a focus on learning disabilities. After several years in the classroom, she worked as a K – 12 principal. She left teaching and administration for many years to work as a school psychologist and director of exceptional student services for 13 school districts. She ended her career in education as a 6th – 12th grades English and history teacher and freshman-level community college teacher.

Kaye is fortunate to spend a lot of time with her family. Many rescued and homeless animals have found a home with her, and more are always welcome. Learn more about Kaye, her books, and where to find her on social media at www.kay espencer.com.

Also by Kaye Spencer

Kaye's Universal Book Link:

https://books2read.com/kayespencer

The Dance

Gunfighters & Ghostriders

Give Me Tomorrow

Gambling with Love

www.ingramcontent.com/pod-product-compliance
Lightning Source LLC
LaVergne TN
LVHW020658110826
845149LV00012B/2042

* 9 7 9 8 9 9 3 0 8 2 3 0 1 *